Fight the Tide

Also by Keira Andrews

Contemporary

The Spy and the Mobster's Son
Honeymoon for One
Beyond the Sea
Ends of the Earth
Arctic Fire

Holiday
The Christmas Deal
The Christmas Leap
The Christmas Veto
Only One Bed
Merry Cherry Christmas
Santa Daddy
In Case of Emergency
Eight Nights in December
If Only in My Dreams
Where the Lovelight Gleams
Gay Romance Holiday Collection
Lumberjack Under the Tree (free read!)

Sports
Kiss and Cry
Reading the Signs
Cold War
The Next Competitor
Love Match
Synchronicity (free read!)

Gay Amish Romance Series
A Forbidden Rumspringa
A Clean Break
A Way Home
A Very English Christmas

Valor Duology
Valor on the Move

Test of Valor
Complete Valor Duology

Lifeguards of Barking Beach
Flash Rip
Swept Away (free read!)

Historical

Kidnapped by the Pirate
Semper Fi
The Station
Voyageurs (free read!)

Paranormal

Kick at the Darkness Trilogy
Kick at the Darkness
Fight the Tide
Defy the Future

Taste of Midnight (free read!)

Fantasy

Barbarian Duet
Wed to the Barbarian
The Barbarian's Vow

Fight the Tide

BY KEIRA ANDREWS

Fight the Tide
Written and published by Keira Andrews
Cover by Dar Albert
Formatting by BB eBooks

Copyright © 2016 by Keira Andrews

ISBN: 978-1-988260-05-1
Print Edition

This is a work of fiction. Names, characters, businesses, places, events and incidents are either the products of the author's imagination or used in a fictitious manner. No persons, living or dead, were harmed by the writing of this book. Any resemblance to any actual persons, living or dead, or actual events is purely coincidental.

Acknowledgements

Thanks so much to my wonderful friends and beta readers Rachel, Anne-Marie, Jules, Becky, and Jay. I couldn't do it without you!

Dedication

To the wonderful readers who asked for more of Parker and Adam's journey. <3

Chapter One

S ALVATION CALLED AS dawn whispered along the unbroken horizon.

The voice from the radio beyond the cabin held Adam rigid where he knelt on the bed, staring out the horizontal porthole as the sailboat rocked gently. He looked over his shoulder at Parker sprawled on the mattress on his belly, his lips parted as he murmured in his sleep, the sheet tangled around his bare, lean hips.

"—here. All are welcome. Join us as we build a new home. We can be found on this—"

Static burst from the radio as it automatically switched to the next frequency, and Adam scrambled off the mattress to fiddle with the radio's settings.

They'd programmed it to scan at ten-second intervals, keeping the volume down so the static was white noise that didn't bother Adam, even with his acute hearing. But after the warmth of the woman's voice, the crackling set him on edge, his fangs pressing for release.

He jabbed the button to scan back, goosebumps sweeping over his skin. But there was only more static. Exhaling, Adam peered at the radio's green-lit dashboard as if he could will the voice into existence again. He switched off the auto-scan and waited, glancing back at Parker and turning up the volume a bit.

Their queen-sized bed was in the cabin at the front—no, the bow—of the sailboat, taking up the whole space but for maybe a foot on either side near the bottom of the bed. Adam's motorcycle, Mariah, was wedged into the other cabin at the stern.

Parker's dark blond hair stood up in clumps, and Adam's fingers itched to smooth it down. Or to grab his little digital camera and start filming, even though he'd taken a few minutes of Parker mumbling in his sleep the other morning, his hair mussed in ridiculous spikes, the little moles on his pale neck stark in the early light.

Not that there was any point in filming footage at all, let alone a repeat of Parker sleeping. Adam imagined being back in the editing studio in the basement of one of the arts buildings on campus. The musty concrete and tile, rows of private editing bays off the hallway with multiple screens and a control board of the latest equipment, everything digital now. No windows, and time had passed in huge slices.

He'd forget to eat—forget everything else but cutting the footage together, fixing the audio and making it perfect. Making it permanent. *Real.* There was nothing else waiting for him outside that box of a room and building.

Aside from Tina, the first real friend he'd ever made, there was only his camera and his footage, observing life around him without touching. He'd held his TA office hours twice a week and had usually spent them alone.

Until the day Parker had marched in.

Parker rolled over and muttered, never able to bite his tongue in sleep either. Smiling, Adam took a quick minute of footage before tucking his camera back away. The battery was super long-lasting, but it wouldn't hold out forever. And even if it did, there would be no more documentaries. That part of his life was over—that part of the world. But Parker was here, and he was real.

Adam fiddled with the radio. Maybe he'd imagined the voice. Aside from the odd message and conversation between survivors, there was nothing out there but hissing static. The automated emergency messages from the Coast Guard had ceased broadcasting the week before as Parker and Adam had sailed down the coast after leaving Provincetown.

Smacking his lips, Parker mumbled something about peanut butter. It was hard to fathom that it'd only been a couple of months since Parker had appeared at Adam's office demanding a better grade. Adam wouldn't have believed that entitled rich kid was going to change everything. Sure, the virus had changed everyone's lives, but Parker's impact was just as enormous for Adam.

Despite the horror, the world was a strange, wonderful place.

Parker shifted restlessly, exposing a round ass cheek. Naked, Adam tugged idly on his dick for a few seconds, stretching his foreskin and sending faint tingles over him as he thought about licking that skin and dipping his tongue into the shadowed crevice.

Hard to believe Parker was actually still a teenager. Adam sometimes thought he should feel guilty about that, although he was only twenty-three himself. But this strange, wonderful, terrifying new world had new rules, and they were a million miles from Stanford and its code of conduct.

They'd covered many of those miles riding Mariah, getting out of California and crossing the desert, traveling into the mountains that split the country, an oasis appearing from the thin air in Colorado.

The memory of waking on a narrow cot under fluorescent lights filled his mind. The only other wolf he'd met aside from his family had betrayed him. The bruises had burrowed deep.

He struggled to forget what had happened at the Pines—the powerlessness and terror, made better only by Parker's presence, his hand brushing back Adam's hair, voice shaky but determined.

Stumbling out of the lab, not going to make it. Telling Parker to leave without him.

"Oh my god, shut the fuck up and run!"

In the dawn, Adam's smile let him breathe a little easier, and he crawled back to bed, pressing a kiss to Parker's shoulder, tasting the faint tang of sweat-salt.

The older woman's voice returned. "This is Salvation Island. We are twenty-nine point-nine-six-five-three degrees north and seventy-eight point-zero-eight-five-seven degrees west."

"What the fuck?" Parker pushed himself up on one hand, his shoulder blade connecting with Adam's nose.

"Ow. Shh." Adam listened intently, rubbing his nose absently, his mouth going dry.

"We have plentiful food and water. We are free from infection and violence. It is safe here. All are welcome. Join us as we build a new home. This is Salvation Island. It is November seventh."

Low static filled the void as Parker demanded, "What did she say? Who was that?"

"I'm not sure." Excitement thrummed through him, something about the woman's calm voice plucking a string that vibrated deeply within.

Parker's breath whistled faintly in his nose, his heart tapping out a staccato, too-quick rhythm that echoed in Adam's ears. Adam leaned against the pillows of their wide bed, pulling him back to sit between his legs. He smoothed his palm over Parker's chest.

If Adam's own heart drummed too sharply too, Parker didn't need to know.

"What did she say?" Parker whispered. "Something about an island? I thought I was dreaming."

"Salvation Island. She said it's safe there."

Water splashed gently against the *Bella Luna*'s hull. A gull cawed hungrily, soon joined by another. The sparse hair on Parker's chest tickled Adam's hand as he rubbed slowly.

When the woman spoke again, Parker clambered off the end

of the bed. Adam followed as Parker cranked up the radio volume. The woman gave the same message and date.

As she finished, Parker stood there naked, his hair still sweetly sleep-rumpled, brown eyes wide, staring at the radio, which was tucked into a control panel above a padded bench outside their sleeping cabin.

"Wow, do you think...?" He breathed rapidly, mouth working. "That recording is from today. It's new."

"It is."

"Maybe it could..." Parker raked a hand through his hair, making it stick up even more. "But there's no way. Right?"

Adam ran his hand over Parker's head and down his back. "We know there are more survivors out there. Maybe it's a good idea to band together."

"But they're not safe." Parker leaned into him, his breath a warm gust on Adam's neck. "No one's safe."

The woman's voice had been so calming, though. It still echoed through him, smoothing jagged edges like water over rocks. "We don't know that for sure."

"Don't we?" Sighing, Parker stepped away and rubbed his face. "It has to be a total trap."

"We don't *know* that."

"Sure we do." Parker snorted cynically. "How could it be anything else?"

"Her voice just sounds so...soothing."

His eyebrows shot up. "Totally, she sounds like my mom reading me a bedtime story. Super soothing. And guess what? Next thing we know she's hypnotized us or some shit." He flicked off the radio with a snap of his wrist. "Then it's all downhill from there."

Adam had to laugh. "You're so cute when you're a drama queen."

Clearly fighting a losing battle not to smile, Parker shook his head, sputtering, which only made him more adorable. "Dude, you were a cinema major. Don't tell me you never watched zombie movies. The message on the radio calling people to a safe haven? It's always evildoers. Every. Single. Time." His smile vanished, a tremble rippling through him. "And you remember what happened at the Pines."

White light. Helpless.

"I know." He drew Parker close, nuzzling his cheek. Some nights, Parker woke sweating and wild-eyed, his nightmares of the things Adam couldn't remember rocking him with tremors that lasted until morning.

"Adam, we're not going near this place and its bullshit bedtime stories."

Hope still tugged, low and insistent. "But what if they're on the up and up?"

Parker stepped away with a brittle smile. "Then great. I wish them all the best and many happy returns in building their little community. And when it all goes to shit, we'll be hundreds of miles away. Safe and sound."

And alone.

The woman's voice echoed, like a loose thread begging to be pulled. Parker had good reason to be afraid, and he was probably right that they should give Salvation Island a wide berth. But still…

"We have an advantage they won't expect since I'm a werewolf."

"Yeah, because that turned out really well at the Pines. No. It's too risky."

"How far away are we? Just out of curiosity."

Parker shot him a skeptical look but switched on a light and padded over to the map spread on the dining table in the main area of the boat, which he referred to as the "saloon." There was a little kitchen outside their cabin, and a shower and toilet (or "head," as Parker insisted) on the starboard side. Soon, the sun would beam through durable skylights that gave the saloon an impressive amount of natural light during the day.

It was remarkably spacious, with almost a half-foot of clearance above Adam when he stood. Still, as the days ticked by, the boat seemed more cramped. He loved being with Parker, but would this be their life? He missed the solid ground beneath his boots, the purr of Mariah's engine, the open road.

Of course, roads now teemed with the infected, who seemed unable to swim or survive in water. It was safer at sea, especially since Parker wasn't immune to the virus like Adam.

But he couldn't help fantasizing about finding a home with Parker somewhere. Maybe even a community. In all the years since his family had died, he'd hidden himself away, and now he ached for more.

Head bent, Parker examined the map, muttering to himself. "She said twenty-nine and seventy-eight, yeah? That's…hmm. Too far north for the Caribbean."

"Have you been?"

Parker's brief smile was too sharp. "No. Dad and Eric sailed down the winter after Eric graduated college. Dad said I was too young. I followed their progress on a map." He ran his fingertip down and across to the Caribbean. "Eric loved the Caymans. Always joked that he'd run away there once he made his fortune trading stocks."

Adam went close and wordlessly rubbed his hand over Parker's hip. They'd discussed investigating the Caymans when they presumably made the Caribbean. Since leaving Cape Cod, progress down the coast had been relatively slow since Adam still had a lot to learn about sailing.

It was possible Eric was still alive, although Parker rarely talked about it. Adam knew Eric had called the night the virus took hold and had been escaping into some kind of bunker with his billionaire boss in London.

Sometimes Parker would pore over charts, which to Adam looked like maps with extra stuff on them, scribbling notes on a transatlantic voyage. But when Adam asked about it, Parker always scoffed and said it was a daydream—that sailing south in good conditions was one thing, but crossing the Atlantic would be much more difficult. And even if they did, finding Eric would be a challenge to say the least. If he was even alive to find.

Still, Adam often found him staring at the maps, and all he could think to do to help was take him to bed, holding him and making him come so Parker could fall asleep.

Parker jabbed a blue swath. "East of Daytona. That doesn't make any sense. There's nothing there."

"How far from where we are now?"

Parker gave him a long look. "We're not falling for these people's crap. Right?"

"But why would they try to lure us out into the middle of the ocean?"

"To steal our shit? Take *Bella*? Eat us for dinner? The possibilities are endless."

"Or maybe they want to help. We've met some good people. It's possible."

"My dad always used to say, 'If it sounds too good to be true, it is.' And some message on the radio telling us exactly what we want to hear? That there's a safe, awesome place out there? Is too good to be true. Since when are you gung-ho to trust strangers? After what those fuckers did to you—" He clenched his jaw, his eyes shadowed.

"I'm fine, Parker." Adam tried to draw him close, but he spun away.

"Let's keep it that way." He scrubbed at his hair, pulse jumping as he stalked to the kitchen and chugged a bottle of water from the little fridge. "We have to be smarter."

He was right, but Adam still wanted to find out more. It couldn't hurt to have more information. "Agreed. I'm just curious how far it is. Just so we know our options."

"Okay, solely for the record, we're off the coast of Virginia now." Parker returned to the table and pointed to a spot on the map. "The naval base is here. Well…was."

Adam's stomach clenched at the memory of the acrid smoke choking his senses, still not enough to mask the rancid smell of the swarms of infected on shore, the eerie chattering sound they made so loud even Parker could hear it drifting over the placid water of the bay.

They'd hoped perhaps the Navy would be organiz-ing…something. Anything. Some kind of official response. But if there were Navy ships at sea that could help, they remained silent.

Parker swallowed hard and dragged his finger lower. "So, we're about here." He lowered his finger. "Daytona Beach. This supposed island is about here, on the other side of the Gulf Stream."

Adam peered at the map. "You've never heard of any islands there?"

"No." Parker scratched his belly, and Adam's gaze followed the trail of dark hair to his groin before forcing his focus back on the map.

"But there could be?"

"I guess so. A private island. I don't remember ever seeing any mention of it, though."

"Would you have?"

"Maybe. My dad said when I graduated high school, we'd sail down the coast. I did a bunch of research into it. But when senior year rolled around and it was time to actually plan, he was too busy at work, so." He snorted.

"I'm sorry." Adam ran a hand over Parker's head and kissed him softly.

"Yeah." Parker's eyes went distant like they did when he remembered the time before the virus.

Adam understood grief and the waves in which it came and went. It had been more than fourteen years since his parents and sisters had died, but sometimes the pain struck like a two-by-four, merciless and blunt. Other moments it slithered in unannounced, insidious and endlessly patient.

"I'd come out by then, and I think he was terrified of a summer of awkward silences. He tried, but me being gay made him so uncomfortable. It was like he didn't know what to say, so he basically stopped talking to me altogether except for surface stuff."

Pulling Parker into his arms, Adam traced the knobs of his spine with his fingers.

"I just wish we'd gotten the chance to… I don't know. A chance for him to really know me. As a grown-up." He forced a laugh. "It's stupid."

"It's not. Not even a little."

Parker clung to him. "I know you understand. And it was so much worse for you, being there in the car when they died. I just—" He sighed. "I'm sorry."

Screeching tires and shearing metal. Glass exploding. The terrible silence and so much blood he could taste it, choking on death.

They stood in each other's arms as the cabin brightened inch by inch, until Adam quietly asked, "Have you thought any more about our route?"

Swiping at his eyes, Parker stepped back and returned to the map. "Okay, so there are pros and cons to sticking closer to shore. Another storm could blow in like last week. And that was nothing, not a real nor'easter. Always a risk to go offshore. But if we do, we're not going near this Salvation Island."

Adam nodded, but the woman's low tenor echoed in his mind: *It is safe here.*

Since taking to the sea, avoiding contact with creepers and

survivors alike had been far easier. When the radio did crackle to life with reports from ham radio operators and other watercraft, the news had not been heartening.

The sickness apparently spread unchecked, with more and more people either dead or infected. There were more rumors of the religious zealots who'd allegedly brewed the virus and unleashed it in coordinated attacks across the world. The Zechariahs had apparently claimed responsibility, but Adam and Parker hadn't heard anything from the group itself.

It was impossible to know what was true, and he supposed it didn't really matter in the end. What mattered was surviving. Keeping Parker safe.

Adam said, "We don't have to decide today which route to take."

"Nope." Parker yawned, stretching his arms over his head and flexing his lean muscles, his soft cock swaying. He shuffled to the small fridge and took out another bottle of water, passing it to Adam wordlessly before sticking his finger into a bowl of chocolate pudding they'd made with powder and boxed almond milk.

The *Bella Luna* was equipped with both a hydro generator below the surface of the water and a wind generator high on the main mast. Parker had explained that each one worked best under different sailing conditions while Adam tried to cram the information into his head along with all the other things he was learning.

He was just grateful they had electricity. Out on the deck with a cool breeze over the water and a frosty beer in his hand, sometimes he could forget about the rest of the world.

Sometimes.

Leaning a hip against the table, Adam said, "They might have medicine there. A doctor, even. At Salvation Island."

Parker exhaled noisily. "And they probably have lies and betrayal and sex slavery. With bonus cannibalism."

Pulling at the moist label on his water bottle and ignoring Parker's hyperbole, Adam looked at the map. "If something happened to me and you were alone, you'd need people. Even if nothing happens, it would be good, don't you think? For us not to be alone?"

His eyes on the pudding, Parker's heart skipped, reaching Adam's ears. "What, I'm not enough for you?" He tried to smile.

"That's not what I meant. Of course you are. You're everything. But we don't know what'll happen. Maybe we could check them out from a distance. With my vision and the binoculars, we could be miles away."

"Nothing's going to happen to you as long as we stay smart." Parker abandoned the pudding and hugged him, pressing his face to Adam's chest.

He was several inches shorter than Adam's six-one, and he fit so perfectly. Adam held him close, breathing in the salty scent of sea air and sweat from Parker's skin.

"You're a big, bad wolf, remember?"

Adam chuckled as Parker rubbed against his chest with his stubbly cheek. Parker was like a cat and Adam his willing scratching post. As he ran his hands over Parker's back, the woman's voice echoed in his mind again.

It is safe here. All are welcome.

"But if we—"

"Dude!" Parker jerked out of Adam's grasp. "We just went over this. Like, I didn't imagine the shit show that went down at the Pines, right?" He stalked to the head and flipped on the shower, waving his hand under the water as if he could will the generator to heat it faster. "Did you wake up with selective amnesia today?"

Adam chugged the rest of his water, biting down a retort. When he swallowed, he calmly said, "No. But there were pros and cons to the Pines."

Parker yanked the shower curtain closed after him. "I'll grant you that movie night and the palatial suite were awesome, and the chef knew his stuff. But my fond memories of our time there are just a tiny bit tainted by that part when the batshit scientist guy and Ramon the werewolf and professional bag of dicks held you captive and did tests on you. Aka *tortured* you."

"I heal quickly." When he thought of Ramon, Adam's anger and hurt were tempered by regret that he hadn't found out more from him about being a werewolf. There was so much he'd never had a chance to learn from his parents. Would he ever have the opportunity again to meet someone else like him?

"Oh, so what they did was okay?" Parker's voice rose as he switched off the shower and stormed out, a few curtain rings flying off the rail. "I guess we'll have to agree to disagree."

"No, no." Adam hugged Parker from behind, wrapping around him tightly as Parker tried to get by. "I'm sorry. I'm not saying it was okay. It wasn't. I just worry. We might need allies. We don't know what's coming. We're even more vigilant now than we were then. We won't be fooled." He pressed his lips to Parker's damp hair.

Parker relaxed a bit against him. "I want to believe that, but…"

"Shh. It's okay." Another day was beginning, and it could be their last. Adam didn't want to fight. Still hugging him close, he inhaled Parker deeply, holding his essence in his lungs until there was nothing else, the fear and uncertainty fading away.

He rubbed against Parker's ass, the adrenaline from their argument quickly transforming into desire. Here, pressed against Parker's warmth, Parker's heartbeat filling Adam's ears and drowning out any other voices, nothing else mattered.

Here, together, they were safe.

Kissing his way down the side of Parker's neck, Adam stroked over his chest and lower to his cock, which thickened quickly in his hand.

"No fair," Parker whined. "You play dirty."

Growling low in his throat, Adam whispered, "And you love it."

Parker moaned as Adam nudged him the short distance to the cabin and pushed him face down on the bed. Adam wanted to drop on top and cover him completely, keeping the rest of the world at bay.

When Parker spread his legs, Adam knelt between them. He licked the water from Parker's flushed skin, kissing and teasing. He hadn't shaved in weeks, and he rubbed his scruff against Parker's ass until the skin reddened beautifully.

"Tease," Parker muttered. "My ass can take more than that. *Need* more."

Adam spread Parker's cheeks and blew across his hole before kissing it ever so lightly, his lips barely touching the puckered flesh.

Parker groaned. "If you're trying to get me to beg, it's working."

The sun filled the cabin through the long and narrow portholes, and sweat dripped down Adam's spine as he chuckled and briefly flicked with his tongue.

Parker's little cries of pleasure joined the gulls circling overhead, and the boat rocked gently as the tide swelled. Adam kissed Parker's inner thighs now, caressing his hips in teasing circles.

With an impatient huff, Parker pushed his knees under him and jutted his ass in the air, reaching back to spread his cheeks. "Come *on*."

"Hmm. I'm not sure what you want."

With a growl of his own, Parker glared over his shoulder. "*Adam*." His eyes went soft and vulnerable, and his voice was barely a whisper. "Need you."

The urge to hold Parker close and never leave their little cabin again swelled, and Adam leaned over to kiss Parker tenderly before whispering in his ear, "You want my cock? Want me to fill you up with my cum? Hmm? You like that, don't you?" He stroked Parker's hips harder now.

"Yes," Parker hissed. "I love it."

"Or do you want my mouth today?" He kissed Parker's hole. "My tongue?" With a long swipe, he licked along his crack.

Shuddering, Parker gasped. "All of it. Please."

Closing his eyes, Adam took a deep breath and let the transformation begin, hair spreading thickly over his face and around his eyes—just enough so he knew Parker could feel it. Could feel the slight prick of claws on his hips and the tip of fangs against his hole too.

Parker trembled with a groan, and Adam could smell the pre-cum that flooded Parker's dick and surely dripped from the end.

"All of you," Parker muttered.

Adam's cock throbbed, but he didn't touch it. With his face buried in Parker's ass, he went to work licking into him, careful to only tease with his fangs and not cut. Parker cried out, writhing and panting. Adam supposed it was their own form of edging— seeing how much of the animal he could let out without going too far.

"Oh, fuck yes. Feels so good. You feel so good."

That it was *all* of him Parker felt—not just his human side— made Adam's blood sing. He'd never dreamed of revealing himself to a lover, and certainly not during the act itself. But Parker wanted it; he came so hard when Adam let the wolf out. Adam had to breathe deeply and rein himself in so he didn't leave cuts on Parker's hips.

He stabbed in with his tongue, which grew rougher and slightly longer when he transformed. He held Parker's ass open and fucked him as Parker begged for it.

"Yes, yes. Like that. Right there—fuck! Adam!"

Parker shouted and came, jerking as he shot over the sheets without his dick being touched. It filled Adam with a primal pride. Heat flamed through him. He sat back on his heels to stroke himself, coming on Parker's flushed ass and wet hole after only several tugs.

Parker pushed up on his hand to watch over his shoulder, his chest heaving. They collapsed together in a tangle on their sides, kissing roughly as Adam's fangs and claws retreated, his werewolf features fading away.

Parker took Adam's hand, uncurling his fingers. Adam hadn't even realized he'd cut his own palm with his claws when he'd jerked himself off. The wounds were already shrinking, leaving tiny smears of blood behind that Parker ran his fingertip through so gently.

He pressed a kiss to Adam's palm before burrowing into his arms, his breath damp and comforting. Adam nuzzled Parker's growing hair. The boat's previous owner had left an electric razor, but they hadn't bothered trimming anything yet.

The boat's previous owner. As if it had simply been sold.

Despite himself, Adam thought of the framed pictures they'd tucked away carefully in a drawer in the spare cabin. His name was Richard Foxe, they knew that much. He'd had a husband or partner whose name they didn't know since it hadn't been on any of the paperwork or permits stashed near the radar console.

But the husband was in the framed pictures. They assumed Richard was the older man, with gray creeping back from his temples. His husband was a good ten years his junior, his smile almost blinding as he held up an enormous fish.

Adam had considered unscrewing the picture frame to see if there was anything written on the back of the snapshot, but in the end had just put the photos out of sight. Richard and his husband would never sail the vessel again, even if they were somehow still alive. Still, it'd felt wrong to erase them completely.

Parker's hot whisper was muffled against Adam's neck. "They cut into you."

Shutting away his thoughts of the *Bella Luna*'s ghosts, Adam frowned. "Hmm?"

"They *hurt* you. At the Pines. I couldn't stop them. I know you were knocked out for most of it, and you heal, but… I don't." He shuddered, his voice scraping out. "I remember. I remember it all."

Holding Parker too tightly as if it could erase his memories of pain, Adam kissed his head. "I'm sorry. It's okay. We're okay."

"I can't deal with that happening again." He shivered in Adam's arms despite their sweat-slick skin in the warming cabin. "We can't trust anyone. We can't go to that island."

Adam relaxed his grip and smoothed his palms over Parker's body until they breathed in a slow unison. "It's okay. We won't."

He pushed away the echo of the woman's bedtime-story voice and listened intently to their surroundings, his eyes closed. No other heartbeats reached his ears. They'd anchored in sight of land, but if anyone had spotted them bobbing on the tide, they kept their distance.

He and Parker should have gone up and caught some fish while they were biting, but the world was out there, and it could wait.

Chapter Two

"HELLO? SENDING A warning to anyone listening."

As the man's voice rang out over the emergency channel, Parker's heart skipped. He finished tightening the sail sheet and returned to the radio by the metal wheel, the wooden deck warm under his bare feet. Adam perched by the bow with his little digital camera, and he looked over, waiting.

The man spoke again. "Warning to avoid Hilton Head. It's infested. Barely made it off."

Shit.

Parker had hoped islands would be able to stay uninfected. They needed to do a supply run soon. Would have to do their best to avoid creepers in the Outer Banks of North Carolina.

Picking up the transmitter, he pushed up his sunglasses on his nose with his other hand. He couldn't resist asking, even though it was pointless. "Thanks for the four-one-one. Have you heard any news from England?"

The man's voice crackled over the radio. "Heard they were hit bad. Any sign of the military where you are?"

Parker and Adam shared a look. "No," Parker answered honestly. "No sign." He hesitated to give any hints of their position, but they were far enough away. "Naval base in Virginia is toast."

The guy on the radio sighed. "I figured. Keep hoping someone's going to come and—I don't know. Fix this shit."

"You and me both, man."

"Heard those terrorist assholes made sure they infected the

capitals and military bases. CDC in Atlanta. The rest of us are left with our dicks in our hands."

"Truth. Stay safe."

"You too."

The radio hissed into silence. Better not to talk and give too much away to any stranger who might be listening, but it was still good to hear another voice. Especially one that wasn't trying to sell a load of horseshit about a magical safe place.

He knew there were still good people out there, but when Parker closed his eyes, he saw the jars in that makeshift lab—blood and chunks of Adam's flesh, Dr. Yamaguchi marveling at how quickly Adam healed. Adam so pale and still. Helpless.

What if other people found out he was a werewolf and wanted to make him their lab rat too? For all his strength and speed and advantages, Adam wasn't immortal. Parker had to protect him.

A little conversation on the radio was fine, but it couldn't go further. It was asking for trouble, and they had fuck-loads of that already. If they went for the Caribbean, he knew they couldn't avoid people forever, but they'd cross that bridge later. And maybe if Eric...

He shook his head. No point in fantasizing about seeing his brother again. For now, he and Adam were safest on their own.

The voice returned. "Hey, you still there? Did you hear those messages earlier? Went out on a bunch of channels. Salvation Island?"

Parker gripped the transmitter. "Yeah. Sounds a little too good to be true if you ask me."

"That's what I was thinking. Maybe it's those Zechariah bastards trying to wipe out the rest of us."

Giving Adam a meaningful look, Parker agreed, "Could be."

"Well, hang in there. Over and out."

He returned the transmitter to its perch. The auto-scan was disabled for the moment since he didn't want to deal with the look Adam got on his face when Salvation Island sent its BS messages.

Parker watched the fabric telltales fluttering on the mast. The wind was changing direction, and he prepared to angle the bow. "Tacking! Watch the boom." A spray of seawater flecked his sunglasses.

Adam looked up from the camera and shifted back even though he was already beyond the boom's reach. As Parker turned the bow, the horizontal pole attached to the bottom of the mainsail swung across the boat. Like the mast, it was made of carbon and was lighter than traditional booms, but could still pack a hell of a punch if it nailed you.

"Do you need any help?" Adam called.

"Nah. Got the wind aft quarter now. We're good."

"Am I supposed to know what that means?"

Parker laughed, some of the tension in his gut ebbing. "Wind is to our back and side. A broad reach. Feel how we're going faster now?"

"Uh-huh. We need to think about supplies."

"I know. We'll be at the Outer Banks tomorrow. We can evaluate."

Adam nodded. "Anything else I can do in the meantime?"

"Just look pretty." Through his sunglasses, Parker winked, knowing that even from the bow, Adam would see it.

With his camera in the pocket of his cargo shorts, Adam stretched his arms over his head, showing off his bare chest. With a flick of his ridiculously glossy black hair, he leaned back on his elbows and let his legs splay a little wider.

"Baby, you are so good at looking pretty," Parker murmured.

Adam's shoulders shook, and he couldn't hide his smile. The temptation to abandon his post to go lick Adam all over was strong, but they were catching the wind perfectly, and Parker had to keep watch. His father's voice filled his mind.

"*A good captain is always watching.*"

Of course, he'd often say that to justify all the paperwork he brought home, and Mom would roll her eyes and mutter, "*Aye-aye.*" But when it came to sailing, he was right.

Parker checked the telltales, fluttering in the wind just as he wanted them to, and his gaze returned to Adam, still spread out in the sun. He wondered what his parents would have thought of his boyfriend.

They'd probably be surprised I could bag such a hottie.

If not for the creeper apocalypse, he surely never would have. Despite the sun beaming down from a cloudless sky, Parker shivered. He shouldn't be glad in any way that so many people were dead or infected. He shouldn't be glad for any of it.

Yet the thought of not being with Adam made the bottom of his stomach drop, and he couldn't deny that the changed world had brought him something so incredibly amazing.

"Okay?"

Blinking, Parker realized Adam had lifted his head and was frowning at him across the *Bella Luna*'s deck. "Yeah. Just thinking. You know how I get." He breathed in even, deliberate inhalations and exhalations to calm his heart. "It's fine. Go back to work. That's it—arch your back. Mmm, perfect."

Adam smiled, and Parker turned his attention back to the sails. Still, thoughts of his parents ricocheted through his mind. He knew they were dead. It was extremely unlikely they survived the destruction of Boston. They'd been heading for the Cape house but had never made it. Judging by the carnage and cars blocking the highway, hardly anyone had.

Closing his eyes for a moment, he thought of the creepers hovering around the lighthouse in Chatham. His parents could have been part of that frenzied herd, with bulging eyes and grasping fingers like talons, blood staining their wordless mouths.

"Hey." Adam had crossed the deck, and he wrapped his arm

around Parker's waist at the wheel.

Eyes still closed, Parker leaned into him. "I'm okay. I know, I shouldn't think."

"Is it Eric?"

"Partly." Sighing, he straightened up and eyed the billowed sails. He loved the way Adam stroked his hip with his big hand. He kissed Adam's shoulder. "My parents too. I know they're dead, but then I wonder... But I can't. I'll drive myself crazy. They're gone, though Eric could still be out there."

"He very well could."

"He could still be in that bunker. They could live down there for years, right? Maybe this virus will die out." Parker snorted. "That's stupid, huh? Because viruses often die out on their own. Yeah, that's the direct opposite of how they work. I did actually ace bio and chem in high school, for the record."

"No C-minuses?"

Laughter warmed Parker from the inside out. "Not until you, Mr. I Expect Students to Actually Do Their Work Even on Electives."

"It was very demanding of me, I know."

They kissed softly, tongues caressing without heat.

Parker pulled back gently, glancing at the sails and checking the wind. "I just... I hate to think that my family's totally gone, you know?" *Fucking DUH.* "I'm sorry. Of course you know." Changing his grip on the wheel to his left hand, Parker snaked his other arm around Adam's back. He was Adam's family now. Was he enough?

"If Eric's alive, we'll do everything we can to find him. And hey, maybe there will be a cure. Our old pal Dr. Yamaguchi might pull it off."

They shared a sardonic smile, and Parker said, "Maybe. At least you're immune. I guess the werewolves will inherit the earth."

Shadows crossed Adam's face, his hazel-gold eyes unmistakably sad. "Doesn't seem like there will be many of us."

Parker had to grip the wheel with both hands as the wind gusted. He nudged Adam playfully with his hip, making his tone light. "You're sure there are no vampires or yetis out there? Abominable snowmen?"

A smile lifted Adam's lips. "Pretty sure. Although we'd better watch out for sirens luring us onto the rocks."

The radio hissed, and the same woman from that morning spoke again. "This is a message from Salvation Island."

"Speak of the fucking devil," Parker grumbled, flipping the volume completely off.

"Maybe we should hear what she has to say." Adam reached for the knob.

"Wind's changing. We've got to head up. Remember how I taught you to trim the sails in tighter? Can you go do it?"

After a moment's hesitation, Adam complied, and Parker pushed everything but the wind, the sails, and the wide-open sea from his mind.

"ARE YOU SURE I shouldn't come with you?" Parker paced across the stern as Adam lowered the dinghy into the choppy water. The day had dawned gray and blustery with a sudden dip in temperature, and Parker zipped up his hoodie, jamming his hands in the pockets. His bare feet and legs below his shorts were cold, but he didn't feel right wearing shoes on deck. It made him feel less connected to the boat somehow.

Adam wore his jeans, leather jacket, and sturdy boots. "I'm sure. If I have to worry about you, it'll take longer. There's no dock, and the tide isn't low enough to wheel out Mariah. There are definitely creepers here, and possibly uninfected too. I can't tell for sure at this distance. There's no sense in you taking any chances. I won't be long."

Parker squinted at the shore. They were just north of the Outer Banks of North Carolina. "See if you can get some water. Just
in case." The *Bella Luna* had a rainwater collection system that fed
into filtered storage tanks, but they could never have too much.
He passed Adam the collection of canvas tote bags they'd found
stashed in the kitchen.

"Will do. I'll be back soon. You have the gun?"

He nodded to the bench of the little seating area beyond the
boat's wheel. "Locked and loaded. I can't believe I just said that."

With a smile, Adam kissed him quickly. "I'll be back soon,
Dirty Harry."

Parker watched Adam pilot the dinghy to shore, the small
motor sounding incredibly loud. They'd anchored in the curve of
a natural harbor, and Parker looked left and right, peering into the
trees once Adam had disappeared. He could only see branches and
thinning leaves, yellow amongst the green.

After retying the sails, he waited and watched, shivering in the
wind and stubbornly refusing to go below deck for the scuffed
Topsiders he'd found under the bed, or at least a pair of socks. He
waited.

And waited.

And waited.

Pacing again, he scanned the trees restlessly, shivering in the
blustery morning. "Come back, come back, come back," he
muttered, wishing he had a watch so he'd know how long Adam
had been gone. It'd been at least an hour now, and Parker's
stomach knotted into another clove hitch. A slide show of horrible
things that could have happened to Adam tumbled through his
mind.

Adam was immune to the virus, but what if there were too
many creepers and he couldn't fight them off? Sure, he had super
werewolf strength, but what if there were hundreds and he got

trapped—and they overwhelmed him and actually tore him apart? What if he was hurt?

"I have to go find him," Parker muttered as he squinted into the distant trees. "But I need the bike. Have to wait for low tide. If he's not back in another hour, I'll…"

What? What the fuck am I going to do?

The wind whipped, flapping the sails, and Parker frowned. He'd tied them down, but—

Turning, his heart just about exploded right out of his chest at the sight of another sailboat—even bigger than the *Bella Luna,* probably sixty feet—closing in. It approached without the telltale hum of a motor, sails still up. Parker had only heard the luffing sails over the wind and choppy sea when the boat was practically on top of him. He'd been so focused on the shore he hadn't looked behind.

Stupid, stupid, stupid!

Two men pulled the sheets off their winches, and the boat jolted nearly to a stop. A younger woman around thirty stood on the bow, casually holding a shotgun, its muzzle pointed down. Parker's gaze darted to his pistol on the bench. It was a good three steps out of reach. He raised a hand in greeting, his frozen smile threatening to crack, pulse galloping. "Morning."

The other boat drifted right into *Bella*'s hull, rubbing up with a horrible screech. Parker spread his legs and kept his footing as the boat rocked and settled again. A short balding man smiled broadly, showing crooked teeth.

"Mornin'. You all alone out here, son?" A handgun stuck out from his waistband. He was small, but all coiled muscle.

Parker wanted to say no, but perhaps it was better for Adam to come as a surprise. As he nodded, he considered the odds again on going for his gun. There was no way. These people looked rough and tumble, as his mom would have said. A grizzled woman leaned against the wheel, chomping on gum and cracking it like gunfire.

Shorty smiled again. "Well, it's a good thing we came along and spotted ya. No one should be alone out here."

The younger woman of about thirty tucked a long lock of reddish hair behind her ear. She smiled, and Parker's knotted stomach flipped. "It's not safe," she said.

They seemed to be waiting for a response, so Parker scraped out, "I'm good," his throat suddenly full of gravel. "Don't need any help, but thanks. It's really nice of you guys to stop and check."

Shorty waved a hand magnanimously. "No bother at all. We've got to look out for each other, huh? Some scary shit going down."

"Yeah." Parker tasted bile, the numbness from his toes spreading up his legs. He wanted to glance back at shore to see if Adam had appeared, but he kept his gaze on Shorty.

Maybe they're not bad. Maybe they're just being neighborly. Maybe—

"We're going to have to go ahead and come aboard." Shorty managed to actually sound regretful. "Getting low on food, so we need to borrow yours. You don't mind, do you?"

The other man, paunchy and tall and built like a brick house, was idly chewing something that was probably tobacco. He leaned over and spat into the water. They all watched Parker, apparently waiting for another response. Parker could only shake his head.

Shorty launched himself over both railings and onto *Bella*'s deck in two efficient movements. "Thanks, son. This is real good of ya. Just to be sure, you ain't lying to us, are you? There's no one down below? Because we really don't want to hurt anyone. We just need a little help. You understand."

"It's just me." Parker was proud that his voice didn't tremble the way his knees did. "Go ahead. Take whatever you need."

The redhead and other man clambered on board without

Shorty's finesse. The redhead said, "Thanks, sugar."

Parker inched toward the bench. If he could just get the gun, maybe—

"Now let's not do anything stupid." Shorty strode over and scooped up the weapon.

Parker inhaled a wave of BO. None of them looked as though they'd cleaned themselves in days. He supposed it was apt considering they were basically pirates. They just needed eye patches and peg legs. And maybe a parrot.

"What's funny?" Shorty demanded.

"Nothing," Parker answered, his voice too high, hysterical laughter bubbling up in his throat, his pulse wild. He was going to piss himself.

Adam, where are you?

The pirates' boat rubbed up against the *Bella Luna* roughly as the wind whipped. They stared at him. Parker had no idea what they were waiting for.

The woman asked, "You packin' anything else?"

He shook his head. It was the truth, at least.

"Clothes off," Shorty ordered.

"I… What?" Parker's heart jumped all around, and his voice was practically a squeak.

"Take your clothes off so we know you ain't lyin' about what else you got on you." Shorty shook his head sadly. "Sorry to be suspicious, but we can't be too careful these days."

Willing his hands not to shake, Parker stripped off his hoodie and T-shirt. Humiliation burned his cheeks as he unzipped his shorts and kicked them free. He crossed his arms over his bare chest.

"Undies too," Shorty said regretfully. "Sorry. We want to trust you, but, well." He held up Parker's gun. "If you'd just been honest from the get-go…"

Choking down the urge to scream out the fear and fury ballooning in his chest, Parker tugged at his boxers. He kicked them free and stood there naked, their eyes crawling over his body like a thousand spiders. He kept his hands fisted at his sides, resisting the powerful urge to pathetically cover his privates.

"Don't worry, kid," the old woman called. "It's real cold out, so we won't judge too harsh." She guffawed, a hoarse wheeze that was likely the product of a pack a day.

As they all laughed, fresh shame flooded Parker from his head all the way to his toes. "What the fuck do you want? Just take the food and go!"

Shorty was suddenly in front of him with the gun raised. Pain exploded in the side of Parker's head. He cracked his knees on the deck, his vision fading from white bursts to black, then the worn wood swimming into focus again as he held himself up on his hands.

"Why'd you have to go and be so rude?" Shorty spat. "Here we are trying to be as nice as can be. Don't ruin it for everyone. You hear?"

On his shaking hands and knees, the pain in his head too much, Parker nodded. Something smacked hard against Parker's butt, echoing with a crack. A hand.

"That's a real sweet piece of ass you've got, so be a good fuckin' boy or we'll have to take a bite. You get me?" Shorty slapped Parker again, harder. The sting was nothing compared to the overwhelming ache in his head, burning and stealing his breath.

As they ransacked the boat, Parker could only curl onto his side on the deck, choking down bile and tasting the blood that dripped down from his temple. He wanted to cry for Adam like a pathetic fucking baby, and pitiful tears pricked at his eyes.

"See now? We only took what we needed. Fair's fair."

Parker realized Shorty was talking to him when the man nudged him with his foot.

Fuck you, you piece of shit. I wish you were dead. I wish Adam would come back and tear your head off your stupid little body.

He stayed silent while his mind screamed.

Shorty bent and slapped Parker's ass again. "You did like's you were told, so we'll be on our way. Happy trails."

The younger woman laughed. "You sure, Mick? We could have some fun with this cute little puppy. Bet he's good with that mouth."

Squeezing his eyes shut, Parker curled into a tighter ball, his heart frantic. He could see Mick's musty boots in front of him. The man leaned down, his stale, cigarette-stinking breath wafting over Parker's face. Parker didn't so much as breathe.

Just go. Please go. Leave me alone.

"Nah. Not sick of your mouth yet, sugar-tits."

The woman laughed, and there were wet sounds of kissing before the shuffle of feet. *Bella* rocked as they clambered back over the railing, the hulls groaning against each other. The other boat's engine started, and Parker forced himself to focus. His vision swam, but he made out the name as they powered away through the harbor and out to sea.

The Good Life

Parker's head thunked back on the deck. Shivering, he ordered himself to get up and put his clothes back on.

Up on your feet and be a man. You're fine. Get up.

He spat out blood, his eyes going unfocused. The boat bobbed in the tide, the wind not relenting. He was so cold. He had to move. Had to get up. Had to...had to...

Chapter Three

W*HERE'S PARKER?*

He wasn't standing on the deck watching as Adam steered the dinghy away from shore, leaving a group of infected splashing after him to their doom.

Nearing the boat, the hair on Adam's body stood on end as Parker didn't appear. A cold weight settled in his gut as he concentrated, reaching out with his senses so he could hear Parker's heartbeat. It was there, beyond the roar of the dinghy's motor, but it stuttered and jumped. Maybe he was napping and dreaming. Maybe it was nothing.

"Parker?" Adam dragged the loaded dinghy up onto its resting place in the hollow of the stern. He stood on the little lowered platform and knotted the rope the way Parker had taught him. Then a mess of scents wafted toward him with the breeze. It smelled like...

People.

His heart plummeting, Adam leapt up to the deck. For a moment, he could only stare in horror. Then he was at Parker's side on his knees, a helpless roar screaming through his mind. "Parker?" He touched the blood on Parker's temple and gingerly prodded as Parker opened his eyes.

Thank you, thank you, thank you.

"It's okay. I'm here. You're okay."

"I couldn't stop them." Parker started shivering so hard his teeth chattered, and for an awful moment Adam thought he was infected. But no, he was just freezing. He was naked and hurt and *someone did this.*

Adam could barely see through the red curtain of fury, his fangs and claws extending as a growl ripped from his throat. It took a few moments to regain control and let his human side take over again. He had to. Parker needed him.

Pushing all other thoughts aside, Adam scooped him into his arms and maneuvered him downstairs. It'd been trashed—the now-empty fridge standing open, the cupboards bare and their few belongings scattered. He brought Parker to their bed, placing him down gently and covering him with the duvet and an extra blanket.

The cries and splashing of the infected by the shore hadn't stopped. He hated leaving, but with a cautious stroke of Parker's hair, Adam dashed back upstairs and started the engines. If the tide went out too far, they'd be beached, and the creepers could easily jolt and stagger across the sand. There were no other boats in sight, and once they were out what he thought was a safe distance, Adam dropped the anchor again.

Fat splatters of rain fell, and the boat rocked in the white-capped waves. But the sky wasn't too dark, so he hoped for the best. The fresh supplies were still in the dinghy, and he quickly hauled them downstairs.

Parker was where Adam left him, curled into a ball beneath the blankets, his head barely showing. Adam yanked off his boots and climbed onto the bed, and Parker tensed, his breath catching on a gasp. Adam knelt beside him, wishing he knew the right thing to do or say.

"Parker?" He eased the blankets down. "Is it just your head? Can you hear me?"

"Cold," Parker whispered, trying to pull the blankets back up, his voice a hoarse rasp.

"I know. I'm sorry." Adam cautiously ran his hands up and

down Parker's limbs, trying to warm him and test for injuries at the same time. The rage simmered low in his gut as he saw the red marks on his backside and hip. "Did they touch you?"

Parker tried to pull the blankets up again. "Fine. I'm fine."

Adam couldn't see any signs of injury aside from the swelling wound on the side of Parker's head and the reddened skin on his ass. There were no other cuts or any blood, but it didn't mean they didn't hurt him. He could smell one person in particular, someone who'd gotten close to Parker.

Gotten on his skin.

He had to take a few deep breaths to calm himself before re-trieving the first aid kit, a Tupperware container the pirates had fortunately missed during their ransacking, which seemed to have been focused on food. Dabbing the antiseptic on the wound on Parker's temple, he tried to think of the best way to bandage it.

"Shower," Parker murmured. "I need a shower."

Adam was going to be sick, but he channeled the rage and guilt into action. He turned on the shower and stripped off his own clothes since he didn't think Parker could stand by himself. Both of them barely fit in the shower stall, and Adam held Parker so he was under the stream of hot water.

"Mmm." Lolling his head on Adam's shoulder, Parker clung to him. "Feels good. I was so cold."

They stood there until the hot water ran out, and Adam wrapped Parker in a terrycloth bathrobe Richard Foxe had kindly left behind. Back on the bed, he dressed the wound on Parker's head, kneeling beside him as Parker stretched on his back. The shower seemed to wake him up a bit. He winced as Adam dabbed on a bit more antiseptic.

"Do you know what your name is?" Adam asked.

Parker rolled his eyes—a good sign. "Luke Skywalker. That makes you Han Solo."

He pressed the bandage against the wound, glad to see it had stopped bleeding and didn't need stitches. "I'm trying to make sure you don't have a concussion."

"Oh, right. My name's Parker Osborne. Okay, let's see. It's November…eighth? Maybe ninth or tenth. I'm fine, Adam."

"What's your favorite movie?"

"*Shaun of the Dead*. The irony is not lost on me. And your favorite movie is *Almost Famous* for fiction, *Grey Gardens* for doc. The only thing I remember about the first one is the scene on the bus where they all sing that awesome old song, and I've never seen the second, much to your consternation." His eyes flickered, and he licked his lips, his voice fading. "As I've told you, I'd happily watch it if Netflix was still part of our lives."

Adam had to smile. "You'd love them both. They're—"

"Classics," Parker finished with him.

He caressed Parker's stubbly cheek and pressed a kiss to his dry lips. "Come on, stay awake." Awkwardly, he wound the bandage around Parker's head.

Parker grumbled. "It's not even bleeding anymore, is it?"

The bleeding had slowed, but it still trickled from the gash, and Adam wasn't taking any chances. "Just a little." He attempted an even tone. "What did they hit you with?"

After a few moments of silence, Parker sighed. "My gun. Took it too, probably. Hope they didn't find the other one down here."

"Who were they?" he asked quietly.

"Just people. Four of them—two men and two women. I was looking at the shore, and by the time I saw them coming in another boat, it was too late. They acted all friendly, but it was like this weird game we were playing. I knew they were going to fuck me up, and so did they." He shivered and fiddled with the bandage.

"Did they hurt you? Aside from this?" Adam motioned to Parker's head. Both their hearts pounded, and Adam hated himself so much for being gone too long.

"I'm tired."

"Parker…" Adam swallowed hard. "Did they do anything else? You can tell me." He thought of the faceless intruders, tearing into their throats while they screamed. Ripping their limbs off and sinking his claws into their guts.

Parker met his gaze. "They made me strip after I tried to get the gun. Hit me in the head. They threatened to…you know. But they didn't do it. The leader slapped my butt a few times. That's it."

Adam exhaled shakily, still longing to taste their blood. He cupped Parker's face. "I'm so sorry. I'm sorry I was gone that long."

"Where were you?" Parker sounded so much like a little boy in that moment. Adam wanted to cry and scream.

"I was helping a couple. Their car broke down." He thought of the guy and girl, still teenagers, and the smoking engine of their Ford Focus. He'd helped *them* while Parker needed him. He'd been leaning under the hood of their car with a wrench while Parker had been naked and alone.

"I'm so sorry," he repeated. "I should have been here."

"You didn't know. It's not your fault." Parker licked his dry lips. Adam grabbed a hard plastic cup from where it had rolled on the floor with other scattered kitchen utensils. He filled it with rainwater at the sink and helped Parker drink before dashing up on deck to scan the area.

It rained steadily, and the boat bobbed in the waves, but it didn't seem like a storm would hit. Eyes narrowed, he turned in a slow circle. The creepers on the shore in the far distance had gone or drowned. Closing his eyes, he listened. They were alone.

Back downstairs, he struggled with the lid of an Advil bottle he'd picked up in an abandoned corner store, forcing himself to be patient and push down the childproof cap. "Here." On the bed again, he held up Parker's head and helped him swallow the pills.

Settling back on the pillows, Parker said, "Thanks." He closed his eyes and attempted a smile. "Did you get more food and stuff? I think we're out."

"I found your favorite cookies. Are you hungry?"

His eyes flickered open. "Maybe later." He frowned. "Don't look like that. I'm fine."

Adam swallowed thickly before he could speak. "You were right. There are bad people out there. I shouldn't have left you."

"Creepers are bad too. Rock and a hard place. I know you would never want me to get hurt. You can't be here all the time. We need supplies. But we need to be careful. People suck."

Adam nodded, but... Did it have to be that way? There had to be good people left. Was it more dangerous on their own? If Salvation Island was real, maybe...

He couldn't stop the bloom of hope, fragile and small.

"*Hope for the best, expect the worst, and turn the stereo up to eleven.*"

As Tina's voice echoed in his mind, love and grief washed through him. She'd regularly texted him mish-mashed inspirational quotes that often featured an element from *Spinal Tap*.

That she was dead, he had little doubt. Maybe he was wrong and she'd somehow survived the bloodbath downtown in San Francisco, but it seemed impossible.

It was equally impossible that it had only been months ago they'd gone to their weekly movie, sitting in the back corner in almost-empty theaters and whispering commentary. She'd been the only person he'd ever told about being a wolf, until Parker.

He'd filmed countless hours of footage of her answering his questions with good humor, talking about her family and friends and the people she felt closest to, her short dark curls framing a round face.

"*What about you? You hide behind your camera and never talk about your family or your life. Your documentary's about 'found families,' but you don't really have any friends except yours truly. Sex hook-ups don't count. How are you supposed to connect with people if you're always looking through a lens?" She grinned straight into the camera, cheeks dimpled and eyes sparkling. "Hey, that was pretty deep, huh? That'll be an A-plus soundbite. You're welcome."*

It was lost now, all the video. His documentary. If by some miracle his apartment hadn't burned, the digital files on his hard drive were still there, useless to looters. Of course, they might as well be on the moon. He'd never return to California, not unless things changed hugely. The only way was forward.

And with his videos gone, as time passed, the tinkling echo of Tina's voice would fade, her dimples disappearing with the other little details that made her *her,* like a photograph bleached by sunlight. Like with his family, there would be little snatches of detail and memory, but overall, it would blur into an ache of affection and emptiness.

His hands flexed on Parker's arms, wanting to haul him close but stilling himself, mindful of his injuries.

"Can I take a nap?" Parker asked. "Weather doesn't look too bad?"

"We're good. Sleep. But I'm waking you up soon in case you have a concussion."

"Cool." He reached for Adam's hand with cold fingers. "I'm okay. Just glad you're back. Was worried." His eyes drifted shut.

What if these people had hurt Parker worse? Put a bullet in his head? What if Adam had returned to silence, no heartbeat or sweet laughter, only a body growing cold, flies swarming?

What if it is safe on that island? What if Parker could be safe?

Not able to utter a sound without howling, Adam leaned over and pressed a kiss to Parker's damp hair.

FEET BRACED ON the deck, Adam scanned the empty horizon. The sun was sinking, the sky clear for the moment but for a thin line of clouds. Orange tinged with pink streaked across, and it was a gorgeous shot, the light a perfect warmth. He slipped the camera from his pocket. It was pointless, filming all these little clips, but as he panned across, a few degrees of the tension in his neck eased.

The chill remained, clinging damply. As Parker's breathing hitched downstairs, Adam froze, waiting until it smoothed out again. He'd tuned his ears to monitor Parker like a radio station.

It'd been a day, and Parker was still in pain. Adam wanted to get his claws into the people who did this, but they were apparently long gone. He wondered if they'd been waiting, watching him go to shore. Watching him leave Parker alone. He thought he'd scanned the area thoroughly before he left, but maybe…

Or maybe they just came along and saw an opportunity, and the only thing Adam could have done differently was not leave Parker behind. He'd been thinking about the threat from creepers; about the fear that seized him every time one of them came too close to Parker, missing him by inches with their greedy hands and manic teeth.

The boat rolled on a wave. They were anchored in the same spot, bobbing around. Adam could probably unfurl the sails and guide them farther south, but would rather wait for Parker to take his usual place at the wheel, monitoring the wind and narrating his actions with a bunch of sailing jargon.

He did another scan, part of him relieved when it came up empty, the other half longing for some sign of life. A memory flickered through his mind.

"We have each other. We don't need anyone else." Adam's mother spoke firmly, but Maddie only huffed.

"But why? Where are the other wolves? Why don't you and Dad know any of them? Shouldn't we have cousins or something?"

Adam watched from the kitchen door as his older sisters dug in their heels. He wished they'd just leave it alone already and stop arguing and making everything tense. What was the big stupid deal? But Christine sat at the breakfast table, nodding vigorously as Maddie squared off with Mom.

"Because it's dangerous," Mom said. "We're better off on our own."

Christine gritted her teeth. "You still haven't said why."

Mom slammed down a carton of milk, splashing it over the counter. "Because we said so. Eat your breakfast."

Heart thumping, Adam took his seat, spilling Rice Krispies onto the table as he poured them into his bowl. A few skittered to the floor, and he bent to snatch them up in the heavy silence. When he straightened, Mom ran a hand over his hair and pressed a kiss to his forehead.

"Do you need any money for the museum trip, hon?"

He shook his head, but his sisters still rolled their eyes. When Mom turned to the fridge, Maddie mouthed, "Sucky baby."

Now he'd give anything to know the answer as to why his parents had isolated them from other wolves. He knew they must have had a good reason, but if he'd had someone after they died, someone who understood…

The boat rocked with another set of waves. It didn't matter now anyway. He had Parker, and Parker was everything.

"Join us as we build a new home."

The voice from Salvation Island echoed in him, deep and persistent. It truly was like a siren's song, drawing him in despite his own skepticism and Parker's dogged resistance. And look at what had happened, what other people had done. Still, the thought of a *home* tugged.

Parker's heart rate increased, and Adam got downstairs as he woke with a gasp. "Hey, hey." Adam crawled on the bed and reached out, his hand hovering uncertainly. "It's okay."

Blinking, Parker pushed himself up to sitting. "Had a stupid dream." Scratching at this chest, he wore only his boxers. The bandage around his head had come precariously loose.

Adam sat there with his hands gripped together in his lap, not knowing what to do. "Everything's okay."

"Yeah. I'm fine." He grimaced. "Sleeping too much. I feel gross."

"Headache? Do you want more Advil?"

"I guess." Parker pulled off the bandage and tilted his head. "How's it look?"

Like if he'd hit you a little harder you might never have woken up.

"Okay," Adam lied. It was healing, but seeing how the skin at Parker's temple had bruised a deep purple was anything but *okay*.

"Maybe I'll have a few cookies." Parker rolled up onto his knees.

"I'll get them. You rest."

With a little huff, he crawled off the bed. "I need to piss anyway. I can manage ten steps."

"I can—"

"What? Carry me?" Rolling his eyes, he shuffled to the toilet while Adam waited uselessly.

A few minutes later, Parker sat on one of the long benches in the saloon and munched a cookie. He held out the box, and Adam took one even though the peanut butter tasted like chalk in his dry throat.

"So, we should move in the morning. I feel better." He peered across at the green radar screen. "Seen anything out there?"

"In the distance, another boat. But that was this morning. Miles away and gone now."

It could have been them. I should have followed. Chased.

Parker chewed another cookie. "Heard anything?"

Adam considered saying no, but told the truth. "Another message from Salvation Island. Similar to before."

"Persistent. They're really trying to lure people in."

"Or help people."

"I don't think anyone wants to help anymore," Parker muttered, his gaze skittering away.

Adam thought about shutting the hood on the Ford Focus, the tears in the young woman's eyes as she clutched his hand, she and her boyfriend thanking him desperately.

"I mean—" Parker's nostrils flared. "Those fuckers acted like they were doing me a favor. Should have seen them coming." Shoulders hunched, he shrugged unconvincingly. "Whatever. It's over." He went to the table and the charts. "Let's plan out our route. Time to get serious about a plan. Winter's closing in. Did you get any fuel yesterday? Those assholes took our extra, right?"

Adam joined him at the table. "They did. And no. The station was dry. We'll have to get some in the next day or two." That meant going ashore. His gut churned. He wouldn't leave Parker behind again, but what if there was trouble on land?

Parker consulted a chart. He simply said, "Okay," as though it was no big deal, but Adam could hear his heart jumping.

He wanted to pull him close, but wasn't sure it was the right thing to do. He wanted to kiss Parker and take him to bed, lay him out and hold him. He knew the headache wasn't gone—in fact another wave was probably hitting now judging by the way Parker rubbed the back of his neck. Adam would just make it worse.

He tried to breathe deeply, but could only take in shallow gulps, images of finding Parker dead on *Bella*'s deck sabotaging his mind. Eyes glassy, chest not moving. That kind, loving, suspicious, maddening, beautiful soul just *gone*. Blood heavy in the air...

Dripping onto him, soaking into his skin where he was trapped in the back of the car. The four heartbeats that made up his entire world now silent.

Adam inhaled deeply, hoping the salt air could scrub away the sense memory. No, he couldn't leave Parker alone again, even with the threat on land. But what if... What if they didn't have to scavenge? If they could find a place to make a home somewhere down south, they could grow plants. Maybe even find livestock. Thrive instead of just survive.

What if it was like that on Salvation Island?

After a minute, Parker lifted his head with a frown. "What?"

Blinking, Adam said, "Huh?"

With a huff of impatience, Parker dropped his pencil. "I can feel your eyes boring into me. What's up?"

"Nothing." He stood. "I'll do a scan."

"Cool," Parker muttered. The purple bruise on his temple was a shadow over his face as he bent his head again.

On deck in the falling darkness, Adam looked and listened. With his night vision and the binoculars, he could see for miles. They were still alone, but the air was heavy. As he paced around, his hair bristled, but the horizon remained empty.

THEY DIDN'T GET very far in the morning before the wind that had been moving them along at a nice clip suddenly blustered, the boat leaning on a frighteningly sharp angle. Adam gripped the railing, waiting for Parker to shout instructions. The gunmetal sky unleashed rain, and the sails flapped alarmingly.

"We have to find a harbor!" Parker shouted, then said something about reefing Adam didn't understand. "Take the wheel!"

He did, and Parker pointed to the right. "Keep it going in that direction."

Parker leapt about, untying knots and bracing his bare feet on the slanting deck. He expertly tugged and the sails got much smaller. The boat lurched upright, the boom swinging around.

But Parker ducked before Adam could even call out a warning, and he continued his work, his T-shirt and jeans soaked.

He opened one of the seats and yanked out orange life vests, zipping his up securely before tossing Adam the other. After tying a rope around his waist, he yelled some more, and Adam turned the wheel as he was told.

Unlike the week before when they'd anchored in a harbor and holed up in the cabin, fucking to pass the time and feeling safe in their cocoon, Adam was most definitely not enjoying a moment of this. Salt stung his eyes, and it got darker as the wind grew stronger. The sky churned, a dense gray, and the boat rocked like a toy.

Even with his enhanced vision, he could barely make out land, though they were getting closer. Parker scurried about, doing things with the ropes and rigging, his feet slipping in the torrent of rain. Unafraid and in control, Parker's eyes snapped intelligently, his lips thinned, and he moved without hesitation, strong and capable.

Pride warmed Adam's chest at the sight of him in his element. He clutched the slick wheel as they rode over a too-big wave. Then someone was talking, and it took a few seconds to realize the voice wasn't Parker's. Adam stared dumbly at the radio as a man's voice rang out.

"Mayday, mayday! Please help! Is anyone out there?"

Parker tied a knot with quick hands, then skidded over the deck and stared at the console. The voice cut sharply through the downpour and the whipping wind.

"We're taking on water. Mayday! Is anyone listening? Help!"

Adam's pulse raced. "Do you recognize the voice? Is it one of them?"

Staring at the radio as if he could read the answer, Parker wiped water from his eyes. The boat pitched and rolled with another set of waves, and they held on. "I don't think so." He met

Adam's gaze. "But we can't help anyone. We have to find shelter or we'll be in our own trouble." He blinked. "Why aren't you tied on? Didn't you hear me?" He tore off the lid of one of the seats and yanked out an orange rope that he looped around Adam's waist.

"You said a bunch of stuff!" Adam held the wheel and let Parker do his thing, securing him to the boat. The speed with which he tied complex knots was dizzying. Adam stared at the radio, his fingers itching to pick up the transmitter and offer help. He knew they had to take care of themselves, but sick dread sank through him at the thought of ignoring the call.

The radio blared again. "We're south of Cape Hatteras. Please help!"

Adam shouted, "Are we close?"

Parker slid into him and steadied himself as another set of waves rocked them. He leaned down and inspected the radar screen, gnawing on his lower lip. "Yes, but... Fuck, we can't. What if it's a trap? What if—"

"Is anyone listening? We'll give you food and fuel! We'll give you anything! Please just help!"

In the background, another voice cried out, "*Daddy!*"

The young girl's voice sent a shiver down Adam's spine, and he and Parker looked at each other. Parker grabbed the transmitter.

"Hold on—we're coming."

Chapter Four

A T THE HELM, Parker squinted at the compass, shaking icy water from his eyes. The temperature had plummeted, and his fingers were numb on the metal wheel.

The boat in alleged trouble was fortunately near Hatteras Island, but Parker wasn't sure they'd make it in time. His chest felt hollow, his heart clanging around, adrenaline giving his stiff limbs energy. The pistol Shorty and his pirates had missed, hidden in the bedroom, now pressed into the small of Parker's back, the steel cold.

Whatever happened, he'd be ready this time.

Wind and salt scoured his face ruthlessly as the girl's cry for her father echoed through his mind. A memory thrashed to the surface.

The water churned around him, his lungs burning as he kicked desperately. He'd always been afraid to open his eyes underwater since Eric had told him about fish that ate your eyeballs. But he opened them now, searching for safety and seeing only blackness.

The hands that grabbed him were strong, and when he gasped in air and rain, held afloat by his father, he felt loved, even when Dad screamed at him for not wearing his life jacket.

He couldn't leave a little girl to drown, but...

Shuddering, he flinched as if Shorty was there again, his palm cracking down on Parker's bare flesh. Shorty or anyone else could be out there, wanting to hurt them. Waiting. Using a kid to do it.

It would be a risky trap to set given the storm, but it wasn't out of the question.

But what if the kid was a prisoner?

He glanced at Adam, who peered anxiously off the starboard side. He'd never know if *Bella* changed course. Parker could tell him the boat must have sunk, and they could stay safe, just the two of them. It wouldn't even necessarily be a lie given the ferocity of the growing waves…

In that moment, Parker hated himself possibly more than he ever had in his life, and that was saying something.

"There!" Adam pointed into the swirling gray.

He pushed his horrible thoughts away. He wasn't going to trust anyone, but he wasn't going to become a sociopath either. "Take the wheel!"

After cranking the winch and bringing down the sails completely, Parker peered at the dangerously listing boat to starboard. He cursed these people for still having the sails up and luffing wildly, flapping in the howling wind, then shouted for Adam to turn on the engine, giving them as much control as possible as they neared. The boat was smaller—twenty feet long, and it was going to capsize any fucking second.

Scanning the frothing sea, Parker searched for survivors, running through the emergency checklist in his head. There was a flash of orange and blond hair before a wave swallowed it. Muffled shouts echoed dully, and he spotted a man and boy braced on the tilting deck. No sign of a little girl.

"Adam! Cut the engine! There's someone in the water. Throw them the life ring!"

Parker's frozen fingers barely cooperated, but he finally got the knot around his waist undone. Down in the dinghy, it took three desperate yanks to get enough juice to the outboard motor. It was thirty feet to the crippled boat, and he spit out saltwater, practically blind in the relentless rain but trying to spot anyone else in the waves.

"Parker! Come back!" Adam's shout was nearly lost in the wind.

Parker ignored him, because if they were going to risk everything to save these people, he was going to save the hell out of them. They were clearly clueless, and if this was a trap, they'd be sorry.

He pulled up alongside, relief flickering through him as he got a good look at the man: tall and slim, African-American. No one from *The Good Life*. Parker called out, "Uncleat the main and jib!"

The man looked up from a tangle of lines and shouted, "What?" He and the boy were braced on the side of the cabin, the boat tilted and close to capsizing. They were wearing life jackets, at least.

After choking down a surge of irritation that they'd even be at sea, Parker yelled, "Come on! Get in." The sails flapped violently overhead, the mast leaning out at an unnatural angle.

The man nodded and held the boy's arm as the kid tried to walk down the sloping deck without tumbling.

"Get on your butt!" Parker shouted.

The boy, a skinny white kid around thirteen, did as instructed and slid the rest of the way before climbing over the railing. He blinked down at Parker from about ten feet up, gripping the rail, his dark hair in his eyes.

"It's too far!" The boy had one leg over the rail.

"I won't let you fall!" Parker attempted to sound as reassuring as possible.

"Get in the boat!" A woman's voice reached them through the roiling thunder of rain, and Parker spotted the blonde who'd been in the water now stumbling on *Bella*'s deck, Adam at her side. "Jacob! Do it!"

The man was suddenly there, crashing into the railing, taking the impact with his legs. An African-American girl of about eight was wrapped around him. After a suspended moment, Jacob lost his balance, plummeting into the dinghy and bouncing half out. Parker hauled him back and reached up for the girl, who shrieked as her father dangled her over the side.

The mast creaked ominously.

"Let go!" Parker stood and grabbed her calves, his muscles screaming as he tried to keep his balance in the roiling sea. "I've got her!"

Well, he barely had her, but he managed to break her fall and stay in the dinghy, so that was a win. After thrusting her at Jacob, he said, "It's okay. You're okay." He shouted up, "Throw me a rope!"

Parker could hear Adam shouting his name, but he ignored him as he heaved himself up and clambered over the railing. "Get in the dinghy! I've got this." Parker threw himself up the deck toward the winch. He glanced back to see the man still at the railing. "Go!"

He wasn't going to let this boat capsize completely, or worse, turtle and flip upside down. He'd just finished uncleating the sheets and releasing the boom vang when Adam appeared beside him, his golden eyes glowing and fingers digging into Parker's shoulders, claws scraping.

"What the hell are you doing?" Panting, Adam gave Parker a shake. Then he blinked and looked at his hands, stepping back quickly and letting his arms fall.

"What the hell are *you* doing? You swam over? You left those people alone on *Bella*? Jesus fucking Christ!" Blood rushed in Parker's ears as he squinted through the rain. But the people seemed to only be waiting on the deck, watching them.

"They're fine, Parker. They're just a family who needs help."

"No one is just anything anymore! You'd better hope you're right." He turned back to the sails.

"What are you doing? This boat is sinking!"

"Not on my fucking watch." There wasn't much left in the world he could fix.

"This is no time for your stubborn routine!"

"You want to help? Go stand on the centerboard. We're going to lever this baby back upright." He turned to point, but Adam was already climbing up the deck on all fours, and before Parker could do anything else, he was over the other side and pulling. With a groan of wood and fiberglass, the boat came level, Parker holding on to the rigging as it righted. "Or you could just use your freaky werewolf strength. Good call," he muttered.

They were close enough to land to drop anchor, and Parker rushed about, battening down as much as he could and turning on the pumps to drain any water below deck. Hopefully she would withstand the storm. He seemed to be the only one with sailing experience, so she'd have to wait it out alone.

Adam hoisted himself back onto the deck. "What now?"

"We get back to *Bella*. Use the engine and reach land. There has to be some cove or harbor nearby."

The man had returned in the dinghy, and they clambered on from the stern. Parker coughed as another wave drenched them. The abandoned boat rocked in the tumult, but wasn't in any immediate danger in Parker's estimation. If the storm got any bigger, that could change.

When they were back on board and he was behind the wheel, Parker checked his nav instruments and adjusted course. It would burn fuel to keep the sails completely down, but they needed to get to shelter.

"Thank you so much. We're so grateful." The man's voice was suddenly close by, and Parker jumped, whirling around. The man added, "My god, it seemed to come out of nowhere!"

"Stand back!" Parker barked, concentrating on the outline of land getting closer and closer in the gray, the gun still securely tucked into his jeans a reassuring weight. Had to get out of the wind…

There was a commotion and several cries, and Adam was suddenly there. Parker blinked at him and then looked down at the man sprawled on the deck on his ass. It took a moment to process that Adam had apparently come to his defense and shoved the man away.

The woman and kids clung together nearby with wide eyes. Tension rolled off Adam in waves, a growl low in his throat.

Parker gripped Adam's arm. "I'm fine." Adam was a breath away from showing his fangs.

"I just wanted to say thank you." The man held up his hands defensively. "I'm sorry."

Parker cleared his throat. "It's okay. Everything's fine. We're all good. Let's just get out of this storm."

He hoped there wasn't another one brewing.

THE COVE WOULD have to do. Parker had sailed them around to the other side of an island off the main coast, where the rain still pummeled them but at least they were protected from the crashing waves. If his calculations were correct, they'd reached an animal refuge. He couldn't see any other signs of life but asked Adam to make sure. Not that they had many options on where else to wait out the storm.

Adam did his Terminator thing, scanning in each direction with a look of intense concentration, then gave Parker a thumbs up. The newcomers huddled in the little seating area beyond the wheel. After dropping anchor and cutting the engine, *Bella* rocked from side to side.

Parker kept his voice even. He had to act normal. The people were probably fine. And if they had something planned, he was ready for them. Not to mention the fact that Adam could shred them in a heartbeat.

"Let's get below deck," Parker called. "Wait this thing out."

The little girl stumbled by the steps, and Parker reached out automatically to take her arm. She looked up at him and then promptly doubled over, puking on his bare feet.

The man surged forward and scooped her up. "Lilly!" To Parker, he added, "Oh god, I'm so sorry."

"It's okay. In seas this rough even the saltiest sailors can end up feeding the fishes." Parker tried to smile at the kid.

Her father froze. "Sleeping with the fishes?"

He raised his voice in the storm's din. "No, *feeding* them. Puking over the side."

The man's smile was tense. "Ah. Right."

The visitors hurried into the hatch while Parker climbed down to the dinghy platform and rinsed his feet. When he came back up, Adam waited.

"You okay?" He watched Parker carefully. *Too* carefully.

Shoving away a burst of irritation, Parker forced a light tone. He wasn't going to cry over puke for fuck's sake. "Yeah, of course. What self-respecting college student can't deal with a little vomit? Not that I'm a college student anymore, since I guess college doesn't exist. But whatever, it's fine."

"No, I mean…" Adam shook his head, shoving his hands in his pockets. "Well, they seem okay to me."

"Yeah. We'll see. So far, so good."

They shuffled down to the saloon, Parker sealing the hatch behind them. The visitors sat in a single row along one padded bench, still wearing their life jackets. Lilly's was too big, cinched with a belt that had to be her father's. Adam unzipped his, but Parker shook his head. "We should all keep our jackets on until this is over. You never know."

Although it was morning, the light coming through the long portholes and the square skylights above the saloon was murky at best. Parker flipped on a lamp, but then thought better of it and switched it off. "Just in case there are any infected on the island. They're attracted to light."

The woman nodded. "We discovered that. We were holed up with some other folks in a cabin. It... It was a bad night."

Eyeing the transparent plastic openings, Parker mused, "We should cover them up at night all the time, actually. Don't want to attract other people either." He thought of Shorty and how far light could be seen out on the water.

He sat stiffly on the bench across from their guests, who perched uneasily on the banquette. After standing for a few moments and probably doing another silent werewolf radar sweep, Adam joined him.

Everyone was soaked to the skin in T-shirts and casual clothes, and Parker clenched and unclenched his fingers into fists, trying to get some feeling back. He'd need his hands to be functional if things went south. The gun pressed uncomfortably into the bottom of his spine, but he didn't shift it.

The man half stood, Lilly clinging to his side as if he'd disappear. He extended his hand. "I'm Craig Washington. This is my daughter, Lilly, and Abigail Lowenstein and her son, Jacob."

Adam extended his hand and introduced himself, and Parker reluctantly did the same.

The woman stood and leaned across to offer her hand. "Call me Abby. We can't thank you enough." Her blonde hair was plastered to her head, escaping a ponytail, a couple inches of darker roots by her scalp.

She and Craig both looked to be in their late thirties, and when she smiled, her round face exuded warmth in a way that made Parker think of his mother in certain moments, like early Sundays when she didn't blow out her hair and strap on her pearls. Abby's pale cheeks were wind-burned red. She nudged Jacob with her elbow.

Jacob stood and solemnly shook their hands, his hand thin and grip tentative. Knobby knees stuck out of his shorts, and his skin had gone red too. Lilly curled into her father's side, her face tucked into her too-big life jacket, her curly hair pulled into a tight bun and socked feet tucked up under her on the bench. She shivered, her father rubbing her bare arm steadily.

After they all stared at each other for a few moments, Adam cleared his throat. "I'm sorry about what happened on deck. I got carried away. All that adrenaline. It won't happen again."

"He's overprotective," Parker added with an attempted smile.

Oh god, please let this storm end.

The agony of small talk combined with suspicion and fear. It was the actual worst.

Craig held up his hands. "No need to apologize. I shouldn't have startled Parker. Don't distract the driver, right? That's what my dad always said."

Silence descended again, aside from the sweeping rain on the skylights and Jacob tapping a staccato rhythm on the floor with his foot. Abby stilled his leg with a hand on his knee.

"Um, do you want something hot?" Parker asked. "There's a machine. We have hot choc—" Remembering the bared cupboards after the pirates' visit, he flushed. "Sorry, we ran out, actually."

"There's coffee," Adam said quietly. "I picked some up."

"That would be wonderful," Abby said, and Craig nodded.

While the fancy coffee machine built into the counter brewed, Parker settled back down on the bench. "So, um, how did you end up on a boat?" As much as he loathed small talk, the silence was worse.

Craig answered, "We came east from Winston-Salem. First we thought we'd try for DC. Figured things might be better there." He grimaced. "Turned out it was the worst hit, so we went for the coast. Don't know much about boats, as I guess you're well aware.

But we thought maybe... Thought it would be better since the infected can't seem to swim." He sighed. "Thank you again. I really didn't think anyone would answer the radio. At least not anybody who actually wanted to help."

That he'd considered ignoring their distress call made Parker shift uneasily, guilt and shame battling for supremacy, his face going hot. Thank God he hadn't let fear overwhelm him.

He shrugged, going for casual and probably hitting on convulsive. "We weren't too far away, so. It's no problem." It was a massive problem for various reasons, but they were stuck together for the time being.

It was too quiet while the coffee dripped. Parker tried to relax, but there were strangers on his boat, and no matter how harmless they seemed... Nope. No relaxing. He cast about for another question, since he'd never been able to handle silence. "Did you guys meet on the road, or did you know each other before?"

Craig and Abby shared a tired smile, and she replied, "Well, we were just finishing up our third date when the world went to hell in a handbasket. And I guess the rest is history. How about you two? Did you know each other before?"

Parker couldn't help but smile. "Yeah. We'd just met, but we couldn't stand each other. We got over it. Now he's crazy about me. And I guess he's okay." Beside him, Adam snorted softly.

"So, you're a couple?" Craig asked.

Tension zapped back into Parker's limbs. "We are," he bit out. "If that's a problem—"

"No, no." Craig shook his head. "Not at all."

"Of course not," Abby added with what appeared to be a genuine smile. She glanced at Jacob, who jerked his head down.

Parker frowned. "Anyway, amazing how everyone dying or turning into bloodthirsty creepers puts shit in perspective." He glanced at Lilly. "Um, stuff, I mean."

"Creepers," Jacob echoed. He wrapped his arms around his

middle, and now he stared at Parker intensely with dark eyes. A few red pimples dotted his chin and forehead. "Do you know what's wrong with them?"

"It's apparently a virus." Parker shrugged. "Some people say it was engineered by religious nuts. But we don't know for sure."

"Hard to know anything these days." Craig tried to smile. "Never thought I'd miss those darn twenty-four-hour news channels."

The coffee machine's chime filled the air, and Parker leapt up to pour it into mugs. He got water for the kids and opened the box of cookies as well. They passed it around, sipping and chewing and sharing rumors they'd heard on the radio and from other survivors.

"What happened here?" Abby asked, indicating the side of her head and nodding at Parker.

Adam went rigid beside him, and Parker tried to calm the sudden skipping of his heart. "Had a little run-in with some modern-day pirates the other day. Word of warning: If you see a boat called *The Good Life*? Give it a wide berth. They stole most of our supplies, but I'm fine. Adam was on land stocking up." He held up a cookie. "Good thing, huh?"

Shoving it in his mouth, he chewed. Everything was fine. He was *fine*. Yes, his head still dully ached, but he'd hardly noticed it once the storm had set in.

As for the rest of what happened, he was a big boy. He wasn't going to let it get to him. Besides, nothing had really *happened*. It was stupid that his skin itched, and he imagined he could still feel that asshole's grimy hand on him.

"I'm so sorry." Abby's face creased sympathetically. "How awful. We've come across a few unsavory characters, but we've been lucky."

"We were thinking of trying for this Salvation Island. Have you heard their messages?" Craig asked.

The cookie was like a stone traveling down Parker's digestive system. "We're not going near it." Adam was a wall of tension beside him, and Parker could almost hear the *"But maybe..."* in Adam's head.

"Oh, have you heard something bad about it?" Craig's brows rose. "Please tell us."

Adam cleared his throat. "We've only heard the messages they've sent out. Parker's just cautious."

Parker ground his molars together, trying to keep the flash of irritation contained before it sparked into more. "I think we just covered why I'm being *cautious.*"

Don't act like I'm paranoid out of the blue.

He hoped he got that message across with his glare.

Eyes soft, Adam nodded. "You're right. We're both cautious, with good reason."

"It's stupid to drop our guard." Parker motioned across the saloon. "I'm sure Craig and Abby agree."

In the awkward silence, Craig said, "Right." He took a sip of his coffee. "I admit it does sound a little too good to be true."

"Yes! Exactly." Parker nodded vigorously. "Too good to be true. They're probably canni—" He broke off as Lilly's eyes widened. "Um, just... Probably not the nicest people."

Abby shared a glance with Craig, who held Lilly closer. Abby said, "I suppose we hadn't thought enough about it. Want to hope for the best, you know? You really think these people are up to no good?"

Parker said, "I don't know for sure, but I don't think it's worth the risk. Sounds like a trap."

"Then there's the fact that we barely know enough about sailing to get out of the harbor," Craig said. "The darn ropes for the sails got all tangled. Even before the storm hit, we were out of our league. You seem to know a lot, Parker."

Grateful for the change of subject even if it was more small talk, he said, "I know a fair amount. I sailed most summers growing up. Cape Cod."

"You must be rich," Jacob muttered.

"*Jacob*. Don't be rude." Abby smiled at Parker. "That sounds lovely."

"Yeah. It was pretty great. And yes, my parents were totally rich. I was rich. I was really lucky. We had our own boat and a house on the Cape."

A sudden pang of longing for Eric and their parents drove the air from Parker's lungs. Snatches of memories invaded his mind:

On the boat, barely rocking on a perfect summer's day with the sky so blue, Mom declared it "officially cerulean."

Getting his picture taken with a guy in a lobster suit at a clambake.

Falling asleep on Eric's shoulder in the back seat driving home from the marina, his skin tight with salt and sun.

"Are they dead?" Jacob asked flatly.

Nostrils flaring, Abby stared at her son. "*Jacob.*"

"It's okay." Parker met Jacob's baldly curious gaze. "Yeah, I think they are. My parents, I mean. Hoping my brother's still alive. Eric. He was in London. Have you heard anything about London?"

Abby and Craig shook their heads. Craig said, "We've only heard that Europe is overrun. So densely populated..."

Jacob pulled apart one of the sandwich cookies. "Have you heard anything about San Francisco?"

Abby sighed. "Honey..."

"We were there, actually," Parker answered.

Jacob's spine straightened, and he grew a few inches taller, his gaze sharp. "You were? Where? Downtown? Oakland?"

"Palo Alto. We were at Stanford. But the whole Bay Area was hit hard. It was a really bad scene."

Jacob licked his lips. "If we went there, do you think—"

"We're not going there," Abby interrupted. She wrapped her

arm around Jacob's shoulder. "Baby, there's no way we can make it all the way back across the country. We barely got to the coast. Even if we did, I don't see how we'd ever find him."

After shaking off his mother's arm, Jacob sprang to his feet and made for the hatch. "I need some air."

"It's not safe! Sit back down." Abby jumped up after him.

"I'll go with him," Adam offered.

Abby hesitated as Jacob disappeared up on deck, looking between the steps and Adam.

"I could use some air too," Adam added. "But if you'd rather…"

Craig said, "It'll be good for him to talk to someone else. Get another perspective."

She contemplated it for a few moments before nodding and sitting back down, her fingers entwining with Craig's. "Okay. Thank you."

Parker opened his mouth, and Adam rested a gentle hand on his knee. "Yes, I'll make sure we're both tied to a safety line." He looked at Parker intensely. "You're okay down here?"

"We're fine. Go impart some wisdom."

Adam followed Jacob up onto the deck and closed the hatch after them. Parker smiled wanly at Abby. "Don't worry. Adam won't let anything happen to him. I'm sure the storm will ease off soon." As if to call him a liar, a fresh gust of rain splattered the skylights.

Abby scrubbed at her face. "I'm sorry about that. His father lives in Oakland. Well, he did." She laughed humorlessly, whispering, "Son of a bitch left us years ago and moved out there with his new girlfriend. Had a couple kids Jacob's never even met. But now he's obsessed with the idea of finding his father. That bastard wasn't worth it before, and he sure as hell isn't now."

She glanced at Lilly as if she'd forgotten she was there and ran a hand over the girl's shoulder, wincing at Craig. "Sorry, sweetheart."

Lilly's voice was muffled by her life jacket where she slouched against her father. "S'okay. I think Jacob's dad's a jerkface too."

As Craig chuckled and pressed a kiss to his daughter's head, Parker wondered where Lilly's mother was. He resisted the urge to ask, just barely. "You guys definitely don't want to try to go cross-country. We made it, but it sure wasn't easy."

"I bet." Abby smiled ruefully. "I just wish we knew where we could go. Seems like we can't go back, but the road forward's not looking so hot either."

In the silence, they all stared at each other, Lilly's dark eyes examining Parker over the edge of the life jacket. He wondered what Jacob and Adam were talking about on the deck.

He cleared his throat. "Well, we can drop you off on land if your boat's not there after the storm. I'm sure you can find a car."

"Thank you." Craig's smile was strained. "We'd appreciate that."

They all jumped when the radio burst to life with a hiss of static. Parker realized he'd turned up the volume earlier.

"This is Salvation Island. We have medicine and food. It is safe here."

As the woman gave her spiel, Parker fidgeted under Lilly's steady gaze. In the silence that followed, he muttered, "Maybe we can help you find a car. But then we have to be on our way."

"Of course," Abby said. "We're grateful for anything you can do to help. You already saved our lives, and we don't expect anything else."

Parker shoved another cookie in his mouth, trying to savor the creamy peanut butter and ignore the spiral of guilt in his gut and cold steel pressing into his back.

Chapter Five

"YOU'RE SUPPOSED TO be sleeping." Adam didn't need to turn from his spot on the bow to see Parker walking up behind him.

He could smell him, yes, but it was like he could sense him approaching with his whole body, the hair on his arms rising in greeting, his skin singing and a primal awareness filling him. The closest thing he'd experienced to it had been the family bond he'd shared with his parents and sisters, but this was different.

With his hands in the big pocket of his sweatshirt, Parker shrugged, standing beside Adam. "They're crashed out in our bed. Wanted to stay close together, so I said we'd take the other cabin. In the morning, we can go back to their boat. Hopefully it's still there." He tipped his head back. "Can see the stars. Looks like this system has passed by."

It'd stopped raining some hours before, although the air remained damp, the deck still slick under Adam's boots. "Aren't your feet cold?"

Parker traced a wooden seam with his big toe. "Not really."

Adam was struck by a memory of ice, of an endless Minnesota winter and a cabin for the weekend. His parents had transformed into full wolf form and bounded through the snow across the frozen lake while he and his sisters had chased behind, the girls demanding to know when they'd be taught the secrets of changing. Adam had wanted to know too, but was mostly just happy to be together and free, miles from anyone and able to be themselves.

In the cabin after, his parents had sat by the fire with their toes peeking out of a tangle of blankets, Adam and his sisters curled up close by, all heartbeats and warmth.

Now, he could hear the breathing of the family down below, could sense their heartbeats and heat huddled together, their thin whispers of hope piercing the fear and worry growing stronger with each moment that passed in safety. Each moment that passed together.

He scanned the dark hulk of the island. He could see clearly through the trees, and there were no creepers or other people. It was peaceful, the boat rocking gently every so often, the wind calm. The soft, steady breathing downstairs echoing beneath his feet, strengthening his own.

"It's nice, isn't it?" Adam asked. "Having them here."

Parker's brow was creased so often he'd likely get wrinkles there eventually.

If he lives that long.

Adam reached out and ran his hand over Parker's head, needing to touch. Maybe he could film him later, get him talking for the camera. But he sensed Parker wasn't in the right mood at the moment.

Parker answered, "It's—I don't know." He shivered. "It's okay. For now. I mean…" He rolled his neck restlessly, his hands still jammed in his pockets. "What do we do about them?"

Adam watched the trees. "They seem good. Useful that Abby was a paramedic."

"It is. Too bad Craig was a PR manager. Don't think we'll need press releases or image consulting."

Chuckling tentatively, Adam said, "Probably not. But they do seem trustworthy. Don't you think?"

"They do. Although we've been fooled before."

Thoughts jumbled through Adam's head: Ramon's gleaming smile, waking strapped down and helpless, clinging to Parker on

Mariah. He shouldn't have trusted Ramon, but he still ached at the loss of knowing another werewolf. It had been so many years, and for so long he'd shoved it away and told himself he couldn't have it.

Then he'd met Parker, and that was something he hadn't thought he could have either: a lover and partner, someone who filled the cracks in him, someone who was more than a one-time fuck. And now these other people were with them—this *family*, holding each other close and safe, and if Adam could have a partner, maybe he could have a pack too. If they went to that island...

Then more images invaded: Parker naked and hurt, bleeding and alone. The helplessness Adam had felt washed over him anew.

"What?"

Adam realized he was staring at Parker and the shadowy bruise on his temple. "Nothing."

Exhaling with a frown, Parker looked at Adam for another few moments before picking up one of the ropes that lined the side of the boat and wrapping it around his fingers. "They seem like decent people. We can take them back to their boat tomorrow to see if it's still there. Get their stuff. But then what? I told them we could drop them off on land. They don't even know what trimming the jib means. Even you know that now. They'll be dead in the water."

"You could teach them."

"I guess." Parker unwound the rope and started again, wrapping his fingers tightly. "Could give them a crash course and then go our separate ways. Hurricane season should be over. We can head for the Caribbean. We're not that far from Beaufort. It's one of the good places to cross the Gulf Stream."

"What exactly is that again? Aside from the place Dexter dumped his bodies. It's a strong current, right?"

A smile ghosted over Parker's lips, and Adam wanted to haul

him close and take his mouth. But he kept his hands at his sides. Parker was still healing, and he didn't want to do anything…wrong.

Parker answered, "Right, it's a current. It's basically like a river in the ocean that's flowing north. It's narrower down where it starts in Florida. Thirty, forty miles across, I think? Gets wider as it goes north, and it's moving at two and a half knots per hour. That might not sound like much, but if you get caught in it with wind coming from the north, you can be really fucked. Big waves. You want to cross when the wind's blowing from the south or southeast. But we don't have weather reports anymore, so it makes it harder to gauge. Winds can change fast."

Adam pondered it. "So, if we crossed the Gulf Stream up here, then we'd be going south toward the Caribbean? In the middle of the ocean, basically?"

"Yep. We'd try to pick up the trade winds to take us southeast. It's the right time of year for it."

"You know where the winds will be?"

"Roughly. Depends on the season. But like I said, they can change, and with global warming, the patterns aren't as stable as they used to be. We shouldn't have any more hurricanes now that it's November, but I wouldn't rule it out. And it's always a risk sailing offshore. You never know what can happen out there. We can't anchor, so we'd sail through the nights. Staying out of shipping lanes was a big concern. Not now, I guess." He unwound the rope from his hand. "It's weird, isn't it? Hard to believe how fast the world went to hell."

"Everything we thought was important." Adam shook his head. "It feels like another life now. Surreal. I've only known you two *months*."

"That is seriously so fucking weird. I can't imagine not knowing you."

The thought of living through this new world order without

Parker rocked Adam with nausea. He hungered to crush Parker against him and climb inside his skin, but Parker was talking again, and Adam refocused.

"I don't think it's a good idea. I'm not some expert sailor. I know a fair bit, but I could get in over my head fast out there. We've been lucky so far."

"Okay. So we go south along the coast. Stick close to land?"

Parker nodded. "Normally, I'd take the ICW. Sorry, Intracoastal Waterway. It's basically a safer way to get to Florida. It follows along the coast, but it's rivers and lakes and canals."

"Why can't we take it now?"

"There are a bunch of locks. You know, on canals, where the water level changes? I don't think we can open or close the gates ourselves. And some bridges need to be raised since they're too low for masts. There are risks either way we go, but getting trapped in a lock or cracking our mast on a low bridge are not scenarios I want to deal with."

Adam could imagine creepers swarming toward them from either side with arms outstretched, fingers bloody. Even though he could fight them, he'd rather not. "Agreed." He looked up at the Big Dipper arcing through the heavens. "We stick to the ocean. The question is, do we do it alone?"

Parker clutched the rope. "I want to say yes. We do it alone."

He waited. "But?"

With a sigh, Parker shook his head. "They seem like decent people. They have kids. They need our help. Plus, they could help us. Having a paramedic could be really important. Could be strength in numbers."

"I think we can trust them. Jacob didn't say much when we were up on deck, but I got a little out of him. I don't think they've hurt anyone. We'll take it slow. Keep separate boats. And we won't tell them about me."

"Definitely not," Parker said sharply. "They have to earn that.

We'll see how it goes. Any time either of us feels like we should cut the cord, we do it. Snip, snip. Okay?"

"Okay."

Parker blew out a long breath. "Fuck, what a day. I hope their boat is still there." He rubbed a hand over his face.

"Go to sleep. It's late."

"You should too. Come on." He took Adam's hand and pulled, but Adam stayed put.

"I'll keep watch. Not tired."

Parker shoved his fists back into the big pocket on the front of his sweatshirt. He watched Adam for a long moment. "What's—" He broke off, shaking his head. "Okay. Come wake me up in a few hours and we'll switch."

Adam nodded, and Parker disappeared down the hatch. There was no chance he'd wake Parker, and they both knew it. He stifled a yawn and stretched his neck. Sleep would be wonderful, but it was his job to protect. He wouldn't fail again.

As *BELLA* SWAYED on the waves' gentle rolls, Adam spread his feet and cast out again, relishing the sound of the fishing line zipping out from the reel. He'd never fished growing up, but still associated the distinct sounds of it with relaxation.

They were far enough out that he couldn't hear any chattering of infected from the mainland. Along with the plaintive cries of distant gulls and water slapping the hull, the only sounds filling his ears as the day waned were Parker's voice across the span of water between the two boats, and the heartbeats of Abby, Craig, and the kids.

"Okay, so what's the difference between the rudder and the keel?" Parker asked, standing on the deck of the *Saltwater Taffy* with the others sitting near his feet. He'd thrown so many new words at them that Adam would be surprised if they could remember their own names.

But little Lilly raised her hand. "Um, the rudder is for steering, and the keel is for staying steady?"

"Exactly!"

Adam watched across the water, reeling in his fishing line. Now that they'd decided to keep the newcomers around, Parker smiled a little more easily. It had been a long day of recovering the other boat, which had miraculously still been bobbing on the waves. It'd taken hours for Parker to untangle the lines and make it seaworthy once more. He'd taught them what he called "the basics," a dizzying litany of nautical terms and procedures.

They'd finally sailed on and found a secluded cove by a tiny island in one of the sounds of the southern Outer Banks. Adam had splashed ashore and run the length of it, making sure they were well and truly alone. He made sure to take his time, and Craig and Abby hadn't questioned him going ashore alone. They'd only seemed relieved to get the all clear.

The two boats were anchored some distance away from each other after Parker did calculations on depth and "swing radius" and the anchor "rode." Everyone had stared at him blankly until he'd explained that they didn't want to drift and hit each other in the night or get their anchor lines tangled.

Parker had grumbled that he had his work cut out for him in making sailors of them all, and god, Adam had wanted to kiss him. His lips still itched with it.

Instead, he slipped the camera from his pocket and started filming the other boat. No one else noticed, and he ran the camera over everyone on board, capturing their faces and voices.

"Okay, now we'll trim the sail one more time," Parker said. "Uh, Jacob, how about it?"

Jacob's head jerked up. "Me?"

"Sure, why not? The only way to really learn is by doing."

"You got this, sweetheart," Abby said as Craig gave Jacob's shoulder a supportive squeeze.

Parker held down his hand to pull Jacob to his feet. "I've been doing it since I was younger than you. Trust me."

Jacob's heart kicked up as he took Parker's hand, and Adam cocked his head as he watched, the fishing line forgotten for the moment.

"Okay, so remember how the sails are positioned depends on the conditions. Where you're heading, and where the wind's coming from. You have to adjust your sails so they'll work the most effectively. We want to minimize drag and optimize lift. Kind of like the wings on an airplane. Okay, look up at the mainsail." With his hand on Jacob's back, Parker positioned him.

As the lesson continued, Adam flipped off his camera and listened to Jacob's heart skip around like a mariachi band. He smiled to himself. The kid wasn't scared—his sweat smelled fresh, with a distinctive spike of arousal. No, the kid wasn't scared at all, and Adam remembered the same fluttery feelings every time he'd gotten close to Henry Chen when they were lab partners in the tenth grade.

He cast out his line again, focusing his hearing on the lap of the waves and the chirp of birds, Parker's voice a pleasant and indistinct murmur. Over the years, he'd trained himself to narrow his focus so he didn't go crazy listening to other people, especially when he wanted peace and quiet.

He'd managed to catch two decent-sized fish by the time Parker came back in the dinghy. "Lesson went well?" Adam asked.

"Think so. You know you could use a refresher. Or five. Ten, probably." Parker disappeared into the hatch and returned with his nautical charts.

"Yeah, yeah." Adam cast out again. "I don't really need to learn. I've got you. I'm just the cabin boy on this vessel, remember?"

Parker laughed. "Your lack of ambition might bite you in the ass if I'm not around one day."

All the wonderful easiness sucked out of the air, and a stone sank in Adam's gut. "That's not funny."

Exhaling with exasperation, Parker spread out on the deck. "I was joking. Chill."

Adam didn't answer, turning back to his fishing. Parker's pencil scratched over paper where he was sprawled on his stomach in the rosy sunset, examining charts.

The breeze was cool, but despite Parker's sweatshirt and jeans, his feet were still bare. He scratched at the back of his neck, and Adam focused on the drag of Parker's blunt nails over his growing hair, the scuffing sound making him itch to touch. Then, despite his best efforts, Adam's gaze was drawn to the purple bruise on Parker's temple, the angry red edges starting to fade to yellow.

He thought of Parker crumpled on the deck, shivering violently, exposed and alone. Forcing an inhalation, Adam's teeth ached, and he clamped his jaw shut to keep his fangs in check.

"Oh my god, would you stop?"

Blinking, he focused on the thin line of Parker's lips pressed together. Trying to think of what he'd done wrong and coming up blank, Adam raised an eyebrow.

"Stop looking at me," Parker hissed, pushing to his knees and rolling up the charts with jerky movements.

"Stop looking at you?" he echoed. Something tugged at his line, and he reeled it in too quickly, coming up with just the hook and lure. He tried a joke, lowering his voice to a leering tone. "I thought you liked it when I look at you."

Parker stood there staring at him. "You seriously don't get it?" Clenching his jaw, he stalked toward the stern, his feet slapping on the wood.

After dropping the rod into the storage area under one of the benches at the bow, Adam followed, catching him by the hatch with his long strides. He reached for his arm, but let his hand hover. "Parker, what—"

Whirling, Parker stared at Adam's outstretched hand accusingly, then met his eyes. "Stop looking at me like I'm *broken*!"

As Parker's shout rang out over the water, Adam registered the cessation of talking on the other boat. Parker barreled down the steps, and Adam called out, "Everything's fine!" and gave the others a wave before following Parker, who paced up and down the saloon, the faint green light of the radar screen chasing away some of the shadows.

"I'm not..." Adam tried to think of the right words.

"You are!" A few feet away, Parker skidded to a stop, gesturing with his hands. "I'm fine, Adam. I'm fine. It was nothing."

"It was not."

He tapped the side of his head. "I barely feel it anymore, so just stop acting like it's a big deal."

Adam kept his tone even. "You were hurt. They hurt you and I—"

"You what?" He raised his hands.

"I wasn't here! I wasn't here to stop them." His words hung in the damp air.

Green light flickered over Parker's face as he stepped closer. "This is the world we live in now. Creepers and pirates and who the fuck knows what else. It sucked, but it's done, and I'm fine."

"You know what it was like finding you like that?" Adam blurted.

Parker's eyebrows flew up. "Yeah, I do. Because I had to watch you unconscious and helpless in that lab where they cut you up for their experiments. And I fucking hated it, but I know you're strong, and I don't think less of you now."

"What? I don't think less of you either!"

Hurt creased Parker's face, making Adam's heart stutter. "Then why do you barely touch me?"

"What? No. I touch you." Adam reached out as if to prove his point, but Parker dodged.

"Not the same way. It's different now. Like you think I'll fucking shatter. And you haven't tried to fuck me."

"We've barely been alone! Things have been a little busy." He gestured in the general direction of the other boat.

"Or is that just an excuse because now I'm…" Parker swallowed hard. "I'm weak."

Adam strode forward and grasped the back of Parker's head, pulling him into a bruising kiss, their lips mashed together. Parker dug his fingers into Adam's sides, bunching up his T-shirt. They opened their mouths, teeth smashing and stubble scraping.

When Adam pulled back to gasp, he tightened his fingers against Parker's skull. "You're the strongest person I've ever known. And you're *mine*. I want you all the time. Don't ever think I don't."

"So fuck me."

Growling, Adam yanked off Parker's clothes and pulled out the retractable table, bending him over it. The red marks on Parker's ass had faded away, and now Adam ran his hands roughly over that pale skin, up to his tanned shoulders and down to his thighs, leaving his own marks and sucking on the side of Parker's neck.

He could smell Parker's growing arousal, and it made his own cock swell, pressing against the fly of his jeans. Still dressed, he rutted against Parker's ass, making him shudder.

"Stop teasing," Parker gritted out. "Fuck me!"

"Shh. Sound carries over the water."

"I don't goddamn c—"

Adam shoved two fingers into Parker's mouth, and Parker sucked them greedily, his tongue working. Adam groaned. "*Fuck*, your mouth," he muttered. Of course, Parker sucked harder, and Adam's cock throbbed.

Around Adam's fingers, Parker mumbled, "Fuck my mouth, my ass. Fuck all of me."

Adam withdrew his fingers with a wet *pop* and spread Parker's cheeks to tease his hole, sticking his index finger just inside. Humping the table, Parker huffed, and Adam had to laugh. Parker glared over his shoulder, but apparently couldn't stop a smile.

"Are you going to fuck me, or do I have to fuck myself?" He licked his lips. "I can make a dildo out of something in the kitchen. Fuck myself hard with it if you won't. Or are you going to give me what I want?"

The thought of watching Parker use a makeshift dildo certainly had its appeal, but as Adam pushed a finger into his tight heat, his dick ached to be there. "I'm going to give you exactly what you want," he whispered, leaning over close to Parker's ear while he pushed in another spit-slick finger past the ring of muscle. "Because you can take it, can't you?"

Jerking out a nod, Parker squeezed around Adam's fingers. "Give it to me."

It was dark now aside from the radar light, but Adam could see clearly. He stripped off his clothes and jacked himself, pulling his foreskin back from the glistening head. Spreading Parker's ass, he spit onto his hole. "You want it like this? Want it rough?"

"Yes," Parker moaned. "Fuck me 'til your cum drips out and I smell like you all over and—"

Adam couldn't wait another moment before slamming his cock into Parker's hole. They both groaned, and Parker tensed, gripping the side of the table, his muscles bunched and his cheek pressed to the smooth wood.

"Fuck," he muttered. "Love how your big dick feels splitting me open." His breath hitched as Adam pulled back and thrust deeper.

Leaning low, Adam growled, sending a shiver through Parker. He was tempted to let himself transform a little, edge right up to that line. But too many emotions were pressing against his chest—lust, guilt, affection, anger. He didn't trust himself to stay in control, and with his strength he could hurt Parker far worse than he was asking for, no matter how rough they both wanted it.

He stayed human and fucked Parker, clutching his hips, their flesh slapping together loudly. The table creaked and tilted, and Adam lifted Parker off it and dropped them to the floor. On his hands and knees now, Parker pushed back, his head hanging low as he panted.

Sweat glistened on his back, and Adam licked up the dip of his spine, loving the salty tang. Gentle swells rocked the boat, the cabin floor hard beneath their knees. Adam slowed his strokes, experimenting to get the right angle as Parker grunted in frustration.

"Come on. Harder."

Adam ignored him, slowing even more and running a hand under Parker's body to tweak his nipples and skate along his leaking cock.

"*Adam.* I want—" Parker cried out as Adam hit his prostate, and Adam slapped his hand over his mouth, because the kids really didn't need to hear this. Breathing hard through his nose, Parker's hot exhalations flowed over Adam's knuckles, and behind Adam's hand he mumbled, "*Harder.*"

Muffling Parker's cries, Adam pounded him, his other hand digging into Parker's hip to keep him in place. "That's it. Take it. You're strong enough."

He kept Parker immobilized, fucking into him with short thrusts that made Parker shake and groan into Adam's hand, practically lifting him off his knees. Adam reached down for Parker's cock and balls with his free hand, fondling roughly as Parker whined hotly against his palm.

"You need this?" Adam muttered in Parker's ear. "You need to come? Have I fucked you hard enough?"

Nodding desperately, Parker bit at Adam's hand and clamped down around his cock with his ass, squeezing so tight. Adam gasped, almost losing control before reining it in. He stroked Parker's cock and went for his prostate again. Parker seized up, spurting long ropes of cum onto the teak floor, some of it dripping down onto Adam's hand. The muffled cries he made filled Adam's ears like music.

His ass was fire around Adam's dick, and Adam rocked his hips, balls so tight and Parker whimpering wetly against his palm. He let go, coming deep inside him, mouth open on Parker's shoulder in a silent cry, his fangs slipping down just a bit. "I love you," he murmured against the flushed skin, licking the shallow marks his fangs had left, not enough to draw blood.

Arms quaking, Parker mumbled against Adam's palm. Sitting back on his heels and bringing Parker back with him, his softening dick still wedged into Parker's hole, Adam lowered his hand and held Parker around the chest. Parker tipped his head back, kissing Adam's chin and cheek messily, breathing hard.

Adam lifted his sticky fingers to Parker's mouth, his cock pulsing with another pure beat of pleasure as his fingers were licked clean. Adam lifted his hips, trying to stay inside Parker as long as possible.

"*Nnngh*," Parker moaned. His arms hung slack.

"Mmm." Kissing along his jaw, Adam held him close, Parker's chest still rising and falling rapidly. "Shower?"

Parker seemed to contemplate it. "Swim. Wanna see the stars."

When they tiptoed up to the deck naked, Adam didn't spot anyone on the other boat. The night air sent goosebumps over their skin, and the water was cold as they slipped in from the low platform at the rear of the stern.

"Oh fuck, oh fuck," Parker muttered when he climbed down the ladder and his feet touched the water. "Okay: one, two, three." He stepped off the ladder and straight down, disappearing under the dark surface, fearless as ever.

Adam had to swallow hard over the swell of emotion. Gratitude that he was lucky enough to face the world with Parker beside him warmed him as he plunged into the chilly depths.

The temperature soon felt comfortable, and they treaded water lazily. Tangling their legs as he got closer, Adam took Parker's face in his hands and whispered across his lips, "Unbreakable."

After salty kisses, Parker tipped his head back and watched the stars while Adam kept his gaze on the curve of Parker's neck, his pale skin glistening, his pulse throbbing steadily.

Chapter Six

"MORNING." ABBY'S VOICE squawked over the radio. "We're making pancakes over here if you'd like to join us for breakfast?"

"Mmm, pancakes," Adam mumbled sleepily, stretching his arms over his head.

Naked, Parker scooted off the bed and picked up the transmitter briefly. "Thanks, but we're good." He shuffled to the fridge for water, enjoying the sting in his ass. Guzzling from the bottle, he returned to the bed, where Adam watched him with an expression that could only be called "exasperated."

"What?"

"You don't have to be rude."

"Rude? I wasn't rude! I said thank you."

Adam scoffed. "Barely. What's wrong with having breakfast with them?"

Parker screwed the cap on the bottle and back off again. "Nothing. I just don't like pancakes," he lied.

Adam's bushy eyebrows shot up. "Is that so? Because I can smell them, and let me tell you, I bet they taste incredible."

"Then go over and have some. I'm not stopping you." He finished his water, knowing he was being huffy as he flopped down on his back next to Adam. "Be my guest."

"It wouldn't kill you to be friendlier to them."

"I'm totally being friendly!"

Adam popped up one skeptical eyebrow. "Uh-huh."

"I'm teaching them how to sail. Isn't that enough? I thought we agreed we'd stay cautious with them. Not get too close. It's been, like, two days."

Adam sighed. "Fair enough. But it's only breakfast. Don't you... I don't know. Don't you miss it?"

"Dude, we can still have breakfast. They don't have a monopoly on it over there." Adam didn't reply, staring at the ceiling instead. Parker frowned. "What am I not getting?"

After a few moments, he sighed again. "Forget it. We should get moving." He sat up.

Parker rolled over and pushed Adam gently back to the mattress, straddling his hairy thighs. "No. Tell me. Why do you look so sad? It can't be because you like pancakes *that* much." He spread his hands over Adam's chest, rubbing softly. Adam's soft cock curved up toward his belly.

"I can hear Lilly laughing over there." He closed his eyes. "She's teasing Jacob, who's ignoring her. And they're putting chocolate in the pancakes. I can smell it melting."

Eyes still closed, he inhaled and exhaled deeply. "It reminds me of Sunday mornings growing up. Christine would be trying to read her book at the table while we waited for Mom to bring in the pancakes. Sometimes chocolate, sometimes blueberry. Maddie would be bugging Christine, and I'd bug them both. Dad would read the newspaper and sip his coffee, tuning us out. It was all so long ago, but I never stopped missing it. Family."

Swallowing thickly, Parker wished he knew what to say. "I miss mine too. I do. And I'm sorry I'm not enough."

Adam's eyes flew open, and he reached up to cup Parker's cheek. "It's not about you being deficient. Do you hear me?"

He seemed to be waiting for an answer, so Parker nodded. "I didn't mean it in a poor-me way." Well, maybe a little, if he was being uncomfortably honest. "Just... Next time we'll go for pancakes, okay?"

"It's fine. If you're not feeling secure, I shouldn't push you."

Parker leaned down and kissed him. "But you push so good."

With a smile, Adam stroked over Parker's ass, dipping his fingers between the cheeks and gently touching his swollen hole. "Feel all right?"

"Abso-fucking-lutely." Parker was sure a shrink would have a field day with his motivations for wanting rough sex, but all he knew was that he felt stronger and better and in control when Adam took him hard. Maybe it made no sense, but having a sore ass gave him confidence.

A little smile lifted Adam's lips as he caressed Parker's butt. "Good thing." His smile faded and his eyebrows knit together. "You'll tell me if it's too much? Too rough?"

Parker rubbed his cheek over Adam's coarse chest hair. "Mmm-hmm."

"Parker." Adam nudged Parker's head up and watched him with serious eyes. "I mean it. I might—" He exhaled sharply.

"What? I know you'd never hurt me."

"Not on purpose. And I know you're tough. I just…"

"Loooove me?" Parker tickled Adam's ribs with a smile. "I know. You're crazy about me."

Adam huffed out a laugh. "I think it's your modesty that I appreciate the most."

They kissed around smiles, and Parker wished they could stay in bed all day. He sighed. "Guess we should get up. Time for a supply run. I think Mariah's due for a spin, don't you?"

"You're going to come with me." It wasn't a question.

"Yep." He leaned down and rubbed their noses together, and Adam kissed him hard.

A couple hours later, they were docked in a small marina. The sun peeked out from behind fluffy clouds, the wind brisk. On the patio of a restaurant, tables were upended, a large umbrella lolling on its top. At a distance, the spray of blood across the sliding glass doors leading inside didn't look fresh.

Saltwater parked on the other side of the dock, and Parker went over to distract them while Adam lugged Mariah out of the cabin and up onto the pier. Craig's brow creased when he saw the bike, but Parker ignored it and barreled on with his instructions on the quickest way to leave the harbor and get the sails up.

"Hopefully it'll be quiet and you can just wait here for us," Parker said. "You've got weapons? And you know how to use them?"

Abby nodded. "I did some training when I became an EMT. My district was talking about arming us, which was insane, but I guess it's coming in handy now."

"Cool. We'll try not to be longer than an hour." Parker glanced at Adam, who nodded. "Okay, so see you in a few." Adam started Mariah, and Parker climbed on behind him wearing an empty backpack with another stuffed inside. *Bella*'s keys dug into his hip in his pocket. He didn't think Craig and Abby would get any bright ideas about stealing the bigger boat, but...just in case.

"What if you don't come back?" Jacob asked.

Parker turned to meet the kid's serious gaze while Abby swatted his shoulder and hissed his name.

Jacob shook her off. "It's not a dumb question. What if they don't come back? How long do we wait?"

"It'll be fine." Craig slipped an arm around Lilly's thin shoulders. "They'll be back real soon. Right, guys?"

"Right," Adam said. "Don't worry about us."

"Whatever," Jacob muttered, turning away and going to the bow, his arms crossed as he looked out to sea.

Adam turned the key, and Mariah's engine purred to life, vibrating between Parker's thighs. He pressed close to Adam as they drove down the dock and bumped up the steps to the marina. Closer, Parker could see the buzzing flies, and the stench of death singed his nostrils.

Then they were in the half-full parking lot, weaving between abandoned cars, one with doors open and at least one body inside. Adam wore his leather jacket, and Parker leaned his cheek against the warm material, closing his eyes as they hit the road, his arms snug around Adam's waist. The gun was tucked into the back of his jeans beneath his hoodie.

For a minute, he let himself dream. That there was no virus, no eviscerated corpses where people once drank cold beer on sunny days. That—

Parker sat up straight, his eyes popping open when he felt Adam tense. A car approached on the two-lane blacktop, and Parker's breath caught in his throat when he saw the red lights on top. The police car slowed to a stop. Waiting.

Adam had pulled back on the throttle, and he glanced over his shoulder at Parker. "We can't go off the road." Indeed, fences on either side penned in fields of neglected crops. "Hang on tight if we have to make a quick exit."

His gun in hand, Parker flicked off the safety and nodded. He could see a person inside the police car, but couldn't make out anything more than that. Then the car door opened, and a man stepped out. A man actually wearing a police uniform. It was such a strange sight after the past months that Parker could only stare.

The supposed cop was about forty, and he leaned against his car with his hands in his pockets. His brown hair was neatly combed, his uniform well-tailored and badge gleaming. He was only missing coffee and a donut.

As Adam slowed, the man lifted a hand in greeting. Adam stopped the bike a good twenty feet away.

"Morning," the man called. "Nice day for it." He didn't specify what *it* was, and Parker's pulse drummed. Looking around, he couldn't see anyone else, or any obvious signs of a trap. Adam would be listening anyway.

"Morning," Adam replied.

"I'm Officer Hanson. Do you need any help?"

"Just passing through," Adam said.

"All right. If you need supplies, there's a gas station a mile down the road that hasn't been completely stripped yet."

Nice place for a trap. Parker gripped his gun a little tighter and said, "Thanks," with a fake smile.

"Shouldn't be any infected around. I take care of any I spot. Try to keep the area safe for those of us that are left."

The radio in the patrol car crackled. Parker could barely make it out. "Hey, babe. It's me. Can you find some more Claritin after your patrol? Ollie's allergies are acting up."

Hanson leaned in the open window and picked up the transmitter. "Copy that, hon. Over and out." He grimaced. "My son's affected by every tree and weed there is. Don't know what we'll do when the meds dry up. Guess we'll have to figure out some natural hippie-type treatment."

Despite himself, Parker's curiosity got the better of him. "You patrol every day?"

"Yep." He smiled ruefully. "Guess I don't know what else to do. At first, we were waiting for the Army to sweep in, but... Well, now I just try to keep the peace. Rounded up the bodies in the beginning, but it got to be too much."

"Many people coming through?" Adam asked.

"Fewer and fewer." He opened the car door. "I should get back to it. Stay safe, and God bless."

They nodded and were soon back on their way. Outside the gas station, Adam listened intently before giving the all clear. Inside, the dark fridges stood open and empty but for a few toppled bottles of soda. Glossy magazines littered the floor.

Lose weight the Hollywood way! Get a bikini bod in eight weeks! Taylor's secret new romance revealed!

Parker kicked a few aside and moved deeper into the store, pleased to find the shelves were still partially full, as promised.

"We still good for visitors?" he asked.

"Yep." Adam turned in a slow circle. "Let's load up."

Parker was examining a slightly dented can of tomatoes when he realized Adam was standing stock-still by the windows, a box of pasta clenched in his hand.

"Adam? What is it?" He took out his gun and crept up behind. Peering out the dirty glass, he could only see the abandoned gas pumps and the empty road beyond. On the other side of the road, a field appeared empty as well.

Adam breathed shallowly through parted lips, his eyes focused on something in the distance. Parker looked again and still couldn't spot anything. He whispered, "What do you see?"

For a strange moment, it seemed like Adam might burst into tears. Then he blinked and spun away from the window. "Nothing. Let's get back." He strapped one of the backpacks to his chest.

"Wait. That wasn't nothing." Parker glanced out the window again. "Do you sense something?"

Cramming cans in the other pack, Adam said, "Yeah. Creepers nearby. We have to go."

"Shit, really?" Parker grabbed the pack from him and swung it onto his back. "We should get gas, but I bet we can siphon from the cars at the marina. Pumps won't work without electricity anyway."

"Sounds good." Adam was practically running outside to where they'd left Mariah by the door. He gunned the engine, and Parker was barely on when they zoomed back onto the road.

Worry tugged at Parker's gut. Something had spooked Adam, but when he looked behind, no creepers appeared.

"THIS IS DELICIOUS, Parker." Abby dipped her spoon back into her soup. "I love chickpeas."

"Um, thanks. I just threw in a bunch of stuff with the carton of stock and the fish Adam caught. I bet you could make it way better."

"Ha! Nope. I've always been rather challenged in that department." Abby nudged Jacob beside her. "I'm sure Jacob can attest."

"You cook fine," he mumbled.

They sat around the table on *Bella*'s deck, near the wheel. It was spacious enough to fit six comfortably on the L-shaped padded benches, especially since Lilly was so slight. Trying to think of some small talk to make and coming up blank, Parker swallowed a mouthful of the soup he'd cobbled together. It wasn't half bad, although he missed fresh vegetables more than he would have thought possible. A nice big salad would have been incredible. Maybe when they made it farther south.

They'd sailed some miles down the coast, until the wind had died down. Now they were anchored in a cove with the sun sinking. Sunset was coming earlier and earlier as November wore on, and he didn't like the idea of being out on open sea in the dark.

They wanted to stick close to shore, but that came with the risk of shoals and damaging their hulls. It was easier to see markers in the daylight, and there was no sense in taking chances. As long as they made their way steadily south as winter came, they'd be okay.

Parker's back was to the mouth of the cove, and he glanced over his shoulder. It was empty, and he knew Adam would hear or see anyone coming, but he still had to look. They hadn't spotted any other sails that day, but that didn't mean people weren't out there.

When he turned back, Adam was watching him. Parker smiled, and Adam gave him a quick, distracted smile in return before his gaze went distant again.

"Now, Craig is quite a gourmet." Abby frowned. "Or is it

gourmand?"

Craig said, "I have no idea, but thank you, my dear." He and Abby beamed at each other while Jacob examined his soup and Lilly ate steadily, methodically dipping saltine crackers one by one into her bowl, crumbling them up, then eating the results.

"Adam, did you grow up fishing?" Abby asked.

It took a moment for Adam to focus on her. "Sorry, what was that?"

"Did you learn to fish when you were younger? You seem to have the knack."

"Oh. No, I didn't. Guess I'm just lucky."

Craig said, "It's all in the wrist, don't you think?"

"I guess so." Adam took a little spoonful of soup before gazing at the horizon again.

Craig and Abby shared a glance, and Parker jumped in as the silence became awkward. "There was this one time, out on the Cape? My brother caught a fish with teeth."

Lilly gaped. "Like a piranha?"

"Kind of. It was a triggerfish. A tropical storm must have carried it up. I swear, it was the ugliest thing I ever saw."

"Uglier than a snake?" Lilly asked.

"Oh yeah. *Way* uglier. It was wriggling around on the line like crazy, snapping away when Eric tried to get the hook out."

Lilly squeaked. "Did it bite him?"

"Took his finger clean off," Parker said gravely.

"*Really?*" Cheeks flushing, Jacob lowered his head and went back to pretending not to listen.

"Nah, it was just the tip. But it was super gross."

Laughing delightedly, Lilly asked for another story, and Parker obliged. And as he spun a partially true tale about the time he spotted a great white shark—he'd actually been safe on his family's huge sailboat, not in a sea kayak—warmth spread in his chest, and he accepted that despite his best efforts to close himself off, he

liked these people. It was pointless to fight it.

Surely if Craig and Abby had been planning something, they would have attacked by now? They listened to his tall tale with avid attention, and ate his crappy soup as if Jamie Oliver had made it. They teased their children and held hands under the table.

"What was the craziest call you ever answered?" Craig asked Abby.

"Hmm. Well, the full moon and LSD are not a good combination, but how about the most cliché call? I actually had to get a kitten out of a tree. Honest to God! Someone actually called nine-one-one because their kitten was stuck in a tree. The thing was, it wasn't actually a huge tree. It was just big enough to be nicely out of reach, but the branches were too thin for the firefighters. Since I was the lightest one, lucky me got to climb up."

Lilly and Jacob listened avidly, and Parker thought of Jaden and Evie at the Pines. God, he hoped they were still alive. Jacob met his gaze suddenly and dropped his head. He stared sullenly at the remnants of his soup, and Parker wondered why the kid had a problem with him. He probably shouldn't have cared, but found, annoyingly, that he did. Meanwhile, Adam was an island, staring into the distance and clearly not listening.

When dinner was over and the others had left in their dinghy, Parker cornered Adam in the kitchen. "What's up with you?"

He didn't look up from the pot he was washing. "Nothing."

"Oh, come on. I'm playing nice with them like you wanted, and you're being a total space cadet."

Scrubbing, Adam shook his head. "It's not them or you. I'm just tired."

Parker took a deep breath and forced himself to stay calm and not start yelling for answers. "Earlier, at the gas station. What did you hear?"

Adam continued scrubbing. "It doesn't matter now."

"Of course it matters!" He lowered his voice. "It was another wolf, wasn't it?"

Adam finally met his gaze. He nodded.

"Okay. Were they… Did they seem threatening?"

"No. I have no way of knowing for sure. But I could sense it, like… Like a switch had been flipped. I felt alive with it."

"So why did you run?" Not that Parker was complaining; after Ramon, he wasn't sure he wanted to meet any other werewolves. Especially if they were like that asshole and thought werewolves should stick to their own kind and procreate.

"Because that's what I've always done." Adam smiled humorlessly. "That's what my parents drilled into us. We were so isolated, but they always said we didn't need anyone else. We had each other. Our family. Our pack. Then I was alone, and I still ran." His knuckles were white on the pot handle. "Today, part of me wanted to howl and run toward whoever it was out there. But I did what I've always done instead. And besides, I couldn't—"

When Adam didn't go on, Parker gently prompted, "What?"

"I couldn't leave you there alone." He looked up then, his eyes soft. "Wouldn't."

"I don't want to hold you back."

"You don't. You hold me together."

Parker wished he knew the right thing to say, but he rarely did. He eased the pot from Adam's grip and wrapped him in a hug. Rubbing his back, he nuzzled Adam's neck. After a long moment, Adam shuddered and squeezed Parker tightly. It was hard to breathe, but Parker just hung on.

Adam's voice rumbled. "I can't stop wondering why my parents were so insistent we keep away from other wolves. If I'm drawn to them so instinctively, why is that bad? I know it didn't go well with Ramon. But surely there are others out there? Others like me? There have to be. Don't there?"

He sounded so small despite the iron bands of his arms around

Parker. "I'm sure there are. It's okay. We'll… We'll find them one day." The thought sent fingers of fear down his spine, but for Adam, he'd deal with it.

"I shouldn't have run. Why did I run? Why do I always run?"

"Because your parents told you to."

"If they'd known how lonely it was. How there's still—" He shivered and clung to Parker.

"Still what? You can tell me."

"Most of the time it's okay, but then it's like a cavern, endless. It's so much better now that I'm with you. Tina tried to get me to stop running if I sensed another wolf, but I wouldn't. Until you, I didn't know how empty I really was."

You have me. All of me. Aren't I enough?

He mentally rolled his eyes at his own pathetic thoughts. It wasn't about him. It was about Adam. "Like how you don't realize how hungry you are sometimes until you start eating? And then you're like Cookie Monster going to town?"

Adam's shoulders shook with a soft laugh. "Exactly like that. God, I love you. I love you so much." He squeezed Parker so tightly.

"I love you too."

They kissed, sweet and soft at first, the warmth quickly sparking into more. Parker's breath came faster, anticipation skating over his skin.

Adam took Parker's mouth in a rough kiss. "Will you fuck me? Please. I need it. Need you."

"Okay, okay. I've got you." Parker tugged him over to their bed. He'd only stuck his dick in Adam once when they were at the Pines, and briefly at that. He loved being fucked, so it had never bothered him that Adam hadn't seemed to want it.

But as they got naked and Adam crawled onto all fours on the mattress, excitement zinged through Parker's veins. He fumbled for the lube in a little drawer in the sideboard, but Adam shook his head.

"Don't need it. Just do it."

"You sure? I don't want to hurt you." Parker licked his hand and jacked his cock, getting himself hard. Usually they preheated the oven before they stuck the turkey in, but Adam vibrated with need and tension.

"You won't. Do it." Adam's balls hung heavy between his hairy thighs, his broad back flexing.

Spreading Adam's ass, he spit on his hole. Adam was already reaching back, grasping for Parker's thigh. Luckily, Parker could get hard in a stiff wind, so he was ready, and he knew that bone-deep need to be filled.

He lined up his cock and pushed into Adam's ass, past the ring of muscle, groaning loudly at the incredible heat clamping down around him, his fingers digging into Adam's hips.

"Jesus, you feel amazing. Fuck." Parker's breath already came in little gasps.

Adam moaned in response, and Parker pushed the rest of the way inside. Without lube, he was surprised at how easily he fit, his balls brushing Adam's ass already. Sure, his cock wasn't as thick, but it was a respectable size. He loved the sensation of Adam's dick ready to break him into two, and he thrust in and out, trying to give Adam that same feeling.

The bed shook and rattled, and they panted as Parker fucked him as hard as he could, one hand fisted in Adam's thick hair, leaning over his sweaty back. He couldn't shake the feeling that Adam should have been tighter given that he didn't usually bottom.

Even though their skin was slick with sweat and they were both clearly trying, when he reached down for Adam's dick, it was only half hard.

"Dude, are you getting off?" Grunting, he angled his hips and tried to find Adam's prostate. Maybe he was no good at topping.

He rammed in harder. He needed to make it good for Adam—needed to make it right, to be everything he needed.

Adam pushed back hard with his ass. "Keep going. Don't stop."

Parker wasn't sure he believed him, but he pounded away, trying to fuck him the way he liked it. Their skin slapped in the quiet of the cabin, the air humid with their sweat and breath.

"Please, please," Adam muttered, pushing back against the thrusts, his thighs flexing and claws out, shredding the sheets as he strained.

Parker was getting close, his balls tightening, but he couldn't come until Adam did. He had to make Adam come. Had to do this for him. Leaning forward, he pumped Adam's cock as he slammed his hole, so hard he was sure anyone else would be tearing.

I have to be enough.

Grunting, he stroked Adam's shaft roughly, without even spit to ease his grasp. Adam was hard, but not leaking yet, and Parker tried another angle to find his prostate, and then another. Adam shoved back, squeezing, and Parker couldn't stop his orgasm, rushing through him as he spilled in long pulses.

Panting, he pulled out easily, and Adam whimpered, his head hanging between his arms. Parker nudged him onto his back. "I'm sorry. I'm sorry," he mumbled as he pushed Adam's legs open and dove for his cock, swallowing it almost to the root. The need to make Adam come burned through him with a twist of shame. He sucked hard and deep, tears in his eyes and spit dripping from his lips, his nostrils flaring for air.

When Adam came in a few bursts of salty cum and with a quiet moan, it somehow still didn't feel like enough. Parker swallowed as much as he could and licked up the rest, his face buried in Adam's wiry pubes, trying to get every drop.

Adam's hand rested on Parker's head. "It's okay," he murmured. "It's good."

Wiping his mouth, Parker sat back on his heels, his chest rising and falling rapidly. "But it wasn't, was it? What did I do wrong?"

"Nothing, nothing. Shh." Adam reached for him, pulling Parker into his arms. On their sides, they kissed with quiet desperation, Adam caressing Parker's back and ass. "It's not you. I promise. You did so good."

"But it wasn't what you wanted. I know it wasn't. Don't lie to me."

He brushed a hand over Parker's hair. "It's not you. It's me." He grimaced. "As horribly cliché as that is. I guess it's appropriate, since I'm a walking cliché. I feel empty after sensing that wolf, so I tried to literally make you fill that hole."

Parker barked out a laugh. "Okay, good point. But there's more to it. Tell me."

Adam's warm exhalation brushed over Parker's face. "It's something that took me a while to figure out. I don't know why I thought it would be different tonight. I've never been able to come this way."

"Why? I'm not big enough?" He leaned his head on his hand, trailing his toes up and down Adam's hairy calf. "I'm not saying that to be all annoyingly insecure or something. It felt tight at first, but pretty soon it was…too easy."

"That's the problem. You know how I can heal. Well, I think it has something to do with that. My body heals and accommodates too much. I can't get full enough." He brushed his thumb over Parker's lips. "No matter how amazing my partner is."

A little voice still hissed: *I'm not enough.*

Parker tried to banish the self-pity and slivers of hurt. He cleared his throat. "Dude, that fucking blows. And not in a good way. Isn't there something else we could do?"

"It's okay. I love fucking you. Get off every time. I don't usually feel this way. This need. It'll pass."

"Yeah, but there must be something. I'm not giving up on this problem yet." Pondering, Parker drew circles on Adam's arm. "I wasn't really serious about using something as a dildo the other day, but we could. Something big. There has to be a limit to how much your ass can take."

Adam licked his lips and swallowed hard. "We could. Or..." A red blush crept up his neck.

"Or what?" Parker's pulse jumped, his cock stirring already.

"You could use your hand. Fist fuck me."

Apprehension and a hot pulse of *want* sent Parker's heart into overdrive. "Whoa. I've never even watched fisting porn. And fuck, I guess it's too late now. It's times like this I really, really miss the internet." His throat was dry. "Have you done it before?"

Adam jerked his head in a shake. "Thought about it. But I never trusted anyone enough. No way I was letting some stranger shove his hand up my ass."

"But you'll let me?"

He leaned in and whispered across Parker's lips, "I'd let you do anything."

Parker could only kiss him in reply, his heart thundering. He'd get this right—he'd be what Adam needed. He had to be, or Adam would keep looking, even if it was only subconsciously. And that would lead to more people, and maybe even that damn island. No, Parker would protect them. Had to stop them from falling into a trap the way they did before, when Adam had been made helpless.

Neither of them would be helpless again.

He broke away, saliva trailing from his mouth to Adam's. "Let's do it. I'm going to fuck you the way you need."

Adam's smile lit up his golden eyes, and he nuzzled Parker's cheek. "Tomorrow. We'll sleep on it, and I'll make sure I get myself ready. If you still want to—"

"I will. I will want to so fucking much." He dug his fingers into Adam's arms and stared into his eyes. "I promise. I'll take care of you."

Still smiling, Adam hauled him close in a full-body hug that warmed Parker inside and out. "You always do."

Chapter Seven

"BABY, YOU'RE SURE you don't want to go over to the other boat?" Abby asked while Adam waited with Lilly and Craig in *Bella*'s dinghy.

"No. Why would I want to do that?" Jacob's sullen reply was muttered.

Abby leaned over the railing and gave Adam an apologetic look before turning back. "To learn more about sailing."

"I don't feel like it."

Adam pushed off, calling to Abby, "No problem."

After dropping off Lilly and Craig on *Bella*, where Parker was waiting with a bunch of rope he was tying into impossible knots, Adam returned to *Saltwater* and climbed the ladder.

"All right. Looks like it's you and me, Adam." Hands on her slim hips, Abby eyed the mast. "First thing I do is… Oh right, this." She pulled on a rope. "It's this, right?"

"I think so. I guess we'll find out." In his head, Adam went through the steps Parker had taught him. Jacob had apparently hidden away in the cabin, and as the sails caught the wind, Adam thought it was a shame to miss the sunshine and briny breeze.

"There! We got it!" Abby raised her hand, and he high-fived her. "Piece of cake." She frowned. "Oh wait, that's flapping too much. We have to trim now."

As he and Abby adjusted the sails, Adam glanced over at the other boat, which skipped along at a good pace, Parker trimming the sails while Lilly and Craig watched. Parker was talking animatedly about the jib sheet, his words tripping out the way they often did, as if the syllables crowded his mouth and had to spill out.

"Penny for your thoughts."

He jerked his gaze back to Abby, who gave him a knowing smile. He chuckled, still smiling like a lovesick teenager, most likely. "I'm pretty transparent, I imagine."

"You are, and it's wonderful." She looked across the water, and Adam followed her gaze. Seeing Parker with Craig and Lilly smoothed out some of Adam's rough edges. He still yearned for other wolves, a low pull that he didn't think would ever go away, but this muffled it like sound underwater.

Abby said, "We're both lucky as hell. Admittedly, we'd be luckier if the end of the world wasn't happening."

"You win some, you lose some."

They laughed and checked the sails, which seemed to be doing okay. Adam turned in a circle and did a scan, jolting to a stop as he peered out, the hair on his body rising. He fought back his claws and fangs, the urge to protect thrumming through him.

"What is it?" Abby lifted her hands to shield her eyes, joining him by the railing. "I really need to replace the sunglasses I lost in the storm. Do you see something?"

"On the left side." He could hear Parker's voice in his head insist that it was *port*. "A boat. No sails. Looks like…a powerboat of some kind."

"I don't see anything. Man, your mom must have fed you lots of carrots."

He tried to smile, eyes locked on the boat, memories of his mother echoing distantly.

At the stove, winking and letting him as he tried to steal a cookie from the pantry before dinner.

Laughing as he and the girls tackled her into a snowdrift, Dad applauding.

The jangle of her charm bracelet as she leaned over his bed to kiss him goodnight.

He exhaled slowly. "It doesn't seem to be getting closer. But I'll keep watching."

"Okay. Good plan." Abby went back to the wheel, peering up at the telltales. "And sorry, I hope I didn't upset you. Bringing up your mom."

"No, it's okay." Adam leaned on the railing nearby. "She's been gone a long time now."

"I'm sorry to hear that. Mine's in Seattle. Or was." She shoved her hair off her face, the wind refusing to let it be. "At least my dad didn't live to see this. He was a quiet man, peaceful. This new world would have horrified him."

Adam had no idea what his parents would have thought of it. Perhaps they would have welcomed the new world and the strange and terrible freedom it brought. He cleared his throat. "You're from Seattle?"

"No, after Dad died, Mom remarried and they retired there a few years ago."

"It's good to know she found love again."

Abby shrugged, running her palms over the wheel. "Nice guy, my stepfather. They were both lonely, I think. It wasn't some grand, sweeping romance, but they enjoy each other's company."

She darted a glance toward the cabin door and lowered her voice. "Jacob and I were supposed to visit this Christmas. Go up to Vancouver and do some skiing at Whistler. Give Jacob a white Christmas." Her lips twisted up with a bittersweet smile. "He would have loved that. Mom too. She was always asking when we were going to visit. But I was so busy, you know? Work and Jacob. Trying to date again. I kept putting it off and putting it off." She blinked rapidly, her eyes glistening. "Damn it. Sorry."

"Don't be." Adam reached out and squeezed her shoulder.

"Fuck, I hate crying." She swiped at her eyes. "Usually I can rein it in. On the job, I saw some awful stuff."

"I can imagine."

"Yeah." She huffed, shaking her head. "I'd give anything to be able to just hop a flight and see my mom in a few hours. Life felt so hard, and it was so goddamn easy."

"I know what you mean." It'd honestly been pretty hard hiding who he was from everyone all the time, but he'd certainly taken a lot for granted. "I miss movies," he blurted before he could stop himself.

Abby's face lit up. "Oh, man, me too! Movies were the best. Going to the theater and buying stupidly expensive popcorn. Good times."

"Butter in the middle and on top."

"Anything else was amateur hour." She smiled wistfully. "I'd still feel... Not excitement, but satisfaction, maybe? When the lights went down and the previews started. Well, the half hour of commercials and *then* the previews."

"I hated missing the previews. I almost didn't want to see the movie if I couldn't do it right." He realized it had been almost like a ritual. In his mind, he could see the silver light of the screen, the surround sound bass vibrating in his bones, the plush seats soft, Tina's whisper in his ear.

"Yep. And then the movie would start, and if it was a good one, it would carry me away."

"And if it was bad, I'd make snarky comments with my friend. It was almost as much fun as good movies." He laughed. "The last one we saw was a bad horror flick where the characters are so dumb you're rooting for the ghosts. Tina was so annoyed when the girl went into the basement alone when she heard a thump."

"Preach. Never go into the basement! There is nothing good down there! Ever. It's an easy rule to remember."

Adam sighed, watching the horizon. "Nothing's easy now."

Abby glanced toward the cabin door again consideringly. "Sometimes I wonder if I made the right choices. You know, when everything went to hell."

"We all did what we had to do to stay alive. I'd say you did quite well."

"Tell Jacob that." She smiled and shook her head. "Teenagers."

"It's tough."

"So's he. He just doesn't know it yet. But he blames me, you know? When it all happened, I wanted to try for Seattle to find my mom, but the roads north were jammed. Craig's parents are gone, and he thought DC would be better. Hoping the government would be able to take control." She grimaced. "Clearly that didn't happen. But we hoped. I was torn. Thought about going our own ways, getting me and Jacob to the West Coast. He wanted to find his dad." She lowered her voice. "Why is beyond me. The man was never there for him."

"He's family, though. That's important."

"No, he's a walking penis with ears."

Adam had to laugh just a bit. "That's...evocative."

"How I ever married that man is beyond me. I look back and think, was he really different in the beginning? Or was I blind and stupid? How could I ever love someone so selfish? But I did. Oh, I loved him. And he cheated on me a dozen times, probably. I only caught him the once, but that was enough."

Adam couldn't imagine it, betraying Parker like that. Throwing away family for sex.

"Shit, we need to trim," Abby muttered.

Once the sails were repositioned, Adam tried to think of something to say. "Craig seems like a great guy."

Abby's eyes crinkled as she smiled. "He is. Thank God I decided it was too much of a risk to go off on our own. I mean, Craig and I barely knew each other."

"Third date, right?" Adam pulled his camera out of the pocket of his cargo shorts. "Do you mind telling me about it? I was a film major. Need to conserve batteries, but I can't resist filming a bit here and there. It's silly, really. Not like I'll ever get the chance to finish my movie."

"Not silly at all."

"Even if I did, who would see it?"

Abby seemed to ponder it. "Would you still want to finish it? Even if no one ever saw it?"

"Yes." He didn't need to think about it. Even if it never had an audience, his images would be captured. They'd be real. He tried to smile. "Not that many people would have seen it anyway besides my advisor and the film department committee."

"Well, if you make a new one, I'll watch the hell out of it. We'll find a way. With popcorn too. Double butter. I'll churn it myself if I have to."

The urge to hug her had his fingers twitching. "Thank you."

"What kind of movies did you study?"

"All of them, but my master's thesis was on documentaries. I was making one on found families."

"Well, that's an apropos subject." She smiled widely and thrust out her chin with an exaggerated smile. "Do I have anything in my teeth?"

"Nope. You look beautiful." And she did, her light hair caught by the wind and a blush in her dimpled cheeks.

"Okay, I'm ready for my close-up, Mr. DeMille."

Adam switched on the camera and got her in frame at the wheel, bracing himself with one hand on the rail, keeping the focus as steady as possible on the swaying deck. "So, your third date with Craig. What did you do?"

"Well, he picked me up at my apartment. Came right up to the door instead of just texting that he was outside in the car. I was wearing a new dress with daisies on it, and he said I looked like sunshine." She smiled. "It was corny, and Jacob was being a brat and making puking sounds in the background, but I loved it.

Craig has this way. He's always sincere, no matter what. You know what I mean?"

"I do. Where did you go?"

"There was one of those box store malls on the outskirts of town. You know, with a Target and Marshall's, a big movie theater and some restaurants. We went to the Cheesecake Factory. I know, it's not exactly gourmet, but I've always enjoyed a chain restaurant. And cheesecake. Anyway, we were munching away, talking about *House of Cards*, and time just flew. Our first and second dates had been for coffee. You know, during the day, only an hour or two. Low pressure. But things were different that night."

"How so?" Adam asked quietly, not wanting to disturb the flow of her memories but nudging her toward more details.

She laughed. "He kissed me before we left for the restaurant. Usually you wait until the end of the date. Traditionally, anyway. But nope, he opened the car door for me, then went around and got behind the wheel. He leaned over, and I elbowed him in the jaw trying to do up my seat belt. Totally oblivious."

With a grin, she shook her head. "Poor Craig. I really dinged him. He said he was fine, that he could always use another scar on his chin. Said that's what he got for trying to kiss me already. Told him if he wanted to try again, I wouldn't mind." She lifted her hand over her eyes and squinted across at the other boat with a tender smile. "Nope, I sure didn't mind."

"Then you had dinner?"

"Right." Abby swung her focus back to the camera. "We'd been planning on seeing a movie, but we skipped it. Sat in that booth for hours, until we finally had room to share a slice of cheesecake."

"What kind?"

Her arms out for balance, Abby closed her eyes, a blissful smile lifting her lips. "Lemon raspberry. Good god, I miss cheesecake.

Did I mention that? It was divine." She opened her eyes again, her smile fading. "It's a good thing we didn't make the movie. Once we realized something was going on—the servers were all clumped together, looking at phone screens, and you could feel it in the air, that something big was happening. Anyway, we were able to get Lilly from her little friend's house, then get back to my place before the traffic got crazy."

She shivered. "Jacob was alone. When he turned thirteen, he insisted he didn't need a sitter anymore, and he was right. Hell, growing up we'd be out miles from home and no one knew where we were. I decided to start giving him some responsibility, and I figured I knew where he was, so he'd be safe for a few hours. But if we hadn't made it back, if the virus had spread in Winston-Salem that first night... He would have been all alone. Now he's got people. Whether he likes it or not. Thank you, Adam."

He turned off the camera and slipped it back into his pocket. "For what?"

"For saving our lives. For all of this." She waved her hand toward the other boat. "I know it's only been, what, a week? But I'm so glad to know you. Both of you. I think Parker wasn't too keen on us to begin with, but we're wearing him down."

Smiling, Adam looked over to where Parker was teaching Lilly knots, Craig at the wheel for the moment. "You are. He's just... Some stuff has happened. It's hard to know who to trust these days."

"It sure is. But we trust you. Thank you."

"I should thank *you*."

"For what? I haven't churned that butter yet."

"For..." He waved his hand toward her and then the other boat. "For this. It helps. Having you all here. We're better this way." They needed this. Maybe it was silly to call it "family" after knowing them such a short time, but Adam hadn't felt so centered since his parents and sisters had been alive.

Whatever it was—family, community, pack—it helped.

Eyes glistening, Abby took his hands, her small fingers gripping, and pressed a kiss to his cheek.

The wind shifted, flapping the sails, and she stepped back. "Okay, enough mushy stuff for one day. Let's adjust this sail. Avast ye, matey! I have no idea what that means, but I think we should talk like pirates for the rest of the day."

Adam laughed, low and deep. "Shiver me timbers, sounds like a plan."

The radio came to life. "Hey, how are things going over there?" Parker asked. "Your sails are luffing. You need to—"

"Arrrr," Adam growled. "Aye-aye, cap'n."

After a beat of silence, Parker asked, "Are you talking like a pirate?"

"Yo-ho-ho." Adam tried not to crack up as Abby dissolved into giggles.

"And a bottle of rum?" Parker laughed. "Okay, landlubbers. Trim your sails or I'll make you walk the plank."

"Arrrr." He put down the radio and went to pull on the ropes.

Parker's laughter reached him across the waves, and Adam worked contentedly by Abby's side.

"YOU DON'T HAVE to do this if you don't want to." Naked and rubbing a towel over his wet hair, Adam listened to the way Parker's heart jumped all around. "It's not like I don't love the other things we do."

Parker looked over from where he finished drawing the blinds over the last porthole by the kitchen. "No, we're doing this."

"But if you're nervous…"

"Of course I'm nervous." He came over to where Adam stood and picked up Adam's hand, placing it on his chest. "But I want to do this. Okay?"

Adam's fingers splayed on the cotton of Parker's T-shirt, and he listened to his heart grow steady. "Okay."

His mouth was dry, excitement sparking in his veins as he helped Parker undress, stealing kisses along the way. He'd gotten himself ready and had a shower as night fell before six o'clock, and although his stomach growled, it would be worth the wait.

They turned off all the lights but one dim lamp in the bedroom, the radar's green light casting shadows in the saloon. Across the water, he could hear the others playing Clue after their dinner. Jacob insisted on being Miss Scarlet, much to Lilly's displeasure, since Miss Scarlet always went first.

"Adam?"

"Hmm?" He refocused.

"You had a goofy smile on your face. Not really what I expected before I shove my hand up your ass."

He laughed and kissed Parker lightly. "Always such a way with words. I was just listening to the other boat. They're playing Clue."

"Oh." Parker's brow furrowed. "Cool. But you're here with me, right? Just the two of us?"

He kept his tone light. "It would be pretty awkward to have an audience. It's just you and me." He drew him close, resting their foreheads together and trailing his fingers over Parker's arms, raising goosebumps.

Parker swallowed thickly. "How do you want to do this? I think I know what to do."

Adam had drawn a diagram and told him everything he'd learned about fisting from his reading over the years. "You'll be great. You won't hurt me, remember? I'm not normal."

Parker frowned. "You're *special*. There's a difference."

A warm flush in his chest, Adam kissed him softly, then piled up a few pillows and spread a towel over them. "From what I've read, the key is being relaxed. Obviously for me, it's going to be a lot easier, but I think I should still try to let go. We don't have a sling, so…"

He leaned over the pillows, fidgeting until his legs were spread and his knees comfortable, his butt in the air and chest leaning down, his face turned to the side.

"*Fuck*," Parker muttered. "Yeah, this works." He ran his palms over Adam's ass, caressing gently. "Look at you. You're so beautiful."

Adam had never felt more vulnerable yet completely safe at the same time. Parker kissed down his spine, wet and gentle, and Adam didn't try to stop a whimper. He knew Parker understood.

Closing his eyes, he inhaled and exhaled deeply, willing himself to relax as Parker massaged his hole, licking into it slowly. The rough, wet lapping of his tongue sent pleasant tingles to Adam's toes.

He'd always loved rimming, and had wondered more than once if it was something to do with being a werewolf. Not that humans didn't enjoy it, but giving and receiving the act touched a primal instinct deep inside him he couldn't name.

Now he wondered if being fisted was going to touch something even deeper. He'd fantasized about this for so long—had wanted to be truly filled.

But what if I still don't feel it? Whatever it *is. What if Parker doesn't like it? What if—*

"Hey. Relax, remember?" Parker smoothed his hands over Adam's hips and flanks. "I can hear you thinking. Stop."

He nodded against the sheets. "Sorry."

"I'm going to use some lube now. Okay?"

Adam nodded again. He knew some people used Crisco or special lube designed for fisting. But as Parker edged a slick finger on his right hand in, Adam adjusted so quickly he barely needed it. Still, the glide felt nice, and as Parker worked up to three fingers, his limbs felt pleasantly heavy.

"Ready for more?"

"Please."

When Parker tucked his thumb under his fingers and pushed them all in past his knuckles, holding Adam's hip with his left hand, a moan escaped Adam's lips at the wonderful stretch. He knew it wouldn't last as his body accommodated too well, but for the moment he felt deliciously full.

"You like that?" Parker murmured. "I wish you could see how hot you look, all open for me like this." He wiggled his slick fingers, brushing Adam's prostate.

Gasping, Adam could only nod again. His dick was soft beneath him, the pleasure entirely centered on his ass. "More," he whispered.

"My hand's inside you," Parker muttered, as if he couldn't believe it. "Fuck, I never thought this would be so hot. I'm getting really hard."

The way Parker moved his fingers, going in past his wrist, sent pulses of sensation waving through Adam. Lips parted, he concentrated on staying relaxed, on being swept away. But the fullness was fading, and he pleaded, "*More.*" He could hear Parker squeezing out more lube, momentarily retracting his hand.

"You want me to fist fuck you? Can you feel that better?"

"Yes, *yes.*"

The movements of Parker's fingers were magnified inside him, and Adam did feel it wonderfully as Parker made a fist and moved back and forth, stretching his rectum and rubbing his prostate. With a human, it would take much, much longer to get to this stage, and Adam already needed more.

"Farther. Please."

Laughter from the other boat sang over the water like a caress. When he was a kid, he'd liked going to bed early while his parents and sisters still had their lights on, the faint yellow glow around his bedroom door a comfort as he drifted off.

A similar sensation of peace filled him, the laughter a distant balm as Parker pushed into his colon. Parker was breathing hard, and he gripped Adam's hip tighter with his free hand. There was another ring of muscle there at the entrance, and he hesitated.

"This is trippy. I mean, I don't really know what I'm doing." He took short, rapid breaths. "I might hurt you even if you heal. Are you sure?"

"*Yes*. Need it." Tensing, a strange sort of panic clawed at him. Like he was so close to finding something just out of reach, something he'd craved for so long. A connection and peace he'd never been able to name until he met Parker. "Don't stop."

Even though his heart hammered and Adam could smell fear in his sweat, Parker said, "I won't, I won't. Shh. I've got you." With his free hand, he petted Adam's hair, bending over to press a kiss between his shoulder blades. His breath tickled Adam's skin.

As Parker's hand curved to the left into the bend inside Adam, easing into his colon, a tidal wave of bliss left him gasping and breathless, his whole body tingling. "Oh, *oh*, yes." He was probably moaning too loudly given how sound traveled across water, but he couldn't stop himself.

"Fuck, baby," Parker breathed. "My arm's *inside* you. You feel that?" He leaned over, kissing Adam's spine. "You're so good."

Parker was deeper than Adam had ever had anything inside him, all the way to his elbow. Adam had tried in the past with dildos, but it had always felt awkward and wrong somehow, and he'd quickly given up.

Something had been missing, and now he had it with Parker's heavy breath brushing his back and neck, his lips against skin as tender whispers fell from them, his fingers flexing and exploring deep inside, every movement more intense than Adam had even hoped. Adam was stretching, but he still felt amazingly full, the pressure from Parker's arm incredible.

As Parker made a fist again, pumping back and forth so deep inside, Adam's eyes rolled back, the waves of intense pleasure almost too much. His mouth open, he groaned rhythmically, sure that he would levitate right off the bed if not for Parker's hand and arm anchoring him.

Completing him.

His throat thick and eyes burning with unshed tears, gratitude swelled sweet and wonderful—for Parker and the family across the water, for the pack they were building. For the home they would make. They'd find a way. Although he was utterly exposed, his defenses never more down, he was *safe*.

His dick wasn't hard, yet as Parker pushed in even farther— almost using his whole arm, the pressure against Adam's core overwhelming—the pulses of pleasure that rippled through his body could only be described as an orgasm. He rubbed his face against the smooth sheets, muffling his cries, his body and soul flying.

"That's it. Yeah. So good," Parker muttered as he pumped his arm inside Adam. "Take it all."

As the pleasure waned to a peaceful flutter, Adam opened his eyes and licked his lips, the tang of his sweat salty on his tongue. "Oh god." He was wrung out, his body buzzing, the fullness starting to fade. "That was... Wow."

Moaning, Parker tried to rut against Adam's thigh. Adam could feel the hard tip of his dick, but Parker clearly couldn't get the leverage needed. Images from a video he'd seen years ago flitted across Adam's mind, followed by a fresh bolt of desire. His voice was hoarse when he spoke.

"Ease back until it's just your hand again."

Parker tensed. "Does it hurt?"

"No, no. Just pull back, and then get your dick in too. Jack yourself off inside me. Fill me." He imagined Parker's cum would flow deep inside him and stay.

With a groan, Parker's heart pounded even harder, the sound drumming in Adam's ears while his own heart was calm, his body so incredibly relaxed. Parker gently retracted his arm. With another squirt of lube, he pushed the head of his cock against Adam's stretched hole. "Are you sure?"

"Yes," Adam murmured, breathing deeply and letting everything go, relaxing his hole as much as he could.

"Oh, Jesus."

Parker's fingers would leave bruises on Adam's hip that would heal all too quickly. Grunting, he shoved, straining as he squeezed his dick inside. His hips hit Adam's ass awkwardly, and he bent over, hot gusts of breath on Adam's skin. Adam was so full again he might burst, and he shuddered with another glorious wave as Parker started jacking himself, brushing Adam's prostate.

"*Oh fuck, oh fuck,*" Parker mumbled. "I'm going to come."

"Do it."

"Jesus, I'm jerking off inside you. I'm so fucking hard."

Adam pushed himself up to his hands so he could look over his shoulder. He could just see where Parker's cock and wrist disappeared inside him. Parker raised his head where it had dangled, and their eyes locked.

"Give me your cum," Adam pleaded. "I want it all."

With a shout, Parker seized and shook, his head tipping back as his orgasm overtook him, baring his throat. Adam wanted to latch on with his teeth, not biting, but marking just enough to show in the morning.

Panting, Parker was still inside him, staring at where his hand and dick disappeared. "Was it enough?"

"Yes," Adam whispered, his voice hoarse. "Thank you."

Parker eased out, first his softening dick, then his hand. His semen dripped from Adam's open hole, down his thighs. Adam dropped onto his chest, and Parker flopped on his back beside him. When Parker turned his head, his breath caught, eyes widening.

"Does it hurt?" He swiped at Adam's face. "Your ass is so swollen…"

Adam realized tears were falling down his cheeks. He smiled. "No. I promise. It feels perfect. Even though you're not in there anymore, I don't feel empty at all."

Parker wiggled close and kissed him softly. "I never thought… That was amazing. I didn't even know it was possible."

"Takes a lot more work and patience for humans to go that far. Years."

"Yeah. I don't know if I could."

"You don't have to."

"Did you come?"

"Not with my dick. But god, yes. I can't describe it. Having you inside me like that… It was everything I wanted."

When they found a home, they could do it without needing to be quiet. If not Salvation Island, maybe another one, with a house of their own and Abby, Craig, and the kids in their place just far enough away without being too far.

Parker kissed Adam's cheeks, nose, and chin. For long minutes, they nuzzled together, boneless.

After a while, Adam reluctantly pushed himself up on his hands. "We should wash up. Have dinner."

"Hmm." Parker wriggled his sticky fingers. "Yeah, I'm starving, and also pretty gross." Face glowing, he whispered, "Dude, I *jerked off inside you.*"

"You sure did."

They laughed and stumbled to the shower, squeezing in and cleaning each other. Parker washed Adam's hole so gently. It felt as if he was still buried deep inside.

Chapter Eight

WAKING UP TO find he was drooling on Adam was Parker's favorite way to start a day.

"Mmm," he mumbled, rubbing his cheek against Adam's chest, loving the rough caress of hair. He was sprawled across Adam, who was on his back, already awake. Parker could tell by how he breathed and the way he spread his big hand over Parker's ass, just resting it there where they cuddled under the covers. "Morning."

"Hey," Adam murmured. "Rise and shine."

"Uh-huh." Parker blinked at the soft light coming in the porthole on one side of the bed. They covered them with black material and duct tape now to be absolutely certain there was no light betraying their position, but Adam must have reached up and pulled a corner free. "Looks like a nice day for scavenging." Unease rippled through him as he thought of the dwindling supply of food and medicine. Of *everything*.

As the days ticked by, the survivors took more and more. The shelves would never be restocked, and then what? A tendril of hope wound its way through him, and he closed his eyes for a moment, letting himself explore the fantasy that the virus would be cured, the government swooping in to save the day and make the world normal again.

They could go back to Stanford, and Parker would study so damn hard for Adam's film noir class. They'd watch old movies, curled up together on a couch, eating popcorn with extra butter while Adam talked about symbolism and the use of light and shadow or some shit. They'd cheer for football on Sundays and stay in for HBO's latest buzzy show. They'd fight about stupid things like finishing the milk and would make up with kisses.

They'd have the most ordinary, amazing lives.

The pang of loss rang through him like a church bell, soul deep. As if he was cycling through the channels on TV, flashes filled his mind:

Carey's eyes bulging, her teeth crashing together as she jerked.

Tumbling into a swimming pool, the machete slipping from his fingers.

Utterly alone on the empty desert road.

Adam dropping like a stone as the tranquilizer took him.

Naked on the deck, powerless with Shorty looming.

"Parker?" Adam stroked down his spine. "You okay?"

Swallowing bile and inhaling steadily, he opened his eyes, peering at Adam's shoulder. He traced a finger over the veins on the underside of Adam's arm, absurdly proud of how steady his hand was.

I'm fine. See?

He asked, "Can you look for more peanut butter cookies?"

"Hmm-hmm. It's on my list."

As Parker imagined grocery shopping, pushing the cart and debating the merits of zesty Doritos versus ranch, the pang of longing and grief revisited, duller this time. "Thanks," he mumbled.

"Are you sure you'll be okay here? Maybe..."

"We talked about this." He circled a finger around Adam's nipple.

Nice and even. Everything's fine.

"Craig wants to go, and I'll stay with Abby and the kids. I'm good."

I'm not broken.

"I won't be long. I—" Adam froze, tension springing through

his limbs. After listening intently, he exhaled, relaxing. "It was only Craig talking."

"Like we said, you won't be long. We got a great haul of weapons yesterday. Backup machetes for the win. Today you can just do medication and food. Oh, and the fishing lures I mentioned, if possible. It's a fishing town, so here's hoping."

They were off the coast of Georgia now, and the place was overrun by creepers. Smoldering fires burned in the distance, something they were seeing more and more as they made their way down the coast. They had to grab everything they could before the world became ash.

The radio came to life, and Parker braced himself. Salvation Island was still transmitting their bullshit messages to come and end up in their dungeon, but Adam listened intently every time as if there was some answer there.

Thankfully, it was Abby's voice that rang out. "Good morning over there. Can I send Jacob over for sugar? We're out, and my coffee will be so depressing without it."

Relieved, Parker disentangled from Adam and crawled off the bed. He picked up the transmitter. "Sure, no prob. How's your dinghy holding up?"

"Eh, not sure how long the patch job will hold, but it seems okay for now. Oh, and Craig's making pancakes if you guys want to come for breakfast in a while."

"Sounds like a plan. We'll get cleaned up. I'll get the sugar out for Jacob."

"Thanks, hon."

Stretching, Parker scratched his ass. Time for another day. Time to smile and be normal. He tugged on boxers and poked Adam's foot. "You want first shower?"

Still under the covers, Adam yawned. "Go ahead." He got up at least twice a night to go on deck and do a sweep, and Parker wished there was more he could do to share the burden. But

Adam wouldn't budge on sharing guard duty.

Hearing the dinghy's motor, Parker poured out a generous helping of sugar into a Tupperware container, closing the lid with satisfying snaps. Soon, Jacob's voice floated down tentatively.

"Uh, hi?"

Parker realized the hatch was still closed and called out, "Come on down!" as he finished surveying the radar screen and doing an instruments check. When he looked up, Jacob stood there staring at him, frozen.

"Uh, good morning," Parker said. *Why is this kid so weird?*

Jacob opened and closed his mouth, then darted his gaze over to the cabin, where Adam was still in bed, the covers down to his waist and tangled around his hairy legs.

"I…" Jacob swallowed thickly, his Adam's apple bobbing. "So, you guys are really…" His brows drew together.

Stiffening, Parker slid the container across the counter. "Gay? Yeah. You got a problem with that?"

Shaking his head vigorously, Jacob grabbed the sugar and backed up, looking between the bed and Parker with wide eyes. He turned and darted up the steps. A few moments later, the dinghy's motor roared on.

Parker grumbled to himself, "Too fucking bad if you've got a problem."

A deep sigh came from the bed. "Parker."

"What?" He stripped off his boxers and leaned in to start the shower. "No one has time for this shit. I didn't put up with homophobia before, and my patience for it now is less than zero."

Adam pushed himself up to sitting, an eyebrow raised wryly. "Yes, I can see that. But I don't think that's what's going on with Jacob. Parker, he's got a crush on you. Can't you see that?"

He sputtered. "What? Why—what?" He thought about Jacob, with his skinny legs and pimples and intense stare, the way Parker would sometimes turn to find those dark eyes trained on him.

"*Me*? Why would he have a crush on *me*?" The shower was running warm, so he got in and pulled the curtain, frowning as he uncapped the shampoo.

"Why wouldn't he?" Adam called.

"Um, hello?" Scoffing, he added, "You're here."

There was silence in reply, then the curtain opened and Adam squeezed in. "Guess I'm not his type." He ran his hands down Parker's back to cup his ass. "But I think he has good taste. And seeing you practically naked in your boxers gave him an instant boner."

Parker elbowed Adam as he reached for the soap. "No way. Really?"

"Yup."

"You seriously think the kid has a crush on me?"

"I seriously do. I can hear his heartbeat, remember? And I sense things."

"And your boner senses are expertly honed?"

"Yes."

"Well, shit." Parker thought of the way Jacob had scurried away after he'd barked at him. He groaned. "Now I feel like a total asshole."

As he edged under the shower's spray, Adam made a humming noise but didn't say anything.

"This is the part where you tell me I'm wonderful and perfect and could never be an asshole," Parker noted dourly.

"Oh, is it?" Laughing, Adam closed his eyes under the water. "Must have missed that memo."

"Shut up, jerk." He laughed too, then sighed. "I'll talk to the kid later. Make nice."

"Good. Although I wouldn't say anything about the crush."

"Oh my god, I'm not *that* clueless." He pinched Adam's flank playfully. "I wasn't raised by wolves."

"Ooooh, *burn*."

Things soon disintegrated into a tickle fight, and only the lure of pancakes kept them from fucking. *Saltwater Taffy* had a small seating area near her bow, and Parker and Adam squeezed in beside Abby and the kids. Jacob resolutely kept his head down and his arms crossed, and guilt niggled even harder at Parker.

He knew what it was like to be a scared little queer kid, and god, what was it going to be like for Jacob in this new world? Maybe it would be easier since sexuality was the last thing people should be worrying about when surviving was a struggle. But he had a feeling it wouldn't be.

Watching him now, nothing seemed easy for Jacob. A zit on his chin was ready to blow, and he was all angles and sharp edges, hunched in on himself. Lilly was telling a story about trying to catch a fish, and Parker thought about being eight years old, and how his biggest problems were not being allowed to have the latest violent video game and whether Jessica would be able to come on a bike ride to the park with the new jungle gym that was across a major road.

Jessica, with her easy laugh and sly sense of humor, her fashion tips and advice about boys. She was in New York and probably dead, or infected. Shuddering at the thought of those kind eyes bulging, Parker picked up his mug of coffee and gulped.

"Chocolate chip pancakes are served." Craig climbed out of the hatch, brandishing a stacked plate with a flourish. He'd borrowed the electric shaver and removed his beard, shaving his head close too. "Try to go easy on the syrup." He nudged Jacob playfully. "That means you, buddy."

"Whatever," Jacob mumbled, his head still down.

Craig blinked and shared a glance with Abby, who shrugged. He said, "Everyone tuck in. I'll be back with more."

Closing his eyes, Parker savored the warm bits of melted chocolate chips, moaning softly and licking at a smear caught on his lower lip. When he opened his eyes, he found Jacob staring with wide eyes, his knife and fork poised over his plate. Parker smiled awkwardly. "Um, I love chocolate. I mean, who doesn't, right?"

Blushing right to his ears, Jacob nodded in a jerk and ducked his head, shoving a bite into his mouth.

Parker happily took another pancake when Craig returned and squeezed in next to Abby at the table. Motioning with his fork to Craig's chin, Parker asked, "Where'd you get the scar? It looks old."

Craig ran his hand over the groove in his chin, about an inch long. "Ah, yes. It's a pretty rough story. Don't know if it's appropriate for young ears." Jacob scowled into his pancakes, and Lilly giggled. "Well, I guess you guys are old enough to hear it." He lowered his voice to a confessional tone, and despite himself, Parker leaned in. "I was a real bruiser as a kid. I'd get myself into all kinds of trouble."

Jacob blurted, "Really?" He flushed as soon as he asked, dropping his head again.

"Oh yeah." Craig whistled softly and rubbed his chin. "The day I got this, I was in the fight of my life."

Craig looked so serious all of a sudden that Parker wasn't sure it was a joke anymore. "Did you, like, get knifed or something?"

"You could say that. Sliced right open with cold steel."

Abby shook her head solemnly. "That soda machine really had it in for you."

"It did!" Craig objected indignantly. "Son of a gun came out of nowhere!"

"When you tripped into it, Dad." Lilly grinned, clearly having heard this tale before. "In a bowling alley. Real tough."

"Listen, young lady. The Rolling Pins and Gutter Sharks meant business. I needed stitches after I landed on the edge of that soda machine, but I still finished my last frame. Our pride and the Boise Lucky Lanes' under-thirteen championship was on the line, and we were going home champions."

Even Jacob smiled as they all laughed. Beside Parker, Adam's shoulders shook. He had a drop of syrup at the corner of his mouth, and Parker reached up to swipe it clean with his finger. When he went back to his pancakes and Craig launched into another bowling story, he realized Jacob was watching with wide eyes.

Before Parker could smile at him and try to make up for being a dick earlier, Jacob took his plate and mumbled something about starting the dishes. Parker sighed to himself. He'd have to try to talk to the kid later. Maybe he could get him alone while Adam and Craig were gone...

Thoughts of Shorty and his friends whipped through him without warning, and he didn't realize he was jiggling his leg until Adam pressed his palm against his knee gently, warm on the bare skin below his shorts.

Parker gave him a little smile and dipped a square of pancake into syrup. The sun was out, and breakfast was sweet on his tongue. He was with good people. The past was done and the future was probably fucked. There was nothing else to do but focus on the present.

"SORRY JACOB'S BEING surly. Not sure what's gotten into him today," Abby said as she climbed the ladder on the tall pier, a gun tucked into the waistband of her capris below her purple tank top.

"No prob." Parker finished hitching *Saltwater* to a post and followed up the ladder, trying to avoid barnacles crusted on the old wood, his new machete in one hand. "Teenagers, right?"

Abby laughed. "You say that like you're not one yourself."

"Guess I don't feel much like one anymore." He stepped up and stretched. "Oh man, you're right—feels good to be on solid ground. Well, wood."

"Yeah, I just need a break from all that swaying. At least I'm not vomiting over the side all the time like I was when we first got the boat. Got my sea legs, I guess." She raised a hand to shield her eyes, peering back at where *Bella* was anchored in the harbor about fifty feet away.

Jacob and Lilly were at the table by the stern under the canvas shade Parker had taken out of storage, its posts snapping easily into answering brackets on the deck. *Saltwater* didn't have any shade, and as the morning went on, the unblinking sun was getting hotter. He was tempted to strip off his cargo shorts and tee and dive into the water. Maybe later when Adam and Craig were back.

The kids' heads bent over the books they were reading. Abby and Craig were trying to institute a school schedule, which Parker understood, even if he thought it was probably not going to hold. Things had stabilized as they sailed down the coast, and they'd been lucky not to see many creepers on shore, and no other survivors for days.

He scanned the trees beyond the pier and the raised board-walk, along with a marina parking lot with a few abandoned cars still gleaming under the sun. He hoped it would stick. It felt too quiet, but they were in a fairly rural area of the coast.

In the distance, smoke curled into the air, a haze that could almost be clouds but for the gray, toxic tinge. They couldn't smell it here on the shore, the wind coming in salty and fresh from the ocean. For the moment, they could pretend it wasn't there, and the sky was nothing but clear and blue.

Craig and Adam had taken *Bella*'s dinghy to shore, where it waited on the sand. They'd already scavenged the marina and brought back anything worthwhile before going farther afield. Parker surveyed the sea beyond the harbor, watching for move-ment before turning back to the land. He did this little dance automatically now. Always watching. He switched his machete from one hand to the other and back again.

"Jacob is…quiet. Has he always been?" he asked.

"Mostly. Especially after his dad left. Not like this, though."

"Right. Did he have a lot of friends? Um, a girlfriend?"

Super subtle, dude.

Abby smiled softly. "No. And I don't think he wants one."

"Oh. Right, okay. Um…" God, he sucked at this.

She picked up some broken shells from the pier, probably left there by birds, and started tossing them into the water: *plop, plop, plop.* "I've been dropping hints for a while. Talking about LGBT rights and marriage equality, and how important it is." Her face creased. "Is there even a Supreme Court anymore? I guess not. People are free to be whoever they want now. To love who they want. One upside."

"It's surreal, isn't it?" He stared at the gleaming cars in the distance. "When you guys tried for Washington…"

She rubbed her hands over her bare arms. "Couldn't even get close. It was decimated." After a few moments, she said, "I went on the radio last night, looking for reports. Heard someone from Germany. My high school German's rusty, but it didn't sound good."

"If you hear anything from England… Good or bad, I want to know."

"I'll tell you. I promise." She reached out and squeezed his elbow. "Anyway, I'm hoping being around you and Adam will help Jacob. I must be doing something wrong, because he just stays clammed up."

"Nah, you're not doing anything wrong. He'll say something when he's ready. It can be hard, saying it out loud. Especially at first."

She nodded. "Okay. Thank you." Her cheeks puffed as she blew out a long breath. "It's tough, this parenting thing."

"Jesus, I can only imagine." He did another turn, watching

closely for movement in any direction.

"I've always worried about what kind of world we're leaving our kids, and now look at us. I can barely sleep thinking about it."

"Yeah. I'm trying to focus on the present. Enjoy the little things and all that shit."

Smiling, Abby rolled her shoulders. "You're right. Okay, I'm going to focus on the vitamin D I'm getting, and the fact that I can stretch my legs." She walked down to the middle of the pier. "This is good shit," she called back.

Parker laughed, and as a set of waves washed in, the salt in the air intensified wetly. He closed his eyes for a moment, inhaling all the way to his toes. The tide strangely rumbled as it receded, and he could feel it shake along the pier. The sun beamed down, white light beyond his eyelids, bright and perfect on his cheeks. The machete handle was solid in his palm, a reassuring weight. Under his bare feet, the worn wood of the pier was hot.

Sighing, Parker opened his eyes, and the world tilted violently.

For a heartbeat he stood frozen, not comprehending the sight of creepers swarming onto the pier with jerky motions, their limbs stiff and wrong but so fast. Then Abby's scream tore through the briny air, gulls shrieking with her as she raced toward Parker.

Parker's feet were moving toward her, and his brain caught up with his eyes, realizing the creepers had somehow come from *below*. They were rising up from under the boardwalk, and Abby ran, shooting blindly behind her. The awful, wild hum they made iced Parker's spine, their bulging eyes stark and sickening in the light of day.

He was still fifteen feet away when he knew Abby wasn't fast enough.

No one but Adam could have been, and she went down in a sprawl, emptying her gun into the infected grasping at her sneakers. Parker skidded to a stop, digging in his bare toes as he hacked at the creepers and hauled Abby up. They managed to slow the handful of infected at the front of the pack, and the boat wasn't too far.

We can make it.

The pier suddenly seemed a mile longer than before, the chattering filling Parker's ears. Above it screams rose, and Parker thought maybe they were his own until he realized it was the kids watching from *Bella* in the middle of the harbor.

He and Abby leapt down onto the boat, pain exploding in Parker's hip as he struck the deck. She yanked out an assault rifle from where it was tucked away by the wheel, spraying bullets into the infected, holding them back just enough for Parker to hack through the mooring rope and shove off as hard as he could, using every ounce of strength. He turned to start the engine, and a creeper dove at him, all teeth and eyes and fury.

Another round of bullets sent it twisting back, and Abby kicked it overboard. Parker slammed down the throttle and they were away, more infected streaming onto the pier. A couple tumbled off the end.

Heart hammering, choking him, Parker panted with his mouth open, clutching the machete. He pulled back on the throttle barely in time to avoid crashing into *Bella,* then backed up toward the pier, making sure they were between it and the kids.

He stared into the depths, harsh breathing filling his ears. The creepers splashed around the tall piles of the pier, not getting anywhere, a handful left on top milling around, screeching. "Looks like they still can't swim. Just our luck they'd learn or something." He could barely hear his own voice over the rushing in his ears. "Fuck. That was—"

"Close" shriveled and disintegrated on his tongue as red filled his peripheral vision.

Abby crumpled to the deck, her blood staining the sunbleached oak.

Parker slammed to his knees, reaching for her and clamping a hand over her thigh. His mind screamed in denial, but she was bitten. There was no doubt.

Her flesh was brutally torn away from her calf and shin, and how she'd run at all, Parker had no fucking idea. But the worst of it was above her knee, where the blood pumped out too fast, flowing between Parker's useless fingers.

Even if she wasn't infected, she was dead.

"*Jacob*," Abby croaked, terror written on her face. She was mercifully still herself, at least for the moment. "Love him. Tell him."

Nodding, Parker pressed down on the wound, knowing the femoral artery was severed, praying into the void that she would bleed out before he had to kill her.

At first, he could only manage a garbled word, but he cleared his throat, rasping, "I'll tell him. I'll take care of him. We'll protect him. I promise."

"Mom! *Mom!*" Jacob's scream tore over the harbor, and Abby shook her head desperately.

Parker ripped his gaze from Abby's and looked across the bow to see Jacob at *Bella*'s wheel some distance away, turning on the engine. He went up on his knees. "No! Stay the fuck over there! Turn it off! Don't fucking move, Jacob!"

Jacob obeyed, shutting off the engine. "Is my mom okay?" he shouted. "Mom?"

"I'm looking after her! Stay there!" Parker realized Jacob and Lilly couldn't see Abby on the deck beyond the cabin's low roof. "Don't move!"

"Craig and Lilly…" Abby gasped for air, an awful gurgling sound in her throat, her eyes glistening as she grasped Parker's arm.

He knew he had to get away from her in case she turned before she died, but he couldn't fucking do it.

She did it for him.

Abby shoved his hand away from her thigh, letting her blood drain faster. He clutched her fingers, babbling, "They'll all be okay. Jacob will be okay. We'll take care of him. I'll tell him you love him. We'll keep him safe."

As her breathing hitched and sputtered, Parker told her the prettiest lies he could, making promises he desperately wanted to keep. Her other hand reached up to claw at her throat, and Parker wished he could give her water at least. Then he realized she was tugging at her necklace, a delicate little silver dove.

"*Jacob*," she moaned. "My baby."

"I'll give it to him. I understand. It's okay, Abby. It's okay."

A tremble went through her, and she shuddered with staccato gasps, more time elapsing between them until they stopped, her blood still pouring out, a warm pool around Parker's knees.

"*Mom?*" Jacob cried.

Parker stared into Abby's unseeing eyes, useless fucking tears falling from his own. "Stay there!" he choked out. "Jacob, stay there." Parker forced his head up, assessing the threat from the remaining infected on the pier. The ones in the water had apparently drowned, or at least he fucking hoped so.

The sun still beamed down, waves lapping at the beach. His chest heaved, nausea roiling through him, bile stark and ugly in his throat.

It had been a minute, maybe two. Three at the most. He'd just been standing on the pier, thinking how perfect the morning was. He'd been right there, and Abby had been smiling, and—

Wishing he could somehow fix it and knowing it was done, Parker turned back to Abby. Hand shaking, he closed her eyes and then reached behind her neck. It took at least five tries before he could unclasp the silver chain. He tucked the necklace into one of the pockets in his cargo shorts, zipping it closed carefully.

Standing, he almost stumbled, and he spread his legs to get his balance. He looked across the bow to where Jacob and Lilly trembled at *Bella*'s stern. Lilly made a high-pitched whimper that skipped across the water, and Jacob stared, his shoulders rising and falling, his lips parted.

Parker could feel Abby's blood dripping down his legs, wet on his hands as well. Looking down, he saw he was virtually covered in it. Lilly quivered at Jacob's side, and he slung his arm around her. They both looked unbearably young as they stared at him across the bobbing waves, and even though Parker wasn't even nineteen, he felt so fucking old.

Shaking, he croaked, "Stay there."

After pulling out one of the thick plastic sail covers, he wrapped Abby in it securely, the unceasing gnashing of the infected on the pier like nails on a chalkboard.

Caught by the wind, Jacob's sobs echoed with the plaintive cries of the circling gulls.

Chapter Nine

CRAIG'S CONFUSED SHOUTS faded behind Adam as he raced toward the water. There were infected there—not many by the sounds of it, but enough. Rising above their din were sobs, and Adam couldn't focus enough to pinpoint whose.

The thudding of his own heart was deafening.

He raced down the pier, machete in hand, tearing through the creepers, his fangs extending and hair spreading. Their heads thumped down, and he skidded to a stop at the edge of the wooden planks. Parker was bleeding. He was in the other boat, and he was covered in blood.

Adam roared, his claws springing out and hair thickening.

But Parker was on his feet at the wheel, backing up the boat to the pier, and he didn't seem injured somehow. There was so much blood, and—

Through the rage jackhammering, Adam focused on the thing near Parker's bloody feet. A long shape, wrapped in a tarp, surrounded by blood. *Oh god.* He glanced at *Bella*, taking in Lilly at the stern, standing there gaping. Jacob was on his knees beside her, head down.

"Adam!"

Blinking, he realized Parker was there, the boat rubbing the pier's ladder. There was so much blood filling Adam's nose with its metallic, too-sweet stench. But it wasn't Parker's. Relief shuddered through him, followed hotly by grief for poor Abby. With a deep breath, he closed his eyes, taming the wolf, becoming human again.

When he looked again, the world was a little duller. "Are you hurt?"

Parker shook his head. "She's dead. The kids are alone over there. We have to…do things. The right things. What are we supposed to do? Fuck." He was trembling, and Adam climbed onto the boat to take him in his arms.

"It's okay. We'll figure it out."

Craig approached at a run, and when he reached the end of the dock, he surveyed the scene mutely, breathing hard through his mouth. "Abby?"

"I'm so sorry." Parker shook his head. "It happened too fast. I couldn't—I'm sorry."

A tremor rocked Craig, his face crumpling. "Please, God. No." His shoulders shook, and for a horrible moment, he seemed ready to break right in half as he slammed to his knees.

Adam and Parker stood uselessly as Craig sobbed. Then he jerked up his head, staring out at *Bella*. Wiping his face roughly, he took a few deep breaths. "Okay. Let's handle this."

So they did.

Adam went back for their dropped supplies and the dinghy, then they sailed the boats back out to sea, Parker still in his bloody clothes behind *Saltwater's* wheel. Lilly wept in her father's arms, and Jacob curled into a ball on *Bella's* bow. Adam could hear his soft whimpers, and a howl clawed at his throat, claws and fangs pushing to be released, the wolf's impotent fury and sorrow almost overpowering him.

He got Parker clean and into fresh clothes, not able to bear the sight of so much blood on him. Abby was still wrapped up on the red-splashed deck, and they refused to let Jacob see her, keeping the kids on *Bella*. They all gathered there, shell-shocked, both of the boats anchored.

Jacob wrapped his arms around his belly, his eyes red and

puffy, but his voice surprisingly strong. "We have to bury her today. We're not supposed to wait. I remember when my grandpa died. It's supposed to be quick."

Since he could hear that flies had started to buzz, Adam wasn't going to argue. "If you want, we can bury her at sea."

Shuddering, Jacob shook his head violently. "No. That's not the way we're supposed to do it. We have to do it right. Do you think it'll make a difference that there's no rabbi?" He dropped his head, and when he looked up again, his eyes glistened with fresh tears. "I don't know any of the hymns. I barely learned the stuff for my bar mitzvah last year. We hardly ever went to synagogue except on holidays." A sob burst up. "I cheated at Hebrew school. I'm sorry!"

"Hey, hey. It's okay." Craig took hold of Jacob's shoulders, his voice gruff. "God will understand. I promise."

Adam could feel Lilly's gaze on him, and he gave her a small smile. She whipped her head away and edged closer to Craig.

Shit.

The kids had been some distance away when he'd lost control on the pier, but she'd clearly seen enough to scare her. He'd have to tell them the truth about himself, but not today.

The corner of the tarp covering Abby fluttered in the warm breeze on the other boat. The sun was lower in the afternoon sky, and sweat beaded on Adam's neck. He wished they could google Jewish funeral rituals, but of course that wealth of information was lost now.

If the world somehow recovered and the power came back on, would Facebook and websites all still be there waiting, as if they'd only been asleep?

He mentally shook his head, refocusing. He had to take care of everyone. He couldn't space out.

In the end, he and Parker went ashore on a small spit of a peninsula. Adam ran through a forest, racing a mile before he found a shovel in a rickety storage shed. He raced back, and in a stand of trees, out of sight of the water, he powered out a grave from the earth while Parker kept watch. The others would likely be too shell-shocked to think about how quickly he'd dug, and he wanted to get Abby in the ground before too many flies buzzed.

Craig insisted on being the one to retrieve Abby's body in the dinghy, carrying her tenderly, his jaw clenched and eyes dry. Jacob stood with his head bowed, staring at the ground. The sun was setting as they gathered around the long hole.

Jacob had remembered the rabbi giving them little black ribbons to pin on at his grandfather's funeral, and Craig had cut slices out of a black T-shirt. There were no safety pins, so they held the little pieces of fabric.

Adam tried to think of something to say. He thought of the awful day of the memorial for his parents and sisters. He hadn't wanted to bury them in pieces after the truck had sliced them in half, and fortunately his parents' wills had stipulated cremation.

But he'd still had to sit through a service, the church jammed full of neighbors and kids from school, their parents, teachers, and people he only vaguely recognized. His sisters had been popular at their high school. Adam's friends had come too—rows of little boys and girls, shifting uncomfortably in their formal clothes and shiny shoes.

All those people, and Adam had been the only one left in the world who'd actually known his family. He'd been betrayed by his parents' secrets in the end. Left so horribly alone.

Parker's hand stole into his, and Adam realized his eyes were burning with unshed tears. He tried to give Parker a reassuring look, but surely failed. Parker just squeezed his fingers gently, and Adam held on. Probably too hard, but Parker would never complain.

Craig was talking, his voice quavering ever so slightly from time to time. He spoke about how kind and smart and good Abby was, and how much she loved Jacob, and how lucky he and Lilly were to have known her—lucky enough to get some of that love.

Lilly wept quietly, clutching Craig's hand, and Jacob stood too still, his hands at his sides, the piece of black fabric locked in a fist. He stared into the grave. There was a spot on the tarp where blood had soaked through, and Adam wished they could cover it somehow.

Craig cleared his throat. "I don't know any Hebrew prayers, but I know God is good, and that Abby is safe in Heaven. That she loved and was loved, and that we will never forget her. Amen."

There was silence now. Adam needed to say something, but his mouth was too dry, any words shriveled and out of reach. Parker was good at talking—and sometimes so bad at it, Adam thought with a swell of affection that nearly toppled him. But before Parker could say anything, Jacob was on his knees pushing handfuls of dirt into the grave.

They stood there watching him, sharing an uneasy glance. Craig put his hand on Jacob's shoulder, but Jacob shrugged it off, desperately asking, "Will they find her here? They might dig her up." His voice was high and reedy. "They can't find her. We have to hide her!"

"It's okay, they won't. We won't let them," Parker said, dropping to his knees as well. He helped push in the dirt.

They all followed suit, even Lilly. Adam tucked away his piece of black fabric, focusing beyond the sounds of breathing and hearts thumping dully, making sure they were still alone. Across the water, he could hear another boat, this one running on a motor that sounded quite big. He pushed dirt as he listened and peered at the low waves, but the boat passed by, too far away to be seen, even by him.

When the grave was full, they hunted for rocks to cover it to keep Abby safe. It was only after that Jacob realized he'd dropped his makeshift ribbon somewhere below the stones, and he sobbed, apparently convinced of his failure.

"It's okay," Parker said. "It's with her. It's like a little piece of you." He tentatively reached for Jacob, as if to pull him into a hug, but Jacob wrenched away, turning his back on the grave.

"We have to go now. Can we go?" he rasped.

"Yes," Craig answered. "We'll go now." He reached into his pocket and took out his own piece of fabric, staring at it for a few moments before letting it flutter to the churned-up ground.

The rest of them followed suit, Lilly carefully tucking hers beneath a rock like a little secret. Jacob was already trudging back to the dinghy, his shoulders hunched, and it was over.

"MIND IF I join you?"

Adam had heard Craig come up from downstairs and tread quietly to the bow, where Adam sat on one of the benches built into *Bella*'s sides, his eyes closed to the cool moonlight. He opened them.

"Of course not." As Craig sat wearily, Adam asked, "How are you holding up?"

He looked out to sea, clearly drained and shell-shocked. "I'm walking and talking. So I guess I'm okay. Whatever that means. 'Okay.'"

"I'm so sorry."

"I keep thinking that if I'd been here, maybe…"

Adam choked down his own surge of guilt, because it wasn't about him. "I understand."

"Woulda, coulda, shoulda, right?" Craig shook his head. "I want to scream, but the kids… Have to keep it together."

Adam had no idea what to say. He nodded.

"So, here I am. Walking and talking. And she's gone." He squeezed his eyes shut before opening them with a loud exhalation. "You looked deep in thought when I came up."

"Just listening." Adam put his hands into the pockets of his leather jacket. It was surprisingly humid for November, even on the water, but the worn leather was a comfort somehow. The camera was in there, the metal smooth under his fingers.

He pulled it out. "I took some video of Abby the other day. Do you want to see it?"

Staring at the camera, Craig's eyes welled. "I woke up with her this morning. How is she gone? *How?*" He swiped at his eyes. "There's no answer, I know." Looking at the camera, he said, "I do want to watch, but not today. Thank you."

Nodding, Adam tucked the camera away.

After a minute of silence as they stared into the night, Craig asked, "And what do you hear? When you listen?"

Parker playing the world's most depressing game of Go Fish with Lilly in the saloon.

Jacob holed up in the spare cabin with Mariah, the door closed, sobbing quietly so no one will hear.

Ocean currents beneath them, fish and sea creatures.

An animal sniffing around Abby's grave—a squirrel, perhaps.

"Not much," he answered. It had been too late to think about sailing on, so they were still anchored, *Saltwater* bobbing nearby like a ghost ship. The wind had picked up, turning them to face the endless sea.

"Seems so empty," Craig said. "I know it can't be. Hear other people like us on the radio. See them sometimes. Still doesn't feel real. Some days, I wake up expecting to be in my bed, my sweet old dog licking at me with her bad breath." He smiled so sadly before glancing at Adam. "I couldn't go back for her. Got Lilly from her play date, and we went to Abby's for Jacob. Thought it would all be over by morning, whatever it was, but I didn't want to leave Abby and Jacob alone. Just in case."

His gaze was distant, and Adam waited, letting him say what he needed to.

"Police were closing roads. People were panicking, seeing video of the carnage happening in the big cities. The mayor told everyone to stay inside and wait. We went back to hole up at Abby's. Never thought it would actually touch us. The authorities would get it under control long before it came our way. Then morning came."

"Yeah." He thought of that first night in the woods with Parker, the snotty freshman he didn't even like.

It seemed like another life.

"I can see her so clearly." Craig's gaze went distant. "Old Lola, waiting by the door, eager for kisses and scratches. Waiting and waiting, getting hungry. Wondering where I was, where Lilly was. Waiting forever." His voice broke. "But we couldn't get back. Had to get out of the city, and I couldn't risk my child, or Abby and Jacob—not even for that sweet animal. If it had just been me, I'd have tried. But with them, I couldn't risk it. You understand, don't you?" he asked desperately, clutching Adam's arm.

"Of course." Adam patted him awkwardly. "You did the right thing."

Craig looked down at his own hand as if he wasn't sure how it had come to be gripping Adam. He let go. "Sorry." Playing with his hoodie zipper, he said, "Lola wouldn't have understood why we never came home. If she's still alive somehow, she'll still be waiting." He wiped his eyes. "Haven't let myself think about it. Hell." Then he looked around guiltily, as if Lilly might hear him.

"I'm sorry." It wasn't enough, but Adam couldn't think of anything else to say.

"When my wife died, it took a year and a half. Cancer. I don't think Lilly really remembers her. But I watched her go, bit by bit, day by day. Couldn't do anything to stop it, to keep her here. Not a thing." He shivered, zipping up his hoodie tighter. "Now Abby's just...*gone*. How is it possible? If I'd known it would be the last time... I should have told her I loved her when I kissed her goodbye. Should have told her."

"She knew."

"You think so? Lord, I hope. Because I did. I loved that woman. I was so grateful we'd found each other just before the world changed. That we'd been together that night. I always thought it was the one good thing that came from this. And now she's just gone." He turned to the dark peninsula. "I know her body's only a shell. That her soul's in Heaven. But I hate to leave her alone. We'll never see her grave again. The forest will grow over it. I suppose that's right in its own way." He shuddered. "Unless it all burns."

The briny wind had cleared the distant smoke from Adam's nose for the night, at least. For the moment, he could believe that the world in the darkness was peaceful.

Craig turned back to the sea, fresh tears gleaming in his eyes, the stars and moon reflecting there. His chin trembled, voice thick. "I hate to think of it, how scared she must have been. Because I know what she was thinking. I know it like I know my own name. She was thinking of Jacob. That she was leaving him, and there wasn't a thing she could do about it. It was Tanya's biggest fear when she was diagnosed—that she would have to leave her baby behind."

The fear of leaving Parker alone was a visceral nightmare squeezing Adam's gut, and he could only imagine how much worse it was for a parent. He had no comforting words, so he stayed silent.

"I know Abby must have felt the same, and it's so much worse now. Leaving her son to *this* world?" Craig blew out a long breath. "Could be me tomorrow. And then what? What happens to my little girl? To that poor boy? I can't leave them." His heart was rabbiting, and Adam could hear the panic rising. "I can't leave my baby!"

Adam took Craig's shoulder. "You won't. You won't leave

them."

"You don't know that! Who's going to take care of my little girl?"

"We will. I promise." He kept his hand secure on Craig's shoulder.

"You're kids! You're what, twenty-five? And Parker's a teenager!"

He didn't point out that he was only twenty-three since he felt a decade older most of the time. "I know we're young. But we'll take care of your daughter if anything happens to you. Jacob too. We're in this together."

As he said the words, the truth of them filled him with peace and purpose. "I promise we won't let anything happen to those children." And maybe it was a crazy promise to make. One he couldn't keep. But he and Parker would never leave the kids to fend for themselves. Never.

"You can't promise that." Craig shook his head, his breath hitching. "No one can. We could all buy it tomorrow."

"We always could have, even before all this. My family died in an instant. One minute we were driving along. I was fighting with my sisters, and my parents were fed up. Then it was over. They were dead, and I was the only one left. It could always happen. And the world has changed, but we'll do our best. We'll do our best for those kids."

Craig stared at him, his throat working as he tried to catch his breath, his shoulder rigid beneath Adam's palm. In increments, he unclenched, his pulse slowing. He blinked hard a few times. "Yes, we will. Okay."

Adam squeezed gently before letting go. "It's all anyone can do."

"I'm so sorry about your family. That must have been...unbearable. But I guess that's what we do. Bear the unbearable. We keep going." He rubbed a hand over his shorn head. "Abby and I talked about it once. That if either of us got it, we'd take care of the kids. Somehow, I never thought it would be me left behind."

"You're not alone. We're in this together."

Craig looked at him again, a watery smile on his face. "I guess we are. Thank you. Thank you both."

They sat in silence, the boat rocking on swells. Adam listened, tuning in to the cabin below. Parker and Lilly were still playing cards, but Jacob seemed to have cried himself to sleep. That was good, at least.

After a few minutes, Craig laughed hollowly. "Now we need to find a place to go. Need to find…something. Don't you think?"

He thought of Salvation Island's calls, the woman's voice echoing in his head often. "I do."

"We can't just keep floating around. Surviving. There has to be more. Somewhere, there has to be more. Lilly and Jacob need a home. A community. Stability."

A pack.

They had each other now, but Craig was right that they needed somewhere to put down roots. Their own territory. "We'll find a place."

"I know Parker's dead set against it, but what about this Salvation Island? Is there a way to get close? Check it out without sailing right up and walking on shore?"

"We have binoculars. We could watch from a distance. I…" His heart skipped. He should tell Craig everything. Adam would need all his abilities to keep them safe, and there was no sense in hiding anymore.

"You what?" Craig prompted.

I'm a werewolf. Please don't be afraid of me.

But the words caught in his throat, rubbing painfully until he choked them down. "I could scout in the dinghy."

Could watch through the binoculars from even farther away, hear sounds across the water you never could.

"I think it's worth a try."

Craig nodded, sitting up straighter, suddenly invigorated. "Yes. Yes, that's what we'll do. We'll be careful, but we'll find a new home. If not this island, then somewhere else. We can do this." Breathing hard, he slumped again, his face creasing, voice shaky. "We have to."

Adam said a silent prayer to the universe that they could.

IT WASN'T QUITE dawn when he heard it.

The soft sound was some kind of...scraping? Rubbing. He reached for Parker, bolting up when his hand closed over cold sheets. Adam had stayed awake for hours keeping watch, and had finally let himself hide in dreams, the urge to close his eyes just for a little while too much to resist. Parker had been nestled close to him, breathing steadily.

Now he was gone, and Adam reached out desperately, focusing on the heartbeats and breathing nearby. The sliding door to the cabin was half open, and beyond, he could see Lilly and Craig fast asleep on the fold-out bed in the saloon. In his T-shirt and boxer briefs, Adam tiptoed past them. By the stern, the other cabin door was still closed, and he could hear Jacob sleeping fitfully inside.

The scraping was coming from outside, and Adam crept up the steps to the deck.

It was empty.

For a moment, he could only blink in surprise. Fear dripped down his spine in icy rivulets, guilt that he'd slept too soundly like lead in his limbs, the urge to scream Parker's name clawing at his throat.

The next moment, it all locked into place—the strange sound

and Parker's heartbeat, muffled across the waves.

His damp head bent in the darkness, Parker was on *Saltwater*'s deck in his boxers and T-shirt, scrubbing. Both dinghies were hitched, so he must have swum over. Adam did the same now, slipping into the cold water, shivering as he sliced through it. At the ladder, he said, "Parker."

Swallowing a gasp, Parker whipped his head around, still on his knees. "Jesus fucking Christ. Stealth wolf mode again."

Adam pulled himself up, dripping onto the deck. "I could say the same about you."

He smiled faintly. "You were really out for the count. You haven't slept enough."

"I still should have heard you. I thought—" Frustration, fear, and guilt still tugging at him, Adam shook his head.

"Hey, it's okay. I'm sorry."

He focused on the deck. "What are you—" Swallowing thickly, he whispered, "Oh."

"I didn't want them to see this." Parker turned back to the remains of the dark stain on the deck, the jagged edges almost black in the fading moonlight, and picked up a scrub brush. "I can't get it all out. Even with bleach. You can still see it."

For a few moments, Adam couldn't speak past the rush of affection for him—for this challenging, wonderful man who would sneak out in the middle of the night to try and scrub away death.

Parker frowned. "What?"

In answer, Adam sank to his knees and took Parker's face in his hands, kissing him softly. He rubbed their noses together. Finally, he got out, "I love you."

Trembling and kissing him back, Parker murmured, "I love you too. Don't die, okay? Let's not die."

"Deal." Adam wrapped him in a tight, damp hug, and they knelt there for a little while, just breathing, the boat rocking on the early morning tide.

When Parker pulled back, he eyed the deck again. "I don't think we can do it. I don't think we can get it out. There was so much blood, Adam. Didn't think there could be that much."

"Let me try." He took the brush and bent to scrubbing, but Parker was right. Abby's blood had sealed itself into the grain of the wood, and it wasn't letting go.

"Jacob can't see this every day." Parker shook his head. "He can't. Damn it!" He sucked in a breath and blew it out. "I didn't... I didn't want to care. I was afraid to trust them, but it was more than that. It was *this*." He jerked his hand toward the dark stain. "I didn't want to feel this way. I don't want to! I don't want to care, Adam! Because we'll just end up losing it all. The world is fucked." He choked back a sob. "We're fucked."

"Shh. It's okay." He tried to hold Parker close, but Parker squirmed away.

"It's not. Because now she's dead. I watched her die. I couldn't do anything but hold her hand while her life ended. It happened so fast." His gaze went distant. "One second it was... Shit, it was awesome. The sun was out, and I closed my eyes." Another sob shuddered through him. "I'm sorry. I should have been watching. I shouldn't have stopped, even for a second."

"You didn't do anything wrong." Adam ran a hand over Parker's damp tangle of hair.

"I couldn't help her. They bit her, and it was just...over. It was happening, and I couldn't stop it. Like going over the top of a hill on a rollercoaster, and it's too high, and you want to get off, but all you can do is finish it. I watched her blood pour out." He ran a quivering hand over the stained wood. "She was so afraid."

"You were there. She wasn't alone."

"But we're all alone in the end." His eyes glistened as he dug his fingers into Adam's thigh. "Don't you see? I'm going to die too. My luck will run out, and there won't be anything you can do. I'll have to say goodbye to you. I'll have to leave, just like Abby did."

"*No.*" It was practically a growl as he yanked Parker to his chest, wrapping him close. "I won't let that happen."

Parker's voice was muffled in Adam's neck, his breath wet and warm. "It happened so fast. She was right there with me." He shivered. "I didn't want to care."

They were quiet for a few minutes, holding each other while Parker's tears dried.

When Parker eased back, he sniffed loudly. "What the fuck are we going to do? I promised her, Adam. I promised we'd take care of Jacob, and Craig, and Lilly."

"We will. We'll do everything we can. We'll get through this."

He stared at the blood stains. "I don't want Jacob to see this."

"Well, they could stay with us until we find another boat. Until we find a home."

Still staring at the blood, Parker seemed to consider it. "It would be safer to be together. Only one boat to worry about. We wouldn't have privacy, but... Yeah, it's safer. That's what matters for now. I promised her." He shook his head. "But we're not going to find a place where we can stay. It's not going to happen."

Adam took a deep breath and exhaled. "Craig and I discussed checking out Salvation Island." As Parker tensed and opened his mouth, he added, "Safely, from a distance."

"Dude, come *on.*" Parker waved his hands sharply and jumped to his feet. "It has to be a trap. No one starts some peace-and-love commune during the non-zombie apocalypse. It's bullshit."

"We don't know that. It could be a good place. We're going to start running out of food. Gas. The supply is finite. If we can find a safe place to rebuild, to have a community... We need that. The kids need that." Adam got to his feet too.

"A community? How? We need to focus on surviving. I think the best way to do that is to keep moving."

"And then what?"

"I don't know." Parker huffed out an exhalation. "None of us know jack shit. But we're already more vulnerable with Lilly and Jacob. We need to stay vigilant. We can't trust people. It'll only end up biting us in the ass."

"Maybe. But we also can't sail around indefinitely. We need to *live*, not just survive. Lilly and Jacob need stability. The ocean isn't exactly known for that."

Rubbing a hand over his face, Parker groaned. "Using the kids to guilt me is not fucking fair."

"It's the truth. We all need to find a home. And we'll go to Salvation Island with eyes open. Ready to defend ourselves. Ready to attack if need be. But I think we have to at least try." His breath came short and quick, hope and excitement ricocheting through him like pinballs.

After a few moments, Parker's shoulders sank. "Fine. We can check it out. From a distance! Like, a really far distance."

Adam smiled, breathing more easily. "You won't regret it. I have a feeling."

"I already do, but here's hoping." Grimacing, he hobbled over to the open container of bleach and screwed on the cap.

Relief that Parker had agreed was eclipsed by worry. "What's wrong? Are you hurt?"

"Think I've got a few splinters from the pier. Guess I was distracted before, but they're starting to really sting now. I need some tweezers."

"Sit." Adam picked up Parker by his hips, placing him down on the closest seat.

"Whoa. Easy there. I'm fine, you don't have to get all growly."

Kneeling, Adam lifted Parker's right foot. "This one?" He leaned in and prodded.

"Yeah, that's—" He hissed. "Right there."

Extending his claws, Adam gently nicked open one of the

swollen wounds to pry out the piece of wood. "You should have said you were hurt."

"I really didn't feel it. Was just thinking about the kids." His heart skipped around with dull thuds, and his eyes went distant again. "It happened so fast. I keep saying that, don't I? But why were they under the boardwalk? It's dark down there. I never thought—I should have been paying more attention. I heard something, but I thought it was just the waves, and I closed my eyes…"

"Look at me." Adam held Parker's chin, waiting for his gaze to focus again. "No matter how many times you relive it, you can't change it."

"I know, but…"

"After the accident, I tortured myself for years. If I hadn't been bugging my sisters and playing that stupid video game, maybe it would have been different. My parents wouldn't have been distracted. Would have seen the truck in time."

"It wasn't your fault." Parker brushed back Adam's hair. "You were just a kid."

"I know. And you did your best today. We all do."

Nodding, Parker pressed his lips together, blinking rapidly. "Okay." He swiped at his eyes. "I've got to get my shit together." Wincing, he circled his foot. "I think there are a couple more."

Carefully, Adam removed the other splinters one by one. Then he kissed Parker until the sun came up, and it was time to leave Abby and the *Saltwater Taffy* behind.

Chapter Ten

HE COULDN'T GET up.

Parker was on *Bella*'s deck, the wood wet under his bare skin. He pushed with his hands, getting his arms under him, but it was useless, as if he was stuck in molasses. He couldn't find Adam. But Eric was there, out of reach. He was saying something Parker couldn't understand, and Abby was there too, dying at his feet, her eyes going glassy with the last spurts of blood, her heart stopping.

He heaved again, trying uselessly to get his noodle legs under him.

Then Shorty loomed into his field of vision, stale tobacco-stink breath choking Parker. Then they weren't on the boat at all, but back in the Cape house in Chatham, and he was on the kitchen floor, and his family were gone, but Shorty was there.

Parker stared up at the pad of paper on the wall by the phone, an illustrated lobster smiling back at him, a note written in Mom's neat script filling out the edges of the pad, arcing gracefully around the lobster's dangling claws. But he was too far away to read it, no matter how he squinted. His legs still wouldn't work, and Shorty laughed and smacked his ass—

"*Parker.*"

Sucking in salty air, he popped his eyes open. Kneeling beside him on the deck at the bow, Adam brushed a hand gently over Parker's head.

"It was only a dream," Adam murmured. "Could hear your heart. Nightmare?"

Parker pushed himself up on his hand. "No, it's fine," he lied, his pulse still racing. He'd only intended to stretch out on the deck for a few minutes, but the sun was much farther to the west now. *Bella* swayed gently, and Craig waved from behind the wheel.

"Shit. Didn't mean to fall asleep," Parker mumbled. He forced himself to squint up at the sails and shove away the clinging tendrils of the nightmare.

I'm fine. I can do this. I'm not broken.

He managed a cheerful tone as he examined the sails. "They look good. Nice angle to catch the wind."

"We're taking care of everything. You can go back to sleep. Right, sailor?" Adam smiled at Lilly, who sat midship on one of the benches, watching them solemnly. She didn't smile back, dropping her head instead. Adam's smile faded, and he sighed. "We need to talk about that later," he whispered to Parker.

Frowning, Parker nodded. "How's Jacob?"

"The same. He's back in the cabin." Adam was still for a moment. "Sleeping, at least."

"Good. Let me check our navigation." With a yawn, he got to his feet and went to take the wheel from Craig.

"I'll get started on dinner," Adam said. "See what kind of canned vegetables we can hide in that jar of alfredo sauce."

Parker checked the instruments to make sure they were still on course. He'd examined the nautical charts so often he practically had them memorized. They were still heading south, land off to their right. Putting on his sunglasses, Parker watched a plume of smoke rise in the distance before he turned away.

While Craig and Lilly untangled some fishing line, Parker trimmed the sails, the wind changing direction a few degrees. He wondered if Jacob would sleep the whole day away. Probably, and he couldn't blame the kid.

It had been two days since Abby. He and Adam had moved

over everything from the other boat and hoisted the sails at dawn. Jacob had barreled up from below and parked himself at the stern, staring back at the peninsula where his mother was buried.

He'd stayed there long after the coast had curved and Abby was miles gone.

After a few minutes at the wheel, Parker glimpsed a flicker of white. Craig and Lilly were still organizing fishing equipment, Craig keeping up a steady patter and praising Lilly for a job well done a little too enthusiastically. Parker zeroed in on the sail as they got closer, watching and waiting.

It was as if he could smell stale cigarette smoke on the wind, and part of him hoped it was actually them. Because this time he'd be ready, and Adam was there, and Shorty and his pals would be in for a rude fucking surprise once—

"Is that another boat?" Lilly asked.

"Uh-huh." Parker lifted the binoculars. He couldn't see the stern to read the name, but the vessel didn't seem big enough to be *The Good Life*. Its sails were up, luffing madly, and the boat listed to starboard, turned at too much of an angle for the wind. Parker bit down a swell of irritation. More people at sea who had no goddamn idea what they were doing. "We're keeping our distance."

"What if they need help?" Craig asked, peering out.

Then they're on their own.

"We'll see." He said sharply, "Adam!"

"I don't think he can hear you over the wind." Craig motioned to Lilly. "Sweetie, go down and get him."

She froze. "But…"

Adam of course appeared a moment later, having heard just fine. Parker handed him the binoculars. After a minute of Parker's heart pounding, wondering how Adam could stand to hear all the sounds he did at once, Adam lowered the binoculars. He shook his head.

"They're infected. At least one dead. The others are…hungry."

"Are you sure?" Craig asked. "God." He wrapped an arm around Lilly's thin shoulders. "Guess we will keep our distance after all."

"I told you," Parker muttered.

Adam said, "Craig, why don't you go down and finish dinner? Put on some water to boil for the pasta?"

"Yeah, okay. Let's do that." Craig hustled Lilly down below.

Coming up behind, Adam wrapped his arms around Parker's middle. He brushed his lips over the nape of his neck. "It's okay."

Tensing, Parker jabbed at the radar screen. "I know it is. But that boat could have been anyone. Could have been those assholes from up the coast, or someone like them. We can't be thinking about helping people all the time. Craig's way too trusting."

"We might be the ones who need help one day."

He wriggled out of Adam's embrace. "We'll be just fine. I'm not trying to be an asshole, but we live in a different world now. Come on."

Crossing his arms, Adam kept his voice soft. "I'm not saying we don't. Pretty sure Craig isn't either, given his girlfriend just bled to death a couple days ago. We approach people with caution. I'm not an idiot, you know."

"I *know.*" Parker untied and retied a few knots in one of the lines. "But you and Craig are too… I don't know. Optimistic."

"I think you're cynical enough for all of us."

"I'm being real!" Lowering his voice, Parker shook his head. "You guys think we're going to find some utopian retreat where kids can play hide-and-seek and pretend the world isn't fucked. It's a fantasy."

"Maybe it is. But we have to try."

"Even if it gets us killed?"

"I won't let that happen." Adam closed the distance between them and took the rope from Parker's hands, grasping them. "I'll never let that happen."

"You're a werewolf," Parker whispered. "You're not God, and you're not immortal. You can't protect us from everything. Can't protect me."

Craig appeared, bringing a stack of four plates up to the outdoor table. "Thought we could eat up here once we find a place to anchor. Jacob says he's not hungry." He rubbed his eyes tiredly. "I'll let it go for today, but I don't know what I'm supposed to do. After Lilly's mom, we still had all this…stuff. School and work and church and a whole bunch of things." He stared at the plates. "Doesn't feel the same now. I'm trying to keep things normal for their sake, but what the heck is that? Normal."

"I don't know," Adam said. "But we'll figure it out." He clapped Craig on the shoulder.

Craig lifted his head, jolting a bit. His eyes were red-rimmed, his voice weary as he said, "Yeah. Thanks. Sorry, I'm…" He squared his shoulders and took a deep breath. "I'm fine." He disappeared back down.

Adam took Parker's face in his hands, his gaze intense. "I'll protect you. I swear."

Parker could only nod. He knew Adam meant it with every fiber of his being, but the persistent fear that it wouldn't be enough coiled around him, tighter and tighter with every mile closer to Salvation Island.

"ARE THEY STILL there?" Parker padded across the deck, the wood cool under his bare feet. It was after midnight, and Adam stood sentinel on the bow. The moon and stars were hidden under a veil of clouds, and Parker squinted into the dark.

"Yep. But they don't seem to swim, so that's something."

He shuddered, thinking of them tumbling off the pier after

him and Abby. "It's like, the one good thing about them." Listening carefully, he could hear the chattering on the wind.

They'd dropped anchor in a cove just before sunset, and soon infected had swarmed along the beach. Even after Craig and Adam had covered every porthole and made sure there was no light, the infected had splashed toward them, fortunately not getting beyond the shallows.

"They're not trying to get to us anymore. Just milling around."

They were still off Georgia, and Parker thought of Atlanta. "Do you think the CDC is still running? Trying to find a cure? I know that guy on the radio said it was hit, but…"

"It's possible they survived. You never know."

The hair on Parker's bare arms rose in the night breeze, and he rubbed them before tugging at his T-shirt collar. "Where do you think they are? The fucking Zechariahs, I mean. Assuming they're real. Which I think they must be, given the shit show we're living in now. No way this was all just some accident."

"Seems unlikely, given how targeted it apparently was." Adam drew Parker close to his side, rubbing his big hand over Parker's arm. He wore his leather jacket, and Parker inhaled the musky scent with a little smile, pressing his face against Adam's shoulder.

"Wonder if they're living it up in some bunker. Waiting for the rest of us to die, or get infected and *then* die. Sooner or later the infected must starve to death. Or dehydrate. Right?"

"I hope so," Adam murmured.

Parker rubbed his cheek against the leather. "Feels weird to hope all those people will die. Maybe they could be fixed. If there was a cure, we could get the world back. But if we do, that means we've killed people who might have been saved."

"We've only killed to survive. We didn't have a choice."

"I know. It just…" Parker lifted his head, laughing softly. "I was going to say it sucks. Understatement of the millennium."

Adam rubbed Parker's arm rhythmically, warm and steady. "You could say that."

"Are they all sleeping downstairs? I think so? I was quiet when I went past Craig and Lilly in the pullout."

After a few moments of silence, Adam said, "Yes."

"So, what's up with Lilly? After you said something, I was checking her out at dinner. She watches you when she thinks you're not paying attention, but then can't look you in the eye. I never noticed that before?"

Adam sighed. "She saw me. After Abby, when I ran onto the pier. I was so afraid something had happened to you. Could smell the blood, and I didn't think to control myself."

"Oh shit. Well… Do you think we should tell them? Just to avoid having to come up with excuses? I mean, sooner or later you'll probably have to get your wolf on again in front of them. Maybe we should get ahead of it."

Adam stared at the dark sky. "Yeah. It's crossed my mind too."

"But?"

"For so many years I kept it a secret. You remember how badly it went with my foster parents when I tried to tell them. Tried to show them." He took a shuddering breath.

"I know," Parker whispered, soothing his hand over Adam's chest. "I'm sorry."

"Until I met Tina in college, I never thought anyone could know the truth and still want to be my friend. Still want anything to do with me." He angled his head to face Parker, brushing his thumb over Parker's lips. "Never thought I'd have this."

Parker caught Adam's hand and pressed a kiss to his rough palm. "You're stuck with me now. You might come to regret it. Probably already do."

With a laugh that sent warmth through Parker's chest, Adam shook his head. "Nope. You're stuck with me too."

"It's a real hardship. You're all sweet and brave and gorgeous.

Ugh. The shit I have to put up with."

Adam kissed him then, and they moved into each other's arms, Parker's thigh sliding between Adam's, rubbing lazily through their jeans. They kissed softly, tongues exploring, and eventually pulled back, resting their foreheads together. Parker closed his eyes contentedly.

When Adam spoke again, it was a whisper. "What if I tell them and they get scared? What if they think I'm a freak and don't want anything to do with us anymore?"

"Then fuck them. It's their loss." Parker bristled at the thought. "We don't need them. They'd be dead without us. Who cares what they think? What anyone thinks?"

"Down boy. It's okay." Adam smoothed a palm over Parker's hair. "You don't have to make them the bad guys here. I wish I didn't care what people think. But I do."

Softening and kissing his cheek, Parker murmured, "I know. It's easy to say, especially for me. Okay, so let's be real. If they see you go all claws and fangs and fur, they're probably going to freak and be terrified. It's a pretty normal reaction since most of us have no clue werewolves even exist."

"Right. I get that."

"But it doesn't seem like Lilly's said anything to her dad. If we get in front of it and tell them the truth, they're probably still going to freak. Craig will be protective of the kids. They'll have a lot of questions. They'll be afraid."

Adam nodded sadly, and god, Parker wished he could take away the hurt that Adam's foster parents had caused. And what the hell was up with his parents keeping Adam and his sisters so isolated? Were all werewolves like that? Did they have some big fight with their pack? Parker knew Adam didn't know the answers, so he kept his rhetorical questions to himself.

He kissed Adam again. "But they'll see that you're good. That you're, like, *the best*. And if nothing else, we're smack in the middle of the non-zombie apocalypse. And you're immune to the Zechariah virus, and you have super strength and speed and are a total badass fighter. Unless they're criminally stupid, once they process it, they'll be damn glad to have a werewolf in their corner."

Adam smiled. "You think?"

"I *know*. So, I guess we should try and figure out a good time. Maybe give it a few days, what with Abby. They probably don't need any more big shocks this week. Especially Jacob." He smiled ruefully. "I just realized I have no idea what day it is. That's so weird, right?" His smile faded as slippery nausea slithered through him. "I can't believe it's only been a couple days. And we're still sailing, and eating dinner, and…going on. Trying to act normal."

"I guess this is normal now. We have to keep going. No matter what."

As rain began spitting down, Parker pressed his face to Adam's neck, glad that the sound of the rainfall washed away the chattering drone from shore.

"HEY. WE SAVED you some coconut milk. The canned stuff tastes pretty good on cereal. And we have Coco Pops." Parker stood at the cabin door, watching Jacob, who was curled on his side on the port bunk beside Mariah, facing the hull. His lank hair brushed his cheek, and he wore the same shorts and tee he'd had on for days. His knobby knees looked even more painfully sharp.

Jacob gave no indication he registered anyone was even there. Parker tried again. "Why don't you come upstairs with the rest of us? Have breakfast and get some fresh air."

Nothing.

Craig had tried already, Lilly dissolving into tears. Parker thought ruefully that Jacob was made of stern stuff to resist a little girl crying. The kid was in shock, but he at least had to eat. "If you're not in the mood for cereal, I'm sure we could whip up something else."

No response.

Parker sighed and sat on the end of Jacob's bed by his feet. He could see Jacob tense up. "Look, I know this sucks. This is the worst. But you need to eat something. You're going to get sick otherwise." He quietly added, "Your mom wouldn't want that."

"How do you know what my mom would want?" Jacob's voice was a hoarse whisper. It was progress, at least. They'd all been avoiding mentioning Abby, but perhaps it had been the wrong tack.

"Well, first of all, no mom wants their son to get dehydrated and malnourished. That's, like, mothering one-oh-one. Second, she asked me to take care of you. Jacob, you were what she was thinking about. She wants you to be okay. She wants you to survive. You need to get out of bed. I know it's only been a few days that she's been gone, and you're in shock. You're confused." He paused. "About a lot of things, I think."

Jacob still stared at the hull, but was wired with tension.

"I'm sorry I snapped at you the other day. When you asked about me and Adam? Sometimes, I can be..." He laughed darkly. "I can be a total asshole, if you want the truth. I'm sorry about that. If you ever want to talk, or ask any questions, or just...anything, I'm here. Adam too. We want to help you."

"Why would I ask you questions?" he asked stiffly.

Oh, you poor terrified little queer kid. Been there, done that.

"You asked the other day. About me and Adam. If there was anything else you were wondering, ask away. I won't bite this time." He realized with horror what he'd said as soon as the words were out. "I mean, uh..."

Shit, fuck, fuck. I suck at this.

Parker jiggled his leg restlessly. "Anyway, I..."

After a few moments, Jacob said, "I want to go to San Francisco." He still stared at the wall.

Parker thought about making a lame joke about how it was indeed a mecca for queers, but bit his tongue. "I know you do. I know what it's like, to want to find your family."

"San Francisco and then Seattle. My grandmother's up there. I'm going."

"No, you're not," Parker said, as gently as he could.

Jacob finally turned his head to look down at Parker by his feet. "I am too."

He choked down an *are not*. "Okay, what's the plan? We drop you off on land, and off you go? That's Florida over there now. You're going to walk to California?"

"*No.* I'll get a car."

"Okay, sure. Sounds easy. And you'll need to siphon a lot of gas. After you learn to drive, that is. Oh, and find food and water. Fight off the creepers. And of course the other humans, some of whom will be only too happy to come across you on the road. To hurt you."

Jacob clenched his jaw. "You and Adam came across the country."

"We did. This whole thing had just started, and we had no idea what to expect. You know now. You know what's out there. And Adam and I wouldn't have made it out of California if not for—" He exhaled. They really did need to get the werewolf business out in the open. Parker thought of that night on the backwoods road and Adam transforming, clawing apart the creepers that would have overwhelmed them otherwise. "If not for dumb luck."

"Maybe I'll get lucky too."

"Maybe. But probably not. What you'll get is dead or infected. That's the way this world is now. We have to be vigilant every second."

"I can take care of myself," Jacob whispered, his wobbling voice belying his words.

"That's pretty impressive, because I can't. The last thing I want to be is alone." Memories of an empty desert highway under a sea of stars filled his mind. He could feel the asphalt under his feet, the cold night wind relentless on his skin. Hear the absolute silence that came with being utterly alone.

"There was a night when I thought I'd lost Adam. It was the worst moment of my life. I can't put it into words, how afraid I was. How much it hurt that he was gone. And if he hadn't been okay, I don't know what I would have done. We need each other. We all do, Jacob."

"But you didn't want to help us. You didn't like having us around."

Guilt sliced through him. "You're right. I was suspicious. Afraid. But I know now that I can trust you guys. We can help each other. I don't trust anyone else out there, but I trust you. It's not easy for me to do."

"But why would you want *me* around now? Why would any of you?" Jacob's breath caught. "You were only stuck with me because of my mom. Now she's gone. Why would you want me to stay? Craig and Lilly could have their own beds if I was gone. I'm not family."

"Aren't you? I think Craig and Lilly will disagree. They loved your mom, and they love you too. Family isn't just about blood. It's about a lot more than that." Tentatively, he pressed his hand on Jacob's bony ankle. "We're a team. And look, I understand wanting to find your dad and your grandma. I wanted to find my parents. But they're gone."

"How do you know for sure?"

"I don't. Not a hundred percent. But from what we saw of Boston… Standing in my kitchen, I just…felt it. And maybe it hurts too much to hope for some kind of miracle. I made my peace with it. I had to let them go. And normally, the way life used to be, it would take months to process it. Years. But we don't have that luxury now. We have to keep going."

"I miss her so much," Jacob whispered.

Parker wanted to hug the poor kid but was afraid of pushing too far. "I know. I'm not saying you're going to get over your mom. You're still going to miss her and be really fucking sad. We all miss people. Family, friends. But we go on. We keep living. And I would never have given you this speech so soon back in the day, but we had time back then. Or at least we felt like we did. And like I said, it's a luxury we don't have now."

"But you're still trying to find your brother."

Eric's blinding smile, his golden hair gleaming under the sun, filled his mind. "Not so much actively trying to find him as hoping he's still out there. I wouldn't risk Adam or any of you to find him. It's more like a daydream, I guess." He swallowed thickly, a knot of grief suddenly choking him. "Deep down, I know I'll never see him again."

"I'm sorry," Jacob whispered.

"At least we managed to talk on the phone that night that everything went to shit. He was in London, going into a bunker with his crazy rich boss. I was in the forest outside campus with Adam. A total stranger I didn't like. Who didn't like me." He shook his head. "Life is so fucking weird. I guess it always was, but especially now. Anyway, yeah, I still dream I'll find my brother one day, as impossible as I know it is. But I guess stranger things have happened, right?"

"I was supposed to Skype with my grandma," Jacob blurted, his eyes filling with tears. "That weekend before. She'd just learned how it worked, and she wanted to try it. But my friends got the new *Star Wars* game, and I blew her off. Emailed and said I had to study for a test, and she said that was okay and school-work had to come first, and maybe we could do it next weekend."

A sob tore from his throat and he curled into himself, burying his face and muffling his words. "But next weekend never came. I should have told her I loved her."

Parker squeezed Jacob's ankle gently. "She knew. Your mom did too, and your dad. They knew you loved them. I promise. And your mom loved you so much."

After several deep breaths, Jacob nodded, swiping at his eyes. Parker kept him anchored with his hand, wishing he knew if he was saying the right things. For a few minutes, they stayed like that, the boat rocking gently on a set of swells. It was full light now, and they needed to get underway, but Parker didn't want to leave Jacob just yet.

Finally, he said, "You can't go searching across the country. We have to move forward. I know it's what your mom wanted. All right?"

Sniffing, Jacob nodded. Then he bolted upright and pressed his mouth to Parker's in a clumsy, wet, haphazard kiss. He jerked back against the headboard, breathing hard. "Sorry. I just wanted to do that once before I die."

Parker scooted off the bed, taking a deep breath. "Okay. It's okay." He smiled softly. "I definitely remember that feeling."

Jacob smiled tentatively. "Yeah?"

"Oh yeah. Now come on. Time for cereal. No arguments." He turned and walked to the kitchen, retrieving the can of milk from the fridge, as well as a bowl and spoon. "Can you grab the cereal?" He climbed up the few steps to the deck, his pulse ticking up a few notches as he waited.

A minute later, Jacob appeared with the box of Coco Pops, blinking into the morning sun.

Chapter Eleven

"WE SHOULD BE getting close to Daytona, right?" Craig asked. He stood at the kitchen sink, washing dishes and handing them to Lilly to dry.

In the door of the master cabin, Adam ran a towel over his damp hair, trying not to show how chilly he felt. They were anchored in the relative protection of a little inlet, the wind and rain howling, the boat rocking. As the day wore on, he went up to patrol regularly, insisting the others should stay dry. He didn't wear a shirt, and his surf shorts were quick dry, at least.

"Should be," Adam agreed. Lilly peeked at him, and he smiled. She ducked her head, drying a plate vigorously.

She avoided Adam's gaze whenever she could, her little heart beating faster whenever he tried to talk to her. He understood—and needed to fix it—but couldn't help the sliver of hurt from digging in.

He heard Parker's heart skipping as he examined the charts at the saloon table. "Yeah," Parker said. "Pretty soon."

Adam came to sit down beside him on the bench. "Is there an issue?"

"No," Parker answered too quickly.

Raising an eyebrow, Adam asked, "Are you sure?"

Parker kept his gaze on the charts, although his pulse raced. "Yep."

Jacob sat on his bed in the other cabin, staring out a porthole. But at least he was up. Since the previous morning, when Parker had a talk with him, Jacob seemed a little more engaged.

Adam had tamped down the fiery surge of possessiveness when he heard Jacob kiss Parker. He shouldn't have been eavesdropping on their conversation but couldn't help himself. For a moment when he'd heard the unmistakable sound, his vision had gone gold, his eyes glowing before he regained control in the next breath. Fortunately, Craig and Lilly had been focused on a book of crosswords.

Adam watched Parker with a swell of pride at how well Parker had handled the whole thing and how good he'd been with Jacob. But he was distracted now by the way Parker's heart was still beating too fast, agitation obvious—to Adam, at least—in his movements as he examined the nautical charts.

"What?" Adam asked quietly.

With a noisy exhalation, Parker sat back. "This is crazy. Stupid. We should keep sailing south offshore. If we're going to cross the Gulf Stream, do it at its absolute narrowest and head to the Caribbean. Or we just keep going south. There are islands off South America. We have other options."

The radio burst to life. "This is Salvation Island. Calling any and all souls still listening."

"Oh my god, it's like they're eavesdropping!" Parker stalked to the radio and flicked it off, interrupting the woman's now-familiar entreaty. "See? It's creepy."

"Or they send out the messages on a set schedule. It was the same time last night. Parker, we talked about this." Adam glanced at Craig and Lilly, who watched from the sink with dishes in their hands. "We're going to investigate Salvation Island. At a distance."

"But there's nothing there! It's such an obvious trap." He sat down again and jabbed at a chart. "It's too far north to be part of the Bahamas. I've never heard of an island there. For all we know, it's a flotilla of boats waiting for us to show up so they can trap us, throw us overboard, and take *Bella*."

"Throw us overboard?" Lilly whispered. "With the sharks?"

"No, of course not." Craig glared at Parker. "That's not going to happen."

"It might!" Parker ran a hand through his hair. "I'm not trying to be a jerk, but we have to be realistic here."

In the cabin, Jacob was watching now, his eyes wide. Adam raised his hands, trying to tamp down the growing anger scratching at him. "Okay, let's take a breath. Parker, it could be a private island. Couldn't it?"

"I… Sure. I guess it's possible."

"And we agreed that we'd try it. Remember?"

Parker cut him a scathing look. "Yes, I remember. I'm not brain damaged, thank you."

Adam gritted his teeth. "Then why are we having this conversation?"

"Because this is a stupid choice!" He leapt up from the table, scattering the charts, his pencil going flying. "Just crossing the Gulf Stream is dangerous. You have to check the weather reports religiously and keep vigilant and make sure you do it with plenty of sunlight and the right winds. And guess what? We don't have weather reports anymore. At best, we're guessing we'll have a window to cross. If the wind shifts and we're in the middle of the stream, we could be totally screwed. I'm not an expert sailor. Do you know how big the waves can get? You haven't seen anything. That storm that nearly took out the other boat? Those waves weren't even that big."

"It's really that dangerous?" Craig asked.

"Yes. It can be." Parker paced. "It definitely can be. If we still had YouTube, I'd show you videos. The more I think about it, the dumber a decision it seems to take the risk when we can't know the weather. And that's aside from the potential risk at this so-called Salvation Island."

"We have faith in you," Adam said. "You can get us there

safely."

"What if I don't want to? I'm the only one who can get us across the stream. I'm the only one who understands all these charts and nautical terms." Parker jutted out his chin. "What if I say no?"

The simmering frustration boiled over, and Adam's nostrils flared. "You agreed! We have to try. We have to find a home."

"We're never going to have a home again!" Parker shouted. "Not the same way we did before. It's a fantasy."

"Maybe it is!" Adam shouted back. "But we have to try. It was a fantasy that you'd be able to find your parents on the Cape. But we tried."

"That was different." He shook his head. "You're putting your faith in a voice on the radio. We hear plenty of voices. We can't trust these people."

Forcing control, Adam unclenched his hands, his fingers sore from preventing his claws from extending. He stood and spoke calmly. "We're not putting our faith in that voice. We're putting it in you. We trust *you* to get us there safely. And we're not going in blind. You know we have an advantage."

"What does that mean?" Craig asked, holding a quivering Lilly to his side.

Hell, maybe it was time to put all their cards on the table. Adam looked to Parker, but he was still pacing around, too wound up. The boat rocked from side to side in the wind.

Craig added, "And Adam's right, we agreed. We need to find a place to live. To have stability. This is what Abby would have wanted. I know that."

"But it has to be a lie!" Parker stabbed the air with his hands. "Safety and food and water and singing kumbaya. Don't you see? It can't be real. It's impossible. This isn't the world we live in now. We live in a world of death and infection and evil people." He shuddered, and Adam wanted to go pull him into his arms.

Parker shook his head. "If I let myself believe that we could find a good place, and then it all goes to shit? I can't. I won't."

Jacob rocketed off his bed and into the saloon. "You said we were a team. Was that all just bullshit?"

"*Jacob*," Craig bit out.

"What? *Language?*" Jacob laughed with a tinge of hysteria. "Give me a fucking break." He glared at Parker. "You gave me that whole spiel about moving forward. But you're the one who wants to stay in the same place. Sailing around forever might feel like doing something, but it won't actually get us anywhere. You're full of shit." He slammed back into the stern cabin, sliding the door shut behind him with a resounding *clang*.

"Good work," Adam muttered.

Parker pressed his lips into a thin line, but before he could retort, Lilly stepped forward and blurted to Parker, "Don't make him mad!"

Heart sinking, Adam's anger drained away, shame licking at its heels. He dropped his head.

"Lilly, it's okay," Craig said. "Adam and Parker are upset right now, but we're going to work this out. Everything will be all right."

"But you don't understand! He's—" She broke off, and Adam stared at his bare feet on the wooden floor, his face hot. He could hear the words she didn't say as if she'd shouted them.

A monster.

"He's the most amazing person I've ever met, and you don't have to be afraid," Parker said quietly. Adam lifted his head to find Parker watching him, his eyes full of love and his agitation vanished. "Lilly, you saw something, didn't you? After Abby… Afterward, when Adam came back, you saw him looking scary."

She nodded, her wide eyes going back and forth between Adam and Parker.

Craig stared between them. "What on earth are you talking

about?"

Parker nodded, and Adam took a breath, trying to block out the memories of his foster parents' faces, their horror as he'd tried to explain.

First, he called, "Jacob, can you please come back out?"

There was silence but for the driving rain.

Parker went to the cabin door and slid it open. "Please? I'm sorry. And you need to hear this."

Jacob followed, slouching into the doorway, his arms crossed and eyes red. Parker came to stand beside Adam, taking Adam's hand and threading their fingers together. Adam squeezed gratefully. No matter what happened, and no matter how they might disagree sometimes, he knew in his heart he'd always have Parker in his corner. Profound gratitude washed through him.

I can do this.

"There's no easy way to say this, so I'll just... I'm a werewolf." He forced himself to keep his head up and gaze at Craig, Lilly, and Jacob squarely. All three gaped back.

A furrow formed between Craig's brows, and he laughed uneasily. "Is that supposed to be funny? I don't get it."

"It's not a joke. I'm a werewolf. I was born that way. It has nothing to do with the moon, or being bitten. Werewolves are born, just like humans are. We're like you in most ways."

"I don't—" Craig shook his head. "Is this your way of diffusing tension? I'm still not following."

"Werewolves are real," Parker said bluntly. "I know, it's crazy at first. But trust me, this is awesome news. Adam's super strong, and he can see and hear long distances. He can heal almost right away if he gets hurt. When he transforms, he grows claws and fangs, and gets furry. Other than that, he's the same as us. He feels the things we do." Parker squeezed Adam's fingers. "His feelings get hurt just like ours. He's not a monster, or a freak."

Jacob stared. "But werewolves can't be real."

"I saw it," Lilly said quietly. She nodded to Jacob and her father. "After Abby got hurt. He had fangs and claws, and his eyes were glowy. He was hairy all over his face."

Closing his eyes for a moment, Adam let the transformation happen, the change flowing through him. His claws scraped the back of Parker's hand, but Parker held on. When Adam looked again, Craig had shoved the kids behind him and backed up, he and Jacob watching with jaws open and eyes wide, Lilly nodding sagely.

"Like that," she said.

"So, exhibit A," Parker said. "Werewolf. But he's still Adam. Still the same guy who wanted to save your lives when I didn't. When I honestly wanted to pretend we never heard that SOS call. He's good and kind and brave."

Adam let the wolf recede, rolling his neck as it quieted within him and he transformed back. "I understand that I frighten you. But I'd never hurt any of you. Never."

Craig opened and closed his mouth. Jacob edged closer, clearly fascinated.

Parker spoke up. "And I meant what I said, Jacob. We're a team. Or at least we can be. We should be. I didn't want to trust anyone but Adam, but I promised Abby I'd take care of you. All of you. That we'd watch out for you. We're in this together. But you have to accept Adam the way he is. Wolf and all. If you can't, then we'll go our separate ways."

"I don't know what to think." Craig's voice was hoarse. "I never imagined…"

"I know, it's trippy." Parker smiled hesitantly. "I couldn't believe my eyes at first. But it gets normal really fast. You'd be surprised. I mean, we're already dealing with a butt-load of crazy." His smile faded as he turned to Adam, still gripping his hand. "And I'm sorry." He blinked back tears. "You're right. I'm afraid. I'm afraid of the shitty people out there, like Shorty and his pirate friends. And I'm afraid to hope that there might really be a safe place."

"I know. It's okay." Adam pulled him into a hug, holding him tight.

"And it genuinely is dangerous to cross the Gulf Stream," Parker mumbled into Adam's shoulder. "I didn't make that up."

He chuckled. "I know." From the corner of his eyes, he could see the others staring dumbly. Stepping back from Parker, he rolled his shoulders. "I hope you can come to see that I'm not a threat to you."

"Oh, and he's immune to the creeper virus, FYI." Parker gave a thumbs up. "Big plus."

Lilly crept forward, shaking off Craig's hand. She reached out and touched Adam's fingers. "Does it hurt when you get claws?"

"Like Wolverine?" Jacob asked, leaning in.

"No. It's a natural movement. It's like extending your arm, or pointing your toes. Same with my fangs and the extra hair."

"Whoa. This is…" Jacob trailed off, looking Adam up and down. Adam braced himself. A slow smile spread over Jacob's pimply face. "This is *so cool.*"

Adam exhaled in a rush, and as the kids peppered him with questions, Craig tentatively joined in. Parker grinned beside him, and he knew everything would be okay, at least for today.

Chapter Twelve

"IT's BETTER TO go south past Daytona, then cross the stream." At Adam's raised eyebrow, Parker raised his own. "I'm not lying. You know I'm not."

With a small smile, Adam nodded. He, Craig, and Parker were leaning over the table in the saloon, the nautical charts spread out before them in the murky afternoon glow from the skylights.

They'd managed to put some more miles behind them during breaks in the weather system the past couple of days, but it was slow going to the outskirts of Daytona, where smoke rose, almost indistinguishable from the steel sky.

"How can he tell that?" Jacob asked from the kitchen, where he sat on the counter with Lilly eating Jell-O cups. The fish hadn't been biting, and supplies were dwindling. Parker's stomach growled, but he ignored it. They needed to conserve their food.

"He can listen to my heartbeat and tell whether or not I'm nervous," Parker explained. "When someone's lying, they usually give it away to Adam and his supersonic hearing."

"You hear that?" Craig said playfully. "No lying from either of you." He forced a laugh, an actual *ha-ha* sound.

Adam smiled back, and there was a moment of awkward silence. Craig and the kids were trying, and in the days since Adam had come out, they'd gone back and forth between surreptitiously watching him when they thought no one was looking and making lame jokes. The latter was mostly Craig, who really seemed like he could use a beer or five.

Parker wiped the sweat from his brow. It was muggy, and they all wore shorts and T-shirts except Adam, who was shirtless most of the time. Parker wasn't complaining, although maybe he was since he and Adam hadn't been able to do more than snuggle. It was too quiet and close quarters to get freaky with other people sleeping nearby.

"Can you turn into an actual wolf?" Jacob blurted.

"Like in movies?" Lilly added. "Or smaller and with more hair?"

"Guys, don't be rude," Craig admonished. "Although, I admit I'm curious myself."

Adam's close-lipped smile was sad. "No. It is possible, but I've never learned how. Maybe one day."

Parker gave Adam's elbow a squeeze and cleared his throat. "Anyway, here's the thing with the Gulf Stream." He pointed at the map. "It starts down here, around the bottom of Florida. Adam, I think I told you it's around thirty or so miles wide. It's like a river in the ocean, with no banks and no rigid course as it goes north. It meanders. It has eddies that can fool you and take you in the wrong direction. It's also faster where it's narrower."

Craig nodded. "I'm following. You've crossed it before?"

"No. I've read about it, and my dad and brother crossed, so I remember them planning." He pushed away the pang of regret that his father hadn't allowed him on that trip. Regret and resentment—with a splash of guilt for having the resentment in the first place. He grimaced and refocused. "The biggest issue is the wind. If there's any coming from the north, conditions will get rougher. Could be very rough, depending."

"Why's that again?" Adam asked.

"Since the stream is moving north—" Parker slid his fingertip along the worn paper from Florida up past New York. "If the wind is coming from the north, it's moving against the stream." He drew his finger back down. "This makes waves. And remember, even though the stream is closest to shore off Florida, once we're out there, it's still the open sea. No ducking into a harbor if the weather turns."

Craig blew out a breath. "Okay. How do we cross it? Assuming the wind is coming from the south and it's all good." He leaned over the chart. "If we go south, where would we leave from? Maybe Cocoa Beach?" He smiled wistfully. "I always wanted to go there growing up. Thought it sounded so exotic. I used to watch the beach volleyball competitions on TV. It all seemed so glamorous. You know Abby—" He glanced at Jacob, his smile disappearing. "She had a cousin there. Bill, I think?"

Staring at his empty plastic Jell-O package, Jacob shrugged his bony shoulders. "Dunno."

In the silence, flashes of Abby's blonde hair and easy smile filled Parker's mind. He shoved them away and jabbed his finger on the map, on the mark he'd made of Salvation Island's alleged location. "This is our ultimate destination."

Adam jumped in, rubbing a hand over his hairy face. He hadn't shaved in a while, and his beard made a scratching sound against his fingers. "Okay, so if the Gulf Stream pushes us north as we go across, should we go from down here, up across like this?" He drew his finger across the map from Cocoa Beach in a straight diagonal line to Salvation.

"No," Parker said. "That's a rhumb line." At the blank stares from everyone, he tried to remember the actual definition but came up empty. "Basically, when you're sailing, a straight line isn't actually the fastest way, because the earth is curved. In navigation, there's the rhumb line or the great circle, which is usually faster." He drew his finger in a semi-circle around the diagonal. "Anyway, it doesn't matter. If we go across the stream on a rhumb line, we'll be crabbing." At the further blank stares, he added, "Going sideways. We don't want to do that."

"Right. What do we want to do?" Craig asked.

"When we hit the stream, we set our course at a ninety-degree angle. We'll still be going diagonally, but at a much steeper angle. There's no point in trying to fight the current. So we'll end up north of Salvation, and then we can go south again once we're on the other side of the stream. Get it?"

"Yeah. Makes sense," Lilly said. They all looked at her, and she shrugged. "What? It's just algebra."

Craig beamed. "She gets that from her mother. My math skills are limited to figuring out a twenty-percent tip."

"That's useful," Parker teased.

"It sure is. We want to reward good service in the end times."

"This all sounds positive," Adam said, eyeing the chart. "If we end up north of the island, we can approach in the night. How long will it take to cross?"

"Depends. Say we're going five or six knots—probably ten hours. Maybe more."

"Seriously?" Adam scratched his bare chest as he stared at the charts. "Wow."

Parker said, "Yeah. That's what I'm trying to tell you—this isn't nothing. We're going way offshore. We really need to plan for this. Without weather reports, a lot of it will be dumb luck. We need to stock up on fuel in case we have to drop sails and use the engine."

"Can't we just do that in the first place?" Craig asked.

Parker examined the chart. "Maybe. But depending on the conditions, we could really eat through fuel and then end up in the middle of the ocean with dry tanks. I think we should keep it as a backup plan. Either way, we need to hope for a good window in the weather. Southern wind, not too rough. Fifteen knots max, I think."

"You think?" Craig asked.

"I may be the expert on this boat, but I'm not actually an expert. If we had Google to refresh my memory, this would be a hell of a lot easier. And if we had Google, I guess we'd have weather, which would help the most. But we'll just have to pretend it's the olden days."

"It's the 'nolden' days," Craig said. "Get it? New-olden days. If we still had Twitter, we could totally get that hashtag trending."

"Sure, Dad." Lilly giggled and toyed with her empty Jell-O container. "What's for dinner?"

As the others discussed their meal options, limited since the fish weren't cooperating, Parker studied the chart. He had it memorized by now, but he still examined the little markings. The X he'd made on Salvation Island drew his gaze again and again. His stomach twisted, and he tugged at his T-shirt, pulling the damp cotton away from his skin.

"Hey." Adam ran his hand over Parker's back.

"I'm fine." He edged away. "Need to cool off. Too humid today." He ducked into the main cabin and changed into the swim shorts he'd scored in a marina up the coast.

"Good idea," Craig called. "You go for a swim and we'll make dinner. Rice and beans, my specialty."

On his way through the saloon, Parker forced a smile. "Awesome, thanks."

The acid in his stomach roiled as he hurried up to the deck, whispers slithering down his spine.

What if there's nothing there? Where do we go? What if something is there and it's just as bad as I think it will be? What if, what if, what if...

In the fading light, Parker dove off the stern. They were anchored in a harbor with empty docks in the distance, and as he resurfaced, reveling in the cool water, he wondered where the boats had gone.

Maybe they're all at Salvation Island having a barbecue. Maybe we're the only ones left behind.

The lack of other survivors was becoming more and more

pronounced. They still heard them on the radio, but the infection's spread seemed relentless.

"Can I join you?"

Treading water, Parker spun back to face the boat. Adam stood on the rear platform by the dinghy in his swim trunks, which hugged his slim hips and powerful thighs. Parker nodded, letting the frisson of desire ripple through him.

They paddled away idly, but not too far. Parker floated on his back in the bobbing, gentle waves. The sky was finally clearing, and he could see stars twinkling into sight in the pink-red of sunset's final sigh. He let his ears fill with water, reaching out to snag Adam's fingers so they didn't float too far apart.

In the muffled peace, he could hear the faint beating of his own heart and wished he could hear Adam's too. He threaded their fingers together, watching a star that was too bright.

"Imagine being that satellite up there," he murmured as Adam caressed the back of Parker's hand with his thumb. He could almost see it, the Earth looking so peaceful from orbit, like nothing had changed. "I guess it'll stay up there forever, going round and round." He took a shuddery breath. "That could be us on the ocean. Just going forever, never stopping." His breath caught on the swell of loneliness.

With a little splash, Adam sat up and tugged Parker's hand. Trying to shake the water from his ears, Parker rolled from his back and treaded water. Adam watched him with kind eyes, so close that their legs brushed as they kept afloat with rhythmic movements.

Parker inhaled deeply through his nose. "I don't want to be a satellite. But what if this all goes wrong?"

"I know you're scared. Especially after what happened that day I left you alone. We're all scared."

"It's not even just if Salvation Island is a lie. The more I think about crossing the stream without knowing the forecast, the more freaked out I get. I'm not an expert. I'm really not."

"You'll do your best."

"What if that's not good enough? I don't want to be responsible. I promised Abby I'd take care of them. What if they get hurt because of me? What if you do? What if I'm not enough?"

Adam reached out, smoothing a hand over Parker's wet hair. "You'll be your best, and that's all we can ask. We have faith in you."

"But why?" he whispered. "Eric was always better at this stuff. My dad—"

"Your dad underestimated you. And I think he would be so proud if he could see you now."

"You really think so?" Parker knew he sounded pathetic, but couldn't stop himself.

"I know it."

"You sound so sure of it. Of me."

"That's because I am." Adam kissed him with a little splash, awkward as they kept afloat. "I'm afraid of a lot of things. But never when it comes to you. Not since that night you saw my true face."

"But I freaked out."

"For a minute. Then you asked me if the Loch Ness Monster exists too." He smiled, his teeth flashing in the gathering dark. "In that moment, I knew you were different. That I could trust you. And in the morning, we fucked like nothing had changed. Like I was the same." He was silent before whispering, "That meant so much to me."

"Baby, I will always want to fuck you."

Adam's laughter rumbled, and Parker joined in, kissing him messily and letting the worry slip away beneath the water's surface. "Speaking of which, it's safer for us to all be on *Bella*, but it's murder on our sex life."

"Guess we'll just have to do what we can, when we can." Adam tugged open Parker's swim shorts, tearing at the Velcro fastening.

"Uh-huh. Yep." Parker yanked on Adam's trunks. "Get those down."

When both their cocks were out and Parker had narrowly missed elbowing Adam in the forehead, they took each other in hand, jerking roughly as they cycled their legs to stay afloat. Their shafts soon swelled.

Parker groaned. "Fuck, that feels good." A set of little waves passed by, and he blinked the salt from his eyes. "When we have some real privacy again, I can't wait for you to fuck me."

"Yeah?" Adam's eyes gleamed, the moon rising behind him. "Tell me how."

"Mmm, let's see. So many possibilities. First, I'm going to get inside you again." Adam's cock jumped in his grasp. "Yeah, you want that? Fist fuck you until you're coming and coming. You'll be so wrung out, but I won't let you rest. I'll suck you and get your cock hard so you can fuck me. God, I need you to fuck me."

"On your back, so I can see your face," Adam muttered. "So I can kiss you." He did kiss him, and they splashed around, tongues thrusting.

Gasping, Parker pulled back and looked to the boat, hoping Craig was keeping those kids busy in the kitchen. He couldn't see anyone watching, so he kissed Adam again, jerking him roughly as Adam did the same. Fire lit his veins, pressure building wonderfully in his nuts.

"And you'll pound my ass, my ankles up around my ears," Parker whispered. "Bend me right in half. Split me with your huge cock." He squeezed it, stroking harder, teasing the foreskin. "Your cock's perfect. I love it in me. My mouth, my ass."

Groaning, his legs moving faster, Adam reached down with his other hand and caressed Parker's balls, the water and his fingers sending incredible tingles over Parker's skin like electricity.

When they came, they swallowed their moans with kisses, panting quietly in the night. He pressed a wet kiss to Adam's cheek, circling his limbs lazily. "That's one way to feed the fishes."

Adam chuckled, and they bobbed on the tide. As the pleasure faded, worry returned to fill its corners, but as Parker's pulse rabbited, Adam pulled him fully into his arms, taking his weight and keeping them both afloat.

"BUT I CAN see it. It's just sitting there."

Biting back a surge of irritation, Parker glanced from the bow to where Jacob stood by the boat's wheel, the binoculars up to his face as he peered off toward land. Lilly sat at the table, her pigtailed curls waving in the breeze. She was supposed to be doing her times tables per Craig's instructions but was doodling little trees on the blank sheet of paper instead. Parker let her because times tables sucked.

He told Jacob, "We're staying here. Craig and Adam will be back soon."

"But you said we need a lot of gas," Jacob insisted. "It's a gas container. Even if it's empty, we could use it to siphon from a car. The gas is going to run out. We should get every bit we can now." He tugged at the neck of his black tee. His cargo shorts were too big on his narrow hips. "I'm tired of sitting here doing jack shit."

Parker turned back to the mouth of the harbor. "I know. It sucks, but we have to be smart. Too risky to go ashore."

"There aren't any creepers. Come on, just drive back to the dock and let me off. I'll go get it and come right back. It's right over that fence."

"*No.* You heard what your—Craig said. Let me have the binoculars back." He held out his hand. Jesus Christ, kids were a pain in the ass.

"Why should I listen to you?" Jacob grumbled. "You're not that much older."

"Because I'm in charge." He gestured impatiently. "Binoculars."

Muttering under his breath, Jacob stalked across the deck and shoved them into Parker's hand. Parker ignored him and peered out to the gray sea. Adam had spotted two sails on the horizon that morning beneath the thickening clouds, but they hadn't come any closer. Parker couldn't see anything now, but he scanned back and forth, listening to the chirp of birds and scratch of Lilly's pencil.

The splash was so small he almost didn't notice, but when Lilly gasped softly, Parker whirled to find Jacob gone. His feet slapping on the wood, he rushed to the stern to see Jacob swimming to the dock.

"Son of a..." Parker's nostrils flared as he choked down a blue streak. He didn't want to shout too loudly, but called, "Jacob! Get back here."

Jacob ignored him, resolutely powering to the dock with a steady front crawl. Sopping, he pulled himself up the ladder and ran without even a glance back.

Eyeing the receding tide, Parker decided he couldn't get any closer. The dinghy was tied by the dock, waiting for Adam and Craig to return. He'd have to swim. He stripped off his shirt and turned to Lilly, who watched him with wide eyes. She sat frozen, clutching her pencil.

"Parker, don't..." She swallowed thickly, her eyes wet.

Shit.

He glanced back to where Jacob was already scaling the chain-link fence separating a storage shed from the main area of the ramshackle marina that probably hadn't been much to look at even before everything went to hell. The harbor mouth was still clear, but what if he went after Jacob and someone showed up?

Clutching his tee, he sighed.

"It's okay. I won't leave you." He squinted. "He'll be back any minute now."

The seconds ticked by like hours. Jacob disappeared into the shed, and Parker and Lilly stared intensely. Parker made sure to check the sea approach so no one could sneak up.

Tick, tick, tick...

He exhaled when Jacob appeared at the fence, the gas can in one hand as he clambered up. There was movement behind him, and Lilly shrieked, Parker's heart stopping as he spotted the creepers swarming after Jacob, reaching up for his bare feet with bloody hands.

"Jacob!" Parker yelled. "Faster!"

Jacob struggled over the top of the fence, dropping all the way to the ground with the red container still clutched in his grasp. The fence rattled with the force of the creepers, a dozen now grasping for him.

Miraculously, the fence held.

Jacob thundered down the dock, jumping back in the water and swimming hard, the container floating along with him.

"See? That's why we stay on board!" Parker yelled as he climbed down to the dinghy launch platform to haul Jacob up. He grabbed his thin arm and held him steady. "Are you hurt? Did they touch you?" He barely resisted the urge to shake him.

"No." Jacob shook his head. Then he grinned crookedly and hoisted the can. "I got it. There's gas in there too! About half full, I think."

"Was it worth dying for? Because you just about bought it. Jesus fucking Christ. Don't ever do anything so stupid again!" Parker spun on his heel, gritting his teeth as he climbed back up to the main deck. He forced out a breath and tried to smile for Lilly. "He's okay."

Jacob followed, and Lilly launched herself at him and wrapped her arms around his middle. "Please don't die."

With the grace to at least look guilty, Jacob hugged her back. "I won't, Lil. I promise. I'm fine, see?"

Lilly stepped back. "You're bleeding."

Parker's stomach flip-flopped. "Where? Let me see."

"Just scraped my knee on the way down." Jacob shrugged, but there was tension to the set of his mouth. "I'm fine. I'll put a Band-Aid on it."

"You want me to help?" Parker asked.

Shaking his head and flushing, Jacob backed away, hugging himself. "If you want to help, don't tell Craig or Adam. Maybe it was dumb, but I'm fine. And I got the gas."

"It was definitely dumb." Parker clenched and unclenched his hands, adrenaline still pumping through his veins. The whole incident had only taken minutes. By the fence, the creepers chattered, the sound floating over the calm water and setting his hair on end. "You get that, right? Like, you *really* get it? You promise to never do something like that again? Even though you didn't get hurt this time, that doesn't mean next time will be okay."

Jacob nodded. "I promise." With a guilty pinch of his mouth, he patted Lilly's shoulder. "I just wanted to do something to help."

"Look, I get it. I do. But it doesn't help anyone to risk your life like that." Parker's anger ebbed, and he nodded. "Okay, we'll keep this between the three of us for now. But if you ever pull another stunt like this..." He could almost hear his dad's voice echoing in his mind. "I'm not covering for you," he finished lamely.

"Deal." Jacob retreated to the steps to go below decks, wincing.

Parker frowned. "You sure you're okay?"

"Yeah. It just stings. My knee. I'm fine. My mom used to..."

He shook his head. "I'm fine. No big."

He disappeared below, and Parker picked up the binoculars. Lilly stood there, staring at the creepers, who rattled the fence with a drone and the odd shriek. Soon enough they'd go back the way they came, but in the meantime...

"Hey, can you help me out, Lilly? I've got something in my eye."

She turned, a little furrow between her brows. "Are you okay?"

"Yeah, I just have an eyelash. But can you do the sweep for a minute?" He extended the binoculars.

Taking them, she nodded and lifted them to her face. They looked ridiculously huge. "I don't see anything?"

"Pull the sides down a bit to reduce the space. So the eye holes fit better. There, that's it."

"Oh!" She pressed the black plastic against her eyes, moving left and right slowly. "I can see all the way out there."

"Pretty cool, huh? Go back and forth, and tell me if you see anything, like another boat."

"Okay." Lilly did as she was told, clearly concentrating very carefully, her tongue sticking out between her teeth. After a few moments, she said, "I only see water and the red and green things."

"The buoys. Good. Great."

She lowered the binoculars and peered up at him. "Is your eye okay?"

Oh, right. "Yeah, it was just an eyelash. I got it."

"Do you want these back?" She held the binoculars to her chest.

"Nah, why don't you patrol for now? Is that cool?"

With a smile that dimpled her cheeks, she nodded and went back to it. Parker glanced at the shore. The creepers were still there, clawing ferociously, grasping at the air.

Chapter Thirteen

I T WASN'T SO much the number of infected swarming Daytona Beach that made Adam's stomach roil, but the dead.

Flesh rotted in the sun, creepers competing with flies, birds, and other creatures for the spoils of war.

They weren't close enough for the others to be able to see even with the binoculars he held, and they didn't seem bothered yet by the stench that practically singed Adam's nostrils. The decaying of the dead and the infected were distinct, but equally sickening, especially as they combined.

There was smoke spiraling into the sky too, but no one was surprised by that anymore.

Rain had come again for two days, the high winds battering them where they waited in the harbor. When Adam and Craig had returned with as much gas as they could carry, a group of infected had surged toward them, rattling a metal fence.

Adam had let them be, although when the rain had come in hard and fast, forcing them back to the harbor, he'd swum to the dock with the machete and gone to dispatch them, the chattering setting him on edge. They were rail thin, but stronger than they should have been. Adam wondered how long they could go before starving.

Now he wondered what excuse he could give to shoo Craig and Lilly below to spare them. He'd try to spare Parker as well but knew Parker would stubbornly stand fast. Then he remembered there was no need for an excuse now.

What a strange and sweet feeling it was to have so many humans know his secret without running away or treating him like some kind of freak and burden.

Parker called out to trim the jib sheet, and Adam hurried to help Craig, getting close to murmur, "You should take Lilly downstairs. Daytona's bad. Maybe do a food inventory?"

Jacob was still sleeping—fitfully, but Adam figured that was normal. He could barely remember the haze of days after the accident that killed his family, and at least Jacob was eating a bit. If the kid wanted to sleep away part of the day, they'd let him.

Craig peered into the distance. "Yeah, okay. Thanks." His smile was strained. "Does come in handy, huh? Your...you know." He waved his hand.

"Yeah." He didn't take offense at Craig's lingering uneasiness. He and the kids were trying their best, and they'd certainly taken news of the truth better than Adam's foster parents had. Not that they had much of a choice, to be fair. Parker had made it clear acceptance was the only option.

While Craig hustled Lilly down, Adam watched Parker at the wheel. His dark blond hair was growing out over his forehead, and he brushed a hand through it as he examined the fluttering telltales on the mast. He spread his legs wide as they rolled over an ocean swell, his feet bare on the deck as always.

His shorts and T-shirt were getting ratty with use, and Adam wanted to poke his finger into the hole in the cotton under Parker's armpit. He wanted to tear it wide and press his face there, inhaling deeply.

"What?"

Blinking, Adam licked his lips. "Nothing."

Parker gave him a distracted smile before leaning down to peer at the instruments. Adam thought of what Craig had said about Parker being a kid. It was hard to believe this was the same cocky little shit who'd knocked on his office door in September.

Funny how important it had been to both of them, that grade in an intro film class. It was all so meaningless now. God, what a luxury movies had been.

The camera was in the pocket of his cargo shorts, reassuring even though he hadn't filmed anything since Abby. He had to preserve the battery anyway. At least that's what he told himself.

Adam went to stand by Parker's side. "It's bad over there. Keep your distance."

"Will do." Parker squinted at the shore, and then looked back at the sea. "Good idea sending them down. Jacob is having a bad day, I guess."

"Yeah." He focused and dialed in to Jacob, who murmured and slept restlessly. He couldn't quite make out what he was saying but tuned out, not wanting to invade the boy's privacy. "How's the wind? Do you think it'll be right tomorrow or the next day?"

Parker gripped the wheel. "Maybe. It's hard to say."

"We'll make it. I have faith in you."

Laughing sharply, Parker went to adjust a sail, handing off the wheel. "Not that I don't appreciate the vote of confidence, but this is the ocean we're talking about. It will chew us up, spit us out, and then swallow us right down. The wind's coming from the southeast today, which is good. The stream should be calm. Well, calmish. Hard to say what it's like out there. We'll see what tomorrow brings. Well, what the middle of the night brings. The days are so short now. We have to leave well before sunrise. Better to have light when we're out there than closer to shore."

God, the *smell*.

Adam kept the beach in his periphery, sensing the movement, movement, movement. A herky-jerky dance of desperation, the virus turning these people into animals. He wondered if he looked anything like that when he transformed without control, the times when it hit him like a bolt and tore out of him, the wolf refusing to be denied.

Picking up the binoculars, Parker gazed at the shore, his throat working as he scanned slowly. When he lowered them, his hands trembled for a moment, his skin pale and eyes wide. "God. That's…"

"I know. Don't look anymore."

"Yeah." He put down the binoculars on the table and chugged from a bottle of water, his chest rising and falling too fast. "It's not getting better. Just worse and worse. Okay, need to put that out of my mind." With a full-body shake, he went back to work, examining the sails and bustling about.

Even when Daytona was miles behind them, the stench still lingered. Adam snagged Parker's belt loop and pulled him back flush against him, rubbing a stubbly cheek over his head.

Parker laughed softly, still tense, but trying not to be. "You okay there, big boy?"

"Mmm." He tugged Parker's tee over his head, keeping his arms aloft as he leaned down and buried his face in Parker's armpit. The tuft of hair there tickled Adam's nose. He inhaled sharply, one hand snaking down to flatten over Parker's stomach.

Laughing breathily, Parker squirmed a little. "Tickles."

Adam rubbed his face back and forth, breathing in Parker deeply. "Thank you," he muttered. "Need to clear my nose out."

"Ah, so this is a palate cleanser? Okay, good to know." Parker lowered his arm and covered Adam's hand on his belly with his own, leaning back.

"Oh, uh, sorry," Craig said.

Lifting his head, Adam found Craig halfway up the steps. He stepped away from Parker, a hot flush spreading up his neck. "We were just… It's fine."

Craig smiled. "No worries. Just getting a little hot down there. Abby would wink and say it's getting hot up here too." His smile faded, and a number of expressions flickered across his face—guilt, grief, affection, sadness. He came up on deck, rubbing the back of his neck.

Parker bent to grab his tee. "Sorry. Come on up. Is Jacob awake?"

"Still curled up in bed. I thought I'd leave him for a bit longer." He called down, "Sweetheart, are you done with the soup?"

Lilly popped up a minute later. "All done. I wrote them on the list. We have five chicken noodles, three beef barley, one tomato, and six split pea." She grimaced.

"Yeah, not my fave either," Parker said. "Hey, you guys want to cast out a line and catch some fish for lunch? I'll lower the sails."

Standing at the bow after they got out the fishing equipment and worms from the fridge, Adam reeled in slowly, hoping for a nibble. Lilly stood beside him with her own rod, Craig hovering nearby to grab hold of it if something bit.

The wind was calm, and Adam breathed in, frowning. He still couldn't get that damn smell out of his nose. It was hovering just out of reach, a wisp of decay and sickness he couldn't banish.

He reeled in a fish—he had no idea what kind, and didn't care as long as they could eat it—and brought it below to clean right away with Richard Foxe's excellent set of boning knives. But when he stood in the kitchen by the sink, the lingering scent of rot got stronger.

He opened up the cupboard and inspected the trash, but they were careful to keep composting garbage separate to throw overboard. Jacob coughed from behind the closed door of the stern cabin, and Adam heard him mumbling to himself.

Adam's feet were already moving, and he inched open the door. The scent flowed over him, and all at once he realized what it was. He leaned over Jacob, who was curled toward the hull, shivering, the covers tangled around him. Resisting the urge to haul Jacob up and inspect him, Adam closed his hand over the kid's shoulder. "Jacob?"

He jerked under Adam's touch, his eyes opening. "I'm fine," he muttered. "Just want to sleep."

Adam pulled back the covers, ignoring Jacob's protests. The kid wore boxers and a too-big dark hoodie. The scrape on his knee had scabbed over, but there was something else...

Jacob was fully awake now, and he batted at Adam's hands. "What are you doing? Leave me alone."

"Are you hurt?" Adam ran his hands over Jacob's bare legs. "Answer me."

"It's nothing. I'm fine."

He tugged down the hoodie zipper despite Jacob's growing protests, his breath catching at the dark stain on Jacob's blue tee. With one knee on the mattress, he shoved Jacob's hands away again and eased up the shirt. "Jesus. How did this happen?"

"It's nothing!" he squeaked, his face flushed, hair damp on his forehead. "I didn't do anything wrong."

A bandage was taped haphazardly to Jacob's belly, blood seeping through. Not much at this point, but when Adam peeled it back, the small puncture wound oozed pus, the smell of infection so strong Adam tasted bile. "Why didn't you tell us?" A run-of-the-mill infection could easily lead to sepsis. "Parker! Craig!"

"No, don't tell them! I told Parker I was okay. He'll be mad. Please." Jacob clutched Adam's wrist with his clammy fingers. "Please."

"It's okay. He won't be mad," Adam lied. He had no idea what had happened, but Parker getting mad was usually a safe bet.

With Craig at his heels, Parker exclaimed, "What the actual fuck!" He stared around Adam, squeezed into the cabin, his eyes locked on the wound before meeting Jacob's accusingly. "Did you do that on the fence? Why didn't you tell me!"

Adam shifted over in the narrow space between beds, Mariah wedged on top of the other bunk. Craig pushed in, his eyes going wide. "What is this?" To Parker, he asked, "What fence?"

Parker muttered another curse under his breath and rubbed his face. "When you guys went for fuel a couple days ago, he saw a gas can over by a shed. Behind a chain-link fence. He…wanted to help, so he went to get it."

"You let him go ashore alone?" Craig's voice rose sharply.

"No," Jacob said hoarsely. "He told me not to. Don't be mad at him. Please."

Looking as if he was confessing to his own parent or perhaps a teacher, Parker lowered his head. "He swam to the dock and ran down it. I was going to go after him, but I couldn't leave Lilly alone. I'm sorry."

Adam wordlessly squeezed Parker's hand.

Craig blew out a sharp breath. "It's okay. But I wish you'd told me when we got back."

"Ugh, I know." Parker scrubbed a hand over his hair. "I figured no harm was done, so I said I wouldn't." He narrowed his gaze on Jacob. "I didn't realize he was straight-up lying to my face."

The flush in Jacob's cheeks deepened, and tears flooded his eyes. "I'm sorry. I didn't think it was bad. You told me not to go, so I didn't want to… I put iodine on it, and I figured it would be okay. It's not much more than a scratch."

"A scratch? There's a *hole*!" Craig dropped to his knees and reached for the wound on Jacob's stomach before apparently thinking better of it. "Okay, it's done, so let's focus on fixing it. You did this on a fence?"

He nodded, tears staining his red cheeks. "Coming back over, I had to hurry because suddenly there were creepers there. They just came out of nowhere." His voice broke. "Which is why I was totally dumb to do it, I know. Parker told me, but I didn't listen. Mom would be so mad."

Craig brushed back Jacob's damp hair. "Yep, she would. But

look, we're going to fix this, okay? Going to get you better so then I can give you a good talking-to. Parker, can you grab the first aid kit?"

As Parker dashed out, Adam gave Jacob's arm a pat. "Hang in there, pal. You'll be okay." To Craig, he added, "I'll go up and check on Lilly. Do a scan." He squeezed past, briefly gripping Craig's shoulder in what he hoped was a reassuring way.

In the kitchen, Parker pulled out the kit from a cupboard. He scowled and whispered, "I should have told you guys. I know. I was trying to be nice to the kid. He's had such a rough time. I didn't want to get him in trouble."

"It's okay." Adam kissed him softly, wanting to erase the creases in his forehead.

"Hope he was up-to-date on all his shots. I don't even know what tetanus is, but my mom was always worried about it. That fence seemed pretty old." He reached back into the cupboard and pulled out a few bottles. "Dicloxacillin. Is that an antibiotic? Sounds like it. That's what you need for an infection, right? How about Linezolid?" He shook the bottles. "Barely half full, but better than nothing."

"I'm not sure."

"Oh, right. You never get sick." His smile was sharp. "Better hope Salvation Island isn't bullshit, because we might need a doctor real soon."

"GUESS IT'S NOW or never." Parker hoisted the sails, muttering to himself as he apparently followed some kind of mental checklist. "At least there's almost a full moon. Wouldn't be able to see shit otherwise. I guess you could, though."

Parker's heart skip-scattered, and Adam gently took hold of his shoulders, the cotton of his hoodie thick and soft. "You can do this. I believe in you. We all believe in you."

Scoffing, Parker said, "The others don't really have a choice. We need a doctor."

"We. Believe. In. You." Adam squeezed for emphasis.

"Okay. Thank you." He gazed around. "The wind's coming more from the west, but as long as it doesn't switch to north… Normally I'd say we wait another day, but…"

But Jacob's fever had steadily climbed all day at a frightening rate, despite giving him aspirin and starting him on the mismatched antibiotics they'd collected along the way. Now it was three a.m., and Parker had deemed it the right window of time.

Adam said, "Let's do it. I'm ready to be ordered around, Captain."

A smile ghosted over Parker's lips. "You're an excellent cabin boy."

With the sails up and catching the mild wind, they headed out to sea. Adam was on watch, scanning with the binoculars in all directions for other vessels or signs of danger.

When he turned methodically back west and realized he'd lost sight of the shore, he had to admit his stomach clenched like a fist. They'd never been this far out to sea before, and the waves were already bigger.

"How will you know when we reach the stream?" he asked.

By the wheel, Parker nodded with his chin toward the faint glow of the instruments. "Water temperature reading. It was seventy-two when we left. Will probably get up into the eighties in the stream. This is assuming the increase in wind and big-ass waves don't tip us off."

For the moment, Adam couldn't discern any difference. He wanted to ask more questions, but went back to patrolling. Parker squinted at the telltales in the darkness and adjusted the sails every few minutes, concentration etched on his face.

After a time, he asked, "How are they doing down there?"

Adam concentrated. "Lilly's finally sleeping. Craig's awake. Jacob's sleeping, but not well. The fever's bad. He's breathing hard." The pitiful little moans and mutters made Adam wish there was some way he could rock Jacob in his arms and lull him into a proper sleep without fever dreams.

When the wind picked up, at first Adam only shivered and zipped his leather jacket. The waves grew, the water looking far more choppy than it had. Parker rushed around tightening things and rolling up the bottom of the jib sheet, muttering to himself again.

Adam tried to concentrate to see if he could hear the water in the Gulf Stream current flowing north, but the wind was howling now, the splashing as the hull rode the growing waves all melding together.

"Okay?" he called to Parker.

"So far. Let's hope the wind doesn't get any stronger." Grimacing, he leaned down and rapped his knuckles on the deck. "I totally jinxed us. Just...no talking."

Adam zipped his lips and did another scan.

An hour later, he was looking at the biggest waves he'd ever seen in real life. While the water was warm, the air had cooled considerably, and Parker shivered more than Adam liked. When Parker shoved his feet into Topsiders, the gnawing worry in Adam's gut took a big bite.

"There are big waves coming that way." Adam pointed.

"I know. The wind's changing. Northwest. Thirty knots now." Parker gripped the wheel as they rocked up a large swell and down the other side.

"This is what you were afraid of." They were both wearing life jackets and were tied on with rope, but Adam still backed away from the railing, struggling to keep his balance as they rode over another dark swell. "Shit. Parker—"

"Talk later!" He cranked the winch, muttering again. "Keep

watch. If there's anyone else out here, we don't want to hit them."

Bracing himself, Craig appeared at the top of the steps. "Are we okay?" he called tensely.

"We will be. Put on your life jackets and stay below!" Parker shouted. He leaned over the panel of instruments. "I'm going to get us to this goddamn island."

The swell of affection that crashed through Adam mirrored the roiling waves. He held on as another one came.

IN THE END, it took almost twelve hours to make it to the other side of the stream and be released from the unrelenting current. In the steely light of day, the waves had been all the more forbidding, breaking with white froth as the wind hammered from the northwest.

If it had switched completely to the north, Adam was sure they could have been swept over. Even dropping the sails and motoring across had proven more difficult than he'd expected.

As he and Parker sprawled on the benches, letting *Bella* drift with sails down for the moment, he said, "This is the part where you get to say 'I told you so.' You earned it."

Parker managed a small smile. "We made it. That's all that matters." He gazed around at the unending bluish gray. "Well, we made it out of the stream. Now we're in the middle of the ocean. Let's get out the charts."

"In a minute." He snagged Parker's cold hand, brushing their knees together, bare beneath their shorts. "Enjoy this victory."

Fidgeting, Parker's brow creased. "It'll be a victory when we find this island, it turns out to be awesome, and Jacob gets to see a doctor or nurse or someone who knows more than we do."

"You're amazing, you know that?"

He kicked off the shoes, flexing his toes. "Sure. I told you that the first time we met."

Chuckling, Adam lifted Parker's hand and kissed his knuckles. "An A student."

Parker leaned in, sliding his tongue into Adam's mouth. They kissed for a few heartbeats, their stubble rubbing, breath stale and lips salty. Adam heard little feet approach, and he reluctantly eased back to smile at Lilly.

She still wore her too-big life jacket, cinched around her middle with Craig's belt. She smiled shyly, cheeks dimpling.

Adam smiled back. "Hey, kiddo."

"Did we make it?" she asked.

"Through the Gulf Stream, yeah," Parker answered. "We'll head south again in a minute. It'll be dark in a couple of hours, and we can look for the island. How's Jacob?"

Her face dropped almost comically, as if she'd allowed herself to forget for a minute. "Bad. His fever's really high. Daddy's very worried."

"We'll come and check on him in a minute. Okay?" Parker gave her a smile.

"Okay." She turned, but impulsively whirled back and skipped forward to press a kiss to Parker's cheek. "Thank you."

Then she scampered away, and Parker blinked after her. He glanced at Adam. "Kids are weird. But pretty great. Sometimes."

"Sounds about right." Adam kissed Parker's other cheek.

Three hours later, he peered into the binoculars, his heart thumping as he made out the definite shape of land amid the gentle waves. "It's really there," he whispered.

Parker squinted at his instruments. "The latitude and longitude are just about right." He straightened up. "Wow. It actually exists. Well, I guess we'll see what happens."

Craig blew out a long breath. "Please, God. We need…" He didn't finish the thought, and the three of them looked at each other in the moon's ghostly gleam.

The stars were a brilliant field of silver stretching to infinity, and Adam peered toward the island. "You guys stay here. I'll approach in the dinghy like we planned."

"I should go with you." Parker's pulse rabbited, and he tapped his fingers on the wheel.

"Captain stays with the ship," Adam said firmly. "I've got this."

"Let's hope I don't go down with it," Parker muttered softly enough that Adam suspected Craig didn't hear.

Adam determinedly smiled, ignoring how his palms sweat. "I've got this."

Parker kissed him a few beats longer than necessary, and when Adam cut through the sea in the dinghy, he could still feel the pressure on his lips.

As he disappeared into the night, Adam opened up his senses, reaching out toward the dark hulk of the island. Lights shone in the distance, flickering. He realized it was firelight, torches and perhaps bonfires burning on the expanse of sand rimming the island.

Cutting the motor, he lifted the binoculars, still far enough away that anyone on the island would never be able to see him, even with binoculars of their own.

With his enhanced vision, the heat of the island came into focus, and he listened intently, the patter of hundreds of heartbeats echoing in his bones, deep within. But there was something else…

Gasping, Adam jerked, dropping the binoculars, the leather cord pulling on the back of his neck as the black plastic thumped against his chest. Across the salt water, the unmistakable musk reached him with a deep pull of sense memory.

It was as if he could reach out and touch fur, playing with his parents and sisters, nipping with teeth and notching with claws, not hard enough to really hurt.

The hair on his body grew, standing to attention, his vision going completely gold as he transformed, answering the insistent urge. Careful of his claws, Adam fumbled the binoculars up to his eyes. Twisting the dials, he focused in on a jetty lit by flickering torches. His heart leapt as a woman filled his vision. She was facing the shore, her dark hair dangling in a ponytail.

Then she turned, and his heart swelled as she looked right at him.

She howled, and before he knew what he was doing, Adam returned her call across the waves.

Chapter Fourteen

*M*AYBE IT WAS *a bird.*

Parker listened carefully, but the sound didn't come again. He could have sworn it was a howl, and it was Adam. Was Adam hurt? Was he in trouble?

"I should have gone with him." He paced up and down *Bella's* length. "Fuck! You heard that, right?"

Craig hovered by the stern, squinting into the darkness. "I'm not sure what it was. It was far away."

The gun tucked into the waistband of his cargo shorts pressed against Parker's lower back, and his fingers itched to heft its weight and flick off the safety.

What if it's not Adam coming back? What if they got him, and it's someone else? What if...

"I'm sure everything's fine."

Parker wasn't sure who Craig was trying to convince, but he nodded. "Adam can take care of himself." Images of the sound-proofed basement laboratory at the Pines flashed through his mind as if to prove him wrong. The jars containing bloody chunks of Adam's flesh labeled neatly: *Arm, Leg, Back.*

He squeezed his eyes shut for a moment, nausea flooding his mouth with saliva. "As long as he doesn't get hit with a tranq dart or something."

Craig's eyebrows drew together, and he looked back out to sea, shifting his machete from one hand to the other and back again. The kids were downstairs, Jacob out of it with fever. Parker watched the waves, waiting for the dinghy to reappear, saying a silent prayer to whoever that it would be Adam in it, safe and sound.

Parker muttered, more to himself than Craig, "I swear to God, he'd better be okay. He'd better—"

The drone of the dinghy's outboard motor sounded jarringly loud in the darkness. The boat came into sight, and Parker exhaled in a rush. He'd know the slope of Adam's wide shoulders anywhere.

He gave Craig a reassuring smile and clambered down onto the launch platform to haul up the dinghy. He held out his hand, and Adam took it, his grip warm and almost too firm.

Adam was practically vibrating, humming with something Parker hoped wasn't fear. He couldn't quite tell, and asked, "What is it?"

"Wolves." Up on the deck, Adam smiled, tremulous and breathy. "*Wolves.*"

Somehow, Parker thought he should have known, but it hadn't even crossed his mind. "Wait... Seriously? Wow." His head spun.

"Other werewolves?" Craig asked. "You said there weren't many."

"There aren't. Not that I know of. But they're here. Come on, pull up the anchor. It's safe."

"Whoa, whoa." Parker held up his hands. "We don't know that. We don't know shit. Tell me what happened."

Adam did, words tripping out almost faster than he could corral them. He was excited in a way Parker had never seen.

Parker said, "Okay, so she saw you and howled, and you howled back—which we heard, by the way, thanks for freaking us the fuck out. Then you came back here, and...what? We're just going to sail right up and they'll roll out the welcome mat? How do we know they're not evil?"

"It's a feeling." Adam breathed shallowly, his fingers twitching. "I can't describe it. But when she called to me, it was like… It felt like home. I'm not running away this time. And Jacob needs a doctor." He reached for Parker's hand, squeezing. "Trust me."

"I do. It's not you I'm worried about. We can't—"

The unmistakable sound of a motor was a low rumble on the waves, and Parker jerked away from the railing. "It's them." He tried to tug his hand free from Adam's so he could pull out his gun, but Adam hung on.

"It's okay. Let's listen to what they have to say." Adam nodded to Craig. "Okay?"

After a moment, Craig tucked the machete behind a pillow on the bench by the table. "I'll follow your lead."

It was a small motorboat that appeared in the silver-tipped moonlight. Slowing, it pulled up to starboard, not too close, but close enough to speak without raising their voices too much. Parker supposed that being wolves, they could have whispered to Adam. They cut the engine, and a middle-aged white woman raised her hand.

Her dark hair was pulled back in a ponytail, and she wore jeans and a light jacket. She looked completely normal. Average. Unremarkable. Pretty in a way Parker's mom would have called "earthy," which was kind of an insult, since Pamela Osborne had preferred more spit and polish—glossy manicures and Ann Taylor cardigans.

The woman was too far away for Parker to check if her eyes were the same hazel-leaning-toward-gold that Adam's were. He hadn't thought about it until later, but Ramon's eyes had been that color. Adam had confirmed that his family had all had the same eyes, so Parker thought perhaps it was a defining werewolf trait.

At the wheel of the boat was a younger Asian man who was probably twenty-five. His dark hair was cropped short, and he was compact and trim. He gave them a nod, apparently waiting for the woman to say more. *Is he a werewolf too?* Parker couldn't be sure of his eye color either.

"Evening." She smiled, her teeth flashing white. "I'm Theresa. This is Kenny. We're glad to meet you."

Adam spoke, still holding Parker's hand. He introduced them and Craig, and added, "We have two children below deck. Lilly and Jacob."

She smiled again. "Very good. We love children."

Because they taste the best? That succulent young meat? Super juicy. Or maybe you're just huge perverts.

The worst-case scenarios whipped through Parker's mind, and he pressed his lips together to keep from blurting them out.

"My son needs a doctor," Craig said, and Parker swallowed a groan. Way to give them the upper hand.

"I'm sorry to hear that. We can definitely help. If you want to follow us, we can take you in to dock and go from there." She added, "I understand that you likely have concerns, but we only want to help. Salvation Island is a safe place."

Adam gripped Parker's hand even tighter, and Parker snapped his mouth shut. He hadn't even realized he'd opened it. But no, screw it, he had some questions. "Are you all werewolves? Why would you want to help us?"

"We only had wolves here before the virus, but we welcome all survivors now. Before, this was a sanctuary. A place for us to reconnect and be ourselves."

"Like werewolf camp? Or a resort?" Parker asked.

A smile flitted over her face. "Basically. Now it's a sanctuary for everyone. Had a boat arrive from Europe last week."

His breath caught. "Europe? Where, London? My brother Eric…" The odds Eric was on a ship crossing the Atlantic were so infinitesimal that Parker stopped talking, his cheeks burning as everyone looked at him. "Forget it."

But Theresa didn't scoff. "No one named Eric on board. I'm sorry."

"It's okay," he muttered.

You'll never see him again. Stop hoping.

Theresa addressed Adam now. "Your friends know about our kind? Is there anything we need to explain?"

"They know the basics. They know…what I know." He sounded so vulnerable in that moment, and Parker wanted to hide him away and keep him safe.

Theresa gave him an appraising nod, seeming to file away questions for later. "You've heard our messages, I assume? Salvation Island is a safe haven, and from what we understand, there aren't many safe places left."

"How have I never heard of this island before?" Parker asked. "It looks pretty big, but it's not on any of the maps."

"It's a private island. My family paid a lot of money over the years to keep it that way. We encourage you to come see for yourselves. See what we have to offer. You're free to leave anytime."

"Gee, thanks," Parker grumbled.

Adam jumped in. "Thank you. We appreciate your hospitality. If we can see the doctor tonight, that would be good."

Theresa frowned. "Yes, I think you should. He doesn't sound well. We can help the boy. My mother's a nurse."

"Thank you." Craig glanced at Parker. "I think it's worth a try. I can't let anything happen to him."

Kenny addressed Parker. "I was scared too when we first came. But it'll be okay. I swear."

"I'm not scared." It was such a ridiculous lie that Parker flushed as soon as the words were out, going hot all the way to his ears. But they were in the middle of the ocean and Jacob was getting worse, so what the hell else could they do? He nodded, pulling free of Adam's grip to go fire up the engine. "Then what are we waiting for?"

He followed the motorboat with sails down, the engine humming. While Craig went below to get the kids ready, Adam stood by Parker, not touching him.

"I know you're not happy."

Parker had to snort. "What gave it away?"

"You usually have such a poker face."

The laughter was nice and warm in his chest, and he exhaled as Adam leaned close and kissed his cheek, his scruff scratching. Parker whispered, "What if they're big bad wolves and we're the pigs?"

"I won't let them hurt you. Or any of us." He wrapped his arm around Parker's shoulders. "I feel good about this. But I'm still on guard. I promise."

The urge to change course and motor as far away as they could was a cold pull in Parker's gut. The island loomed bigger and bigger, fire dancing in torches along the shore. They couldn't trust these people. They couldn't trust anyone but themselves. They should go and—

He bit back a gasp as Craig emerged from below, carrying Jacob in his arms like a much smaller kid. Jacob moaned and thrashed, barely conscious, and fear slithered icily through Parker's veins. Jacob was so much worse, and for the first time, Parker realized he might really *die*.

As Adam went to help, taking Lilly by the hand as she followed her father on deck, Parker's throat burned, thoughts of Abby and the warmth of her blood pulsing out between his fingers consuming him. He'd promised her. He'd promised to keep Jacob safe. He should have known the kid would try something stupid and go for the gas can. He should have been smarter. Should have been more prepared.

He should have been better.

Salvation Island surrounded them now on three sides, hilly

peaks rising above, black lumps amid the stars. The only way out of the deep curve of the harbor would be back. But to where? Parker's own words to Jacob echoed.

We have to move forward.

With a deep breath, he pulled up to a long jetty, one of a maze of wooden docks holding dozens of boats. He switched off the engine as they rubbed up against the bumpers.

A young woman on the dock called, "Throw me the ropes!"

He did, and it felt like leaping off a cliff. He watched anxiously as she tied *Bella* securely. He would have used a round turn with two half hitches, then whipped the end, but her knots did the job.

After pocketing the keys, he reluctantly followed the others onto the dock, concentrating on keeping his breathing and heart rate steady, counting in his head. He didn't want anyone to think he was scared. Weak.

Adam was nervous and excited, giving Parker an eager little smile. Parker knew how much it meant to him to talk to other wolves instead of running away. How scared Adam was underneath it all.

If these fuckers hurt him, it'll be the last thing they do.

Theresa was speaking. "We have a strict no-weapons policy. You won't need them here. If you have a weapon, please leave it locked in your boat tonight and we'll collect them in the morning, or give them to us now for safekeeping." Her gaze slid over them. Craig had Jacob in his arms, and Adam held Lilly's hand. Parker counted his breath in: *one, two, three, four.* His gun pressed reassuringly against his lower back.

From my cold, dead hands...

Craig said, "I left a machete on the bench there."

Kenny hopped down and grabbed it, resettling the pillows when he found it.

Out, two, three, four. In, two, three, four. Out...

If they wouldn't need weapons, then great. He'd keep the gun tucked away, and no one had to know.

TORCH-LIT PATHWAYS CUT through the forest, palm trees giving way to denser foliage. Craig stumbled over a root, grunting as he hoisted Jacob higher in his arms, Jacob moaning. Guilt tugged at Parker again, low and insistent. Should have kept him safe.

Should have kept my promise.

"Do you want me to take him?" Adam asked, still holding Lilly's hand.

"I got him." Craig cradled Jacob close, muttering, "I got you, buddy. I've got you."

"No electricity?" Parker asked Theresa.

"Don't worry, we have plenty. But the paths have never been lit. We didn't need them to be. But now that humans are here, things are changing."

Parker wondered how she felt about this development, but her tone was even, giving nothing away. "There were no humans at all before?"

"The odd one—a husband or wife, girlfriend or boyfriend. Not nearly enough to install lights on the paths."

"So, what did you do at this werewolf resort?"

Theresa tucked a long strand of dark hair behind her ear where it had come loose from her ponytail. "Same things most people do at any resort. We'll answer all your questions, don't worry."

He wasn't so sure about that, but feeling Adam's gaze on him, he bit his tongue.

The square, single-story infirmary building did indeed have electricity, and Parker blinked at the fluorescent lights and sterile white tiles glaring in stark contrast to the dark forest. A handful of empty beds lined one wall, storage cabinets on the others.

As Craig gently lowered Jacob to the nearest bed, Theresa said, "We have a full store of medicine. You did the right thing bringing him here."

"If werewolves don't get sick, why do you have medicine?" Parker asked.

She frowned. "Who said werewolves don't get sick?"

"My boyfriend." He jerked his thumb at Adam. "The were-wolf."

"We do get sick—just not in the way humans do."

Parker frowned at Adam, who shrugged back. That was potentially disturbing news, but there was no time for it.

Theresa added, "When the trouble began, my cousin traveled here from Miami with his human wife and children. As time went on, more of our number came, and we decided to open our doors to other survivors. We traveled to the mainland and stocked up on medical supplies for all our residents, human and wolf."

Jacob whimpered and cried out, and Parker's heart clenched.

"Mom!" Jacob cried. "I want my mom!"

"I know you do." Craig brushed back Jacob's too-long bangs. "I do too. But she's looking out for you. She's here—you just can't see her. But you can feel her. Hang on. Everything's going to be okay."

He tried to stop the images from coming, but Parker could only withstand it as he relived it all over again—*the dock under his feet, splinters under his skin, Abby's blood pumping between his fingers in the sunshine, her cries and desperate eyes, Jacob and Lilly watching helplessly.*

The door opened, and Parker spun around, certain creepers were going to flood into the white room, their eyes bulging, lurching with bloody fingers outstretched, teeth ready to tear. But it was only a short, older woman entering with Kenny at her heels.

Swallowing his gasp as the danger didn't materialize, Parker looked to Adam, who had reached out to him. But now Adam stared at the new arrival, his lips parted. Parker turned to her again.

Under the relentless fluorescent lights, he could tell her eyes were definitely hazel with flecks of gold. Her gray hair was bobbed around her jaw, and she was plump, wearing jeans and an ugly purple sweatshirt featuring butterflies and flowers.

Theresa said, "This is my mother, Connie. She was a nurse for many years."

Connie nodded to them, but only had eyes for Jacob. "Let's take a look-see."

As she spoke, Parker jolted in recognition. It was the woman from the radio messages—he was sure of it. Adam still stared at her intensely, and Parker wished he could read his mind. But Adam stayed silent, holding Lilly's hand. Craig took her other hand, and a pang of irrational loneliness struck Parker, standing off to the side.

Efficiently and quietly, Connie asked questions in her soothing, even tone, and stitched Jacob's festering puncture wound with a few efficient strokes, cleaning and bandaging it before lifting his head and feeding him a few pills. She wheeled over an IV stand and got a bag out of a little fridge.

Once it was hung and the needle was inserted into the back of Jacob's hand, she stood back and looked at him. "We'll have to wait and see. He's young; he has a good chance. Why don't we let him rest and get you all settled."

"No, I'm not leaving him," Craig said. "Lilly and I will stay here tonight. She can sleep over there." He indicated one of the empty beds.

Connie nodded. "All right. And your name is?" After shaking Craig's hand and getting his name, she said to Parker and Adam, "Let me show you to your cabin, and we can be properly introduced."

Parker shook his head. "We should stay too. I don't want to

leave Jacob."

"He needs rest," Connie said. "How about I show you around, and you can come back in a little while if you'd like."

Part of him wanted to argue just to be contrary, but he managed to resist. After giving Lilly and Craig encouraging smiles, he and Adam followed Connie outside and along another path.

Wooden cabins were nestled in the trees. Most were dark, and Parker swore he could feel eyes watching as they passed by. It sent a chill down his spine, and he had to shove his hands in his pockets to stop from taking the gun out of his waistband.

"Here we are." Connie walked up a few steps to a small porch, crossing it to open the door to the cabin. Inside, she flicked on a floor lamp standing beside a soft-looking blue fabric couch. "Nothing fancy, but it should be comfortable."

Off the main room, a kitchenette lined one wall to the right, with a fridge, stove, and cabinets painted a pale green. A short hall led to what Parker assumed were the bathroom and a bedroom. The medium brown wooden floor was uneven but polished, and simply framed photos of ocean vistas dotted the wooden walls.

He forced a smile. "It's great. Thank you." And it really was nice—provided Connie and the gang weren't luring them into complacency before striking.

Adam nodded, his gaze still stuck on Connie, who smiled kindly. "I'm glad you're here," she said. "Someone will be by any minute to stock the fridge with some essentials. You can drink the tap water; we have a filtration system."

"Cool. Thanks." Parker waited for Adam to say something, but words were apparently escaping him. Having always hated an awkward silence, Parker blurted, "So, you're a werewolf?"

"I am indeed. Just like your boyfriend." She gave Adam a contemplative look, her head tilted. "I was going to suggest you get a good night's sleep before we talk, but perhaps we should have a word now."

Adam only nodded.

"Um, great. Let's sit down, I guess." Parker waved to the couch and matching armchair.

She said, "Why don't you settle in, and Adam and I can go have a chat. I won't keep him long."

Parker opened his mouth to say *no freaking way*, but Adam was nodding and already following Connie to the door.

"Dude." Parker pressed his lips into a line. "I think it's better if we stay together."

Blinking, Adam seemed to remember he was there. "It's okay. I'll be back soon."

"I'll wait outside, Adam. Good to meet you, Parker. Try to get some rest. You're safe here." She disappeared into the night.

Likely fucking story.

He grabbed Adam's arm and hissed, "Is she doing something to you? Some werewolf Jedi mind trick?"

"I don't think so," Adam whispered. "It's... I can't explain it, but it doesn't feel bad. I just really want to go talk to her. Okay?"

"No! Not okay." He knew Connie could hear even though he barely whispered, but whatever. "You're acting like a total space cadet."

"I'm sorry." He took Parker's hands. "But it's okay. Let me talk to her. I *need* to talk to her."

And leave me here alone?

For a moment, his throat tightened, and Parker thought he might cry like a pathetic baby.

Get a grip, loser. Be a grown-up.

He shrugged carelessly. "Okay, whatever. If she offers you any Kool-Aid, the answer's no."

With a half smile, Adam kissed him and followed Connie outside. Parker stood in the doorway and watched them disappear beyond the torchlight.

Crickets or cicadas or something chirped and leaves rustled in the light breeze. Squinting into the darkness, he couldn't see anything but the hulking shadows of trees. But he was certain he could feel eyes on him again, assessing. In the whisper of the leaves, he was sure people were talking about him, getting closer...

Skin crawling, he slammed the door. It didn't lock, because of course it fucking didn't.

Adam, come back!

Parker wanted to run back to the infirmary but realized he wasn't sure which winding path to take.

His shaking hands were clammy, breath short and shallow. What if Adam didn't come back? Parker felt utterly alone and vulnerable. Shorty's grating laughter echoed, and for a moment Parker could have sworn it was real.

The porch creaked, and his heart leapt into his throat. He listened with his ear at the door before slowly edging it open. There was no one there. A wind chime tinkled in the distance, the leaves rustling.

Parker closed the door and leaned against it, his feet braced. After reaching for the gun, at least he could breathe again.

Chapter Fifteen

"CAN I GET you a drink?" Connie asked as she led Adam inside a cabin similar to the one they'd just left but situated at the top of a rise. "Something to eat?"

He shook his head. He had to clasp his hands in front of him to keep from reaching out to her. Every word she said seemed to echo inside him, resonating bone-deep in a way he couldn't understand. He watched as she turned on the stove and filled a kettle.

"I'll go back soon and check on Jacob. Are you sure you don't want a mug of tea?"

He nodded, and as she turned back to him, he realized he'd stretched his arm out to touch. He snatched his hand back. "I'm sorry. I—I—"

She smiled kindly. "You've never met an alpha before." Grasping his hand in both of hers, she added, "Welcome."

Peace and warmth seemed to flow from her callused hands right into his veins. He managed to find his voice, although it was hoarse. "How?"

"I don't know exactly. Something to do with our pack instincts. You must have sensed it when you heard me on the radio, didn't you?"

He thought of the messages, of how compelling her voice had been. "I did, but I didn't realize what it was." His cheeks grew hot at his foolishness. "I just knew I wanted to come here."

She squeezed his fingers kindly. "There's a frequency in our voices, especially strong in alphas. When I was a little girl, I'd follow my father around like a duckling. We all did."

"He was the alpha before you?"

"Mmm-hmm. This was his idea, the island. He was something of a hippie, my dad. A billionaire hippie, so not your usual."

"A billionaire?" She was still holding Adam's hand, and he wanted to drop to her feet and press into her knees. But he stayed standing, looking down at her. Her head just reached his chin.

"Made his money in plastics. Used a lot of it to buy and develop this island. I took over for him when he died."

"Uh-huh." It was hard to concentrate on what she was saying. He just wanted to rub against her, but not in a sexual way.

"Sit. I think some tea would do you good." She patted his hand and let go, and he barely stopped himself from grabbing her back.

As she bustled around, the kettle began to whistle. When the tea was steeping, she urged him to the couch, and they sat side by side, their knees pressing together. She said, "You'll get used to it, and then it won't affect you this way. Tell me where you came from."

Adam gave her the condensed version of his childhood with his parents and sisters, living totally isolated from other wolves and told to avoid them if they ever happened upon any. Then the accident.

"Oh, you poor child. How lonely that must have been." She squeezed his arm, and it tingled with the most wonderful, comforting warmth.

"Yes," he choked out before clearing his throat. "Do you think anyone here knew my parents?"

"It's possible. We'll look into it. What happened after the accident?"

Adam told her about his foster family and how badly it had ended. He cleared his throat, working to keep an even tone. "But I made a friend in college who I told eventually."

"And your young man. Cute one, if a little high-strung." She smiled, taking any sting from her words.

A pang of guilt flowed. He couldn't believe he'd left Parker all alone, but the urge to follow Connie had been too strong. "I should get back to him. He's nervous that this place isn't what you say it is." And maybe Adam shouldn't have actually said that out loud, but there it was, hanging in the air.

Connie only pushed herself up with a rueful laugh and went to pour the tea. "I don't blame him. Hard to know who to trust." She pulled down two mugs. "But you trust him?"

"Yes. Completely. I love him. Is that… That's not a problem, is it?"

Pulling out a bottle of milk from the fridge, she said, "Because he's a boy or because he's human?"

"Both?"

"Well, the answer's no in both cases. Not a problem at all. Milk and sugar?"

"Uh, sure." He never drank tea, but it sounded right. "I'm glad to hear it. We ran into some trouble with another werewolf in Colorado who didn't like wolves and humans mixing."

Handing a mug emblazoned with *Miami is for Lovers* to Adam, she resettled on the couch. "Yes, it can be controversial. Some packs have outlawed it. We became so scattered and fractured in the twentieth century. It was one of the reasons my father created this place—to bring wolves back together. To reconnect packs and give omegas like you a place to come and feel at home. Life happens, and I'm not going to tell anyone who they should love. Parker accepted the truth about you easily?"

Adam sipped the warm tea, not sure if he liked it or not, and thought of that night when he'd revealed himself to save Parker's life. Thought of telling him about the accident, and how Parker had climbed into bed with him in the dark, unafraid. "He did.

The initial shock didn't last long at all. Craig and the kids took it well too. Considering how the world's changed, I suppose it makes it easier now to tell people."

She smiled. "That it does. We have a strict like-it-or-lump-it policy here now. And by 'lump it,' I mean turn around and sail off into the sunset. The time has come that we're not going to hide what we are or apologize for it."

"Wow. I never thought... I never even imagined it." What would his parents think? Would they still shun other wolves and hide away? "It really is a new world."

"Don't think it'll go back to the way it was. The virus is running rampant. There doesn't seem to be anyone in charge anymore, which is why I decided it was time to step up. From what we've heard on the radio, infrastructures have been decimated around the world. Amazing how quickly all those years of building societies can be reduced to ashes."

He thought of the stench of Daytona Beach and nodded. "What about the terrorists who caused this? The Zechariahs?"

"Who knows? There are rumors here and there that they're planning a second wave, but I have a feeling the first wave was a little more successful than they'd anticipated. Assuming they exist at all. This could have been the work of nature. We might never know for sure. Probably won't."

"If no one stops it, I guess werewolves will inherit the earth." He held the mug in his hands, the handle feeling delicate.

"Why would you say that?"

"We seem to be immune. At least I was."

Connie peered at him intently, her tea on the table, forgotten. "How do you know this?"

"I was bitten. Badly, in the neck. But nothing happened. We met scientists who tested my blood. I'm immune—to that strain, at least."

"Scientists?"

"It's a long story."

"Tell me."

Suddenly Adam wanted nothing more than to fill her in on every detail. "We ended up at this exclusive hotel in the Rockies…"

When he finished the saga of the Pines, Dr. Yamaguchi, and Ramon, Connie sat back against the worn cushions. "We did have a report from one of our residents of being bitten on the mainland and not being affected, but we had no idea if it was a fluke or not. Finding out the hard way hasn't been a priority. But if we're really immune…" Her eyes shone gold as she stared into space, contemplating it.

Adam cradled his mug. "We could go ashore. Fight the infected and help the survivors."

Connie refocused on him. "Mmm. Assuming the virus doesn't mutate, and that immunity doesn't vary based on genetics. Werewolves come from all backgrounds. My mother was Mexican and my father Greek." She lifted her mug and sloshed tea on her butterfly sweatshirt, grimacing down at it. "A gift from my grandson. It's apparently 'ironic' because it's what grandmas should wear, but he says I'm a badass."

It was hard to imagine her with fangs and claws, but strength emanated from her like a current. "I can believe it."

Connie gave him a shrewd smile. "Well, thank you." She took a gulp of tea, all business again. "All right, we need to think hard about a long-term plan. We can't make any assumptions about immunity. It could prove fatal if we do, and our kind is already close enough to extinction. Right now, I think we have to concentrate on our safe haven. On helping those that respond to our radio calls." She checked her watch. "Now, let me get back to the infirmary, and you get some sleep. That's an alpha order. I'll put the whammy on you if you don't comply."

"Yes, ma'am." He wanted to reach out and ask her to stay and talk to him for hours—days—but he had to get back to Parker. He followed her outside and along a path, and she pointed him to the cabin. He said, "You'll come get us if something happens with Jacob?"

"Of course. But I think time will tell. There's nothing you can do tonight except rest up yourselves."

"Okay. Thank you. It's great to meet you. I can't... Just— thank you."

She took his hand in hers again, her eyes glowing gold. "Welcome, Adam. Welcome home."

For a minute after she was gone, he had to lean against the porch railing to catch his breath, his eyes burning.

Pushing the cabin door open, he quietly called, "Parker? It's me."

As Adam neared, Parker appeared at the bedroom door, still in his shorts, tee, and sneakers. "Well?"

"She seems great. Nothing to worry about."

"Yet." Parker's fingers twitched. "It's too good to be true. It has to be. We should go check on Jacob and make sure Craig and Lilly are okay."

"Let's get some sleep. Jacob's in good hands. I really think we're safe here."

Grunting, Parker retreated into the simple bedroom and unlaced his shoes. "I'll take this side." He stripped to his boxers and pulled back the thin duvet.

"Sure. I like the right anyway." There was so much more he wanted to say and try to explain, but Parker had already curled away from him.

It was at least an hour later when he startled awake, the rapid staccato of Parker's pulse finding its way into Adam's dreams. He reached out, Parker's soft cries and whimpers grabbing at his heart.

"Shhh, it's just a dream. Wake up."

Parker did, gasping. He was still turned away from Adam, and he buried his face in his arm, shuddering.

"What was it?" Adam asked softly.

"Nothing," he mumbled. "I'm fine."

"I don't think you are." Parker trembled, perspiration beading his skin even though the night was cool. "Please tell me." Adam pressed his lips to the back of Parker's neck, nosing the sweat-damp hair there and spooning close.

"I'm fine," he insisted. "Just a dumb dream." Squirming, he turned, pressing their lips together, his thigh between Adam's legs. He reached into Adam's boxer briefs to take hold of his cock.

Adam groaned, pleasure sparking down his spine, his dick twitching to life at the first touch. The urge to bury himself in Parker and not think about anything else almost overwhelmed him, but he broke their kiss.

"Talk to me," he whispered.

Parker's face creased, and he stroked up and down Adam's length before reaching lower to caress his balls, sending a shiver of desire through him. "There's nothing wrong with me." He kissed Adam again before wriggling lower and licking over the head of Adam's cock, easing down the foreskin.

Adam took hold of Parker's shoulders. "Don't use sex as avoidance. It doesn't feel right."

A slideshow of emotion passed over Parker's face—anger, incredulity, and most of all, hurt. His voice was painfully small. "You don't want me?"

"Of course I do, but..."

"But what?" He yanked his hand free of Adam's underwear and leaned away.

"It's—" Adam groaned in frustration as he tried to find the elusive right words.

Parker rolled away, curling into a ball. "I'm tired anyway."

"So that's it?"

Glaring over his shoulder, he bit out, "You're the one who doesn't want to fuck."

"Because we should talk!"

He flopped onto his back and crossed his arms, the duvet tangled around his waist. "Fine, talk."

"What did you dream about?"

Parker shook his head. "I said it was nothing."

"If it was nothing—"

"God, I had a shitty nightmare about some of the shitty stuff that's happened. It was—wait for it—shitty. Why are you making a federal case out of it?"

"I'm not! I want to help you—"

"Then why aren't you fucking me right now?"

They lay rigid, a few inches between them on the mattress. Adam clenched his jaw and took a deep breath. "I'm not in the mood."

"Why? Maybe you'd rather be with another werewolf."

He sputtered, staring at Parker's profile in the shadows. "What? Now you're being ridiculous."

"Am I?" Parker's chest rose and fell rapidly. "If there are other wolves here, maybe you'll meet one you like better than me. One you have some wolfy connection with that I can never give you."

Softening, Adam reached for him, but Parker squirmed away. Adam sighed. "That won't happen."

"You already took off on me tonight for your little rendezvous with Connie."

"What, now we have to be joined at the hip?"

"No, but we don't even know these people! They could be on their way over right now to murder us in our sleep and eat us for breakfast."

"Can we just try to be positive for once?"

Nostrils flaring, Parker rolled away onto his side. "Whatever. Since *we're* not fucking, let's go to sleep."

Adam wanted to press close and hold him, but he stayed flat on his back, his hands fisted in the sheets. He stared at the logs of the ceiling as the night marched on. They were both wide awake.

THE BOAT WASN'T swaying.

Adam couldn't hear the water or Parker breathing, and where were Craig and the kids? In a single motion, he opened his eyes and shot to his feet. Staring down at the empty, rumpled bed, the pieces fell into place.

Salvation Island. They'd actually made it.

Safe.

The feeling of home surrounded him, flowing over his skin and burrowing beneath. He still felt the warmth of Connie taking his hand in hers. It was different than when he'd met Ramon. The word she'd used returned to Adam: *omega.* A lone wolf. He wondered if his mother or father had been the alpha of their little family pack. He didn't recall one of them being more comforting or powerful than the other. To him, they'd just been Mom and Dad.

Here, it wasn't just Connie and Theresa—he could feel the hum of hundreds of other wolves. But instead of frightening him as it had in the past, it enveloped him in an embrace. He closed his eyes and breathed deeply.

Still, he had to be cautious. He wouldn't accept anything blindly or be too trusting. Parker was right that they needed to be on their guard, even though Adam's instincts told him they were safe. Parker—

Adam opened his eyes. Where was Parker? He realized with a jolt that he couldn't hear him in the cabin. "Parker?"

Silence but for the birds in the trees beyond the cabin and insects and small creatures scurrying in the undergrowth. Adam tugged on his jeans and worn T-shirt and shoved his feet into his boots. Parker had probably just woken early and gone to check on Jacob. He was fine. There was nothing to worry about.

Adam's pulse still raced, his stomach swooping.

He tracked Parker's scent along the paths between cabins, down to the water, spotting him at the foot of the series of interconnected docks and boats. Approaching from behind with a sigh of relief, Adam said, "Here you are."

He reached out, but Parker jerked away from his touch. Irritation flared, and Adam clenched his jaw. "Seriously? You're still pissed? Come on."

But Parker stood stock-still, staring at the harbor as if he hadn't even heard him. His heart skipped, his breathing shallow. Adam frowned. Boats bobbed in the swift breeze, *glug-glugging* against the bumpers. The sun was bright, yet Parker shivered in his thick, too-big hoodie over his cargo shorts.

"I knew it," Parker muttered.

"Knew what?" Adam reached for him again, his hand hovering in the air. He peered around carefully, but the morning was all blue sky and sunshine on his skin. "What is it?"

Then Parker was running, his sneakers squeaking on the wood as he raced down the dock and made a left toward a huge sailboat. Adam followed, trying to spot the danger Parker was apparently running straight toward.

The large boat was docked bow first, and Parker skidded to the end of the jetty, turning to stare at the stern. Lips parted, he stared in apparent horror before gagging. Folding in half, he fell to his knees and retched over the side of the dock. Adam dropped down beside him, his heart thumping so loudly in his own ears it was hard to hear anything else.

"What is it?" He wanted to rub Parker's back but was afraid to make it worse. He stared at the huge boat, which seemed to be empty. "What—" He registered the name with a sinking sensation of dread.

The Good Life

Fury—hot and dark, sticky and thick—spread through him. "It's their boat?"

Parker muttered hoarsely, "See? I knew it. We can't trust anyone. They're here."

Adam ran his hand over Parker's hair. "It's okay. I won't let them hurt you again."

Parker trembled, but his eyes shone angrily. "*I* won't let them hurt me this time. I'm ready for them."

A new voice said, "Hey, what are you—"

They both shot to their feet as a woman appeared on the boat's deck holding a box of Pop-Tarts. Her reddish hair was twisted into a braid, and she wore shorts over a blue bathing suit. Eyes going wide, she stared at Parker and simply said, "Oh."

Parker jerked beside Adam, and the woman stumbled back, crying, "Wait!"

Somehow Parker was pointing a gun at her.

Adam stared at it, utterly baffled. "Where—? Parker, no. Put that down."

"No way. I couldn't get to my gun last time. Not going to happen again." He clutched the pistol with both hands, his finger quivering over the trigger. "Where's Shorty, huh?"

"What?" She shook her head. "Who, Mick? That no-dick asshole's dead." The woman glanced at Adam, wide-eyed. "Look, it wasn't my fault what happened. I'm sorry things got a little messy."

"Liar," Parker gritted out. "You laughed. You said you guys could have fun with me. With—with my mouth," he spat. "You *laughed.*"

The simmering rage boiled up, and Adam realized the growl filling the air had come from his own throat. The woman backed up another step, clutching the box of Pop-Tarts. Adam could jump onto the deck and eviscerate her in a heartbeat, and the urge had him shaking, hair spreading over his body, gold rage narrowing his vision, his claws and fangs growing sharp, tingling.

She trembled. "I'm sorry, okay? I had to go along with Mick or I'd have been the one he hit. I didn't want to. I'm sorry you got hurt, kid. But shit, it could have been worse. You got off light compared to others. That's why I shoved that asshole overboard and left him out there."

"You murdered him?" Adam wasn't sure whether to be glad or sorry he didn't have the chance to do it himself.

The woman puffed up. "He was a bad person! Who are you to judge me? He'd already killed the others over a case of goddamned Coors Light. He was a crazy fucker. I didn't want anything to do with him."

Parker shook his head, his voice wavering but hands steady now, leveling the gun at the woman. "Why should I believe you? You were having fun. You didn't help me."

"I had my own problems. I needed to keep Mick happy so I could stay alive." Her hard gaze slid to Adam. "You're going to let him shoot me in cold blood? Huh?"

Adam had to work to form words that weren't just a growl. "Maybe I'll kill you myself."

She lifted her chin. "Boss ladies won't like that. Ain't supposed to kill here. Have to follow the rules." Her bravado faltered. "And I have! I haven't given anyone trouble. I like it here. Ask anyone. I've done everything I'm supposed to. This is a good place. Don't mess it up!"

"Why should I believe you?" Parker asked, his throat working and his voice strained.

She held up the Pop-Tarts. "I came to get these for the new girl. Lilly? I thought she'd like them. Sweet kid."

"You stay the fuck away from her." Parker's face was frighteningly red, his eyes wild. "All of you stay away from her. From us!"

"I know what you're thinking, okay? That this place is bull-shit? I thought so too. Mick was planning on taking over." She smiled then, bitter and sharp. "I almost wish he'd gotten the chance to try. Would have loved to see the look on his dumb face when he came up against a bunch of werewolves."

"You're sure he's dead?" Adam asked. Vibrating, he flexed his claws, his fangs aching, fur bristling with adrenaline.

"Not a doubt. I waited. Watched with binoculars. Drunk fuck didn't tread water for long. It was a little disappointing the sharks were MIA." She shrugged defensively. "Maybe I should be sorry, but after a few months with that asshole, I know we're all better off."

Adam couldn't argue. Parker apparently couldn't either, and his breathing had steadied somewhat, the panicked mania seeming to loosen its grip as he asked, "Why did you come here? Why didn't you turn back?"

"Back to what? You've been there. You've seen it." Eyes glistening, she blinked rapidly. "It's gone. I figured what the hell. If Salvation Island was a crock of shit, then that would be that. And maybe it wouldn't be so bad, not having to live in this fucked-up world. But when I showed up, they welcomed me." She motioned toward land. "Gave me a cabin of my own. A job. I do shifts milking the cows." Her laughter was thin and tinged with hysteria. "Me, milking fuckin' cows! My momma wouldn't believe her eyes." Tears hung on her lashes.

To Adam, she said, "Look, your kind has been good to me. It's been a real long time since anyone was. I just want to get along with everyone and…and live." Her voice caught. "I want to *live*. Please."

Although her heart thumped, Adam thought it was with fear, not falsehood. Turning to Parker, he kept his tone low. "Do you trust me?"

Parker's gaze slid over to him, and his Adam's apple bobbed as he swallowed. "Yes."

"Then give me the gun. If you shoot her, I think you'll really regret it." He could take the gun, but didn't want to do that to Parker. The choice had to be his.

Parker still held the pistol steady, his heart was anything but. "I've shot people. Killed them. Creepers, but they're still *people*. I don't like to think of them that way. Because I kill them. I'm already a killer."

"To survive, we do what we have to." Adam glanced at the woman, who stood frozen, her heart rabbiting, terror sweat-slick on her skin. Inhaling deeply, he reined in the wolf, his fangs and claws retracting, the gold filter on the world fading back to brilliant blue in the morning sun.

Parker whispered, "I think of them as monsters, but they were just like us. They could be us." He blinked at Adam. "Well, not you. But me."

"I won't let that happen." He had to reach out then—had to touch. He gently grasped Parker's trembling shoulder, trying to infuse his conviction into Parker's skin through the thin cotton of his T-shirt. "I'm sorry I wasn't there that day on the boat when they came. But I'm here now. I won't let anyone hurt you."

Parker's outstretched arms wavered. "I know."

"I don't want to hurt you," the woman said quietly. "I don't want to hurt anyone. We've all had to do terrible things to survive—we fight and kill and hurt. It's true I did awful stuff when I was with Mick and the others. But I don't want to do that anymore. I didn't like who I was with them. That's why I let him die out there. Life has to be more than that. It's got to be better. I want to be better. I know that must sound like a load of horse shit, but I mean it. Don't you wanna be better than you are?"

A shaky little smile lifted Parker's lips. "All the time." To Adam, he whispered, "I want to be what you need. What you want."

Adam pleaded, "You *are*. Why can't you believe that?"

"This place—" He blinked at the woman. "If it's really safe..."

"If it's really safe, we can build a life here. Have a community here. And it doesn't mean I want you any less, or that you're any less important to me. Let's make this place our home *together*. A fresh start."

Parker lowered his arms, the gun still in his right hand. The woman's eyes flicked continually from the pistol to Parker to Adam and back again in a loop, but she was thankfully staying silent.

"I'm afraid." Parker's voice was barely audible.

"Me too. We'll be afraid together." Adam extended his hand.

The metal was warm and slick, and Adam drew back his arm and threw the gun as far as he could into the deep of the ocean.

Chapter Sixteen

THE WORN WOOD dock creaked under his sneakers, water lapping against it and birds squawking in the distance. Parker stared at the spot where the gun had disappeared. There were footsteps approaching, and he turned, bracing. Adam stepped closer, keeping Parker partially behind him.

"Everything okay here?" Kenny asked as he neared *The Good Life* with an older, bearded man Parker didn't recognize. Kenny was frowning at him, and Parker realized he was panting and shaking. Before he could come up with some kind of excuse, the woman said, "Everything's fine." Parker jolted in surprise. She added, "It was my fault. Not theirs."

"Are you sure, Bethany?" the bearded man asked. "I could have sworn I saw a gun and heard threats being made."

Adam said, "There's some prior history here. Parker had a run-in with Bethany and her friends."

The man asked, "Where's the gun?"

"I threw it away." Adam jerked his chin toward the water. "Parker was taken by surprise. He wasn't thinking clearly."

"It's on me, not the kid," Bethany insisted.

The man eyed Parker closely. "And you're thinking clearly now?"

Parker nodded. He hoped it was the truth.

"And don't have any other weapons?"

"I don't," Parker said. That was definitely the truth, at least.

Bethany said, "Gotta get these Pop-Tarts over to the mess

hall." With a little hop, she landed up on the dock. "See you around," she added to Parker and Adam before hurrying away, her flip-flops slapping. Kenny trailed after her, shooting glances back over his shoulder as he went.

"I don't think we've met," the bearded man said as he extended his hand. "Damian Bautista." His hair was dark and shot through with gray, his skin tan, body trim and fit.

Forcing a smile that was likely little more than a grimace, Parker took his hand and introduced himself after Adam did. Damian's palm was cool and his grip strong. Adam stood very still, his gaze locked on Damian.

"I'm sure you've been told weapons are forbidden here on Salvation Island. If you have any remaining on your boat, please bring them to Theresa this morning for lockup."

"We will," Adam said.

"Thank you." Damian's eyes softened as he looked at Parker. "I'm sure this has been a stressful journey. But we're all in this together. If there's anything I can do to help, don't hesitate."

Parker nodded, willing the tears burning his eyes to stay unshed. He blurted, "I was scared." He motioned with his hand. "I saw the boat, and I thought…" Vomit lingered in his mouth and throat, and he tried to swallow it away. "She was with some shitty people before. A bad man. He hurt me, and I thought he was here."

"Ah. Yes, Bethany told us a bit about her former companions. I can understand your reaction. But I assure you they're not here, and people like that will never be tolerated on this island. Bethany has proven herself to be hardworking in the time she's been with us."

It popped into Parker's head and out his mouth. "You really have cows here?"

Damian smiled. "We do. A whole herd, as a matter of fact. Dairy and beef. The goal of the island was always to be sustainable and self-sufficient, but obviously we've upped our game recently. The chickens are doing very well, and we're quadrupling the size of the garden. If you have any experience, we'd love to have you pitch in."

"I don't know anything about it. Sorry." Parker suddenly wished he did, desperately. What did he have to offer? After being scared and resistant for so long about going to Salvation Island, he found he was afraid they'd be the ones that didn't want *him*.

"That's all right," Damian assured. "We're all learning."

"We'll help in any way we can," Adam said. "You can trust us."

Damian nodded. "I'll speak to Connie and Theresa about this incident, and I'm sure one of them will follow up with you later. In the meantime, breakfast is on if you're hungry."

Parker's stomach rebelled at the thought, but he nodded tightly. Adam and Damian shared a look before Damian strolled down the dock, and then they were alone.

Suddenly feeling utterly exposed, he turned back to the water. "I'm sorry. Fuck."

Adam's voice was remarkably calm. "Parker, it's okay. Look at me."

"I can't. I'm such a fuckup." He hugged himself, squeezing his eyes shut. Adam didn't touch him now, and Parker didn't blame him. "I almost shot her."

"But you didn't."

"But I *wanted* to! I wanted to."

"She's fine. Everything's going to be okay."

He whirled around, his arms flying out. "No, it won't! I wanted to *murder* someone! I could have killed her because I couldn't get my shit together."

"You didn't," Adam soothed, his eyes so kind.

Looking at his right hand as if the gun was still in it, Parker wanted to puke again. He croaked, "I lied to you."

"About having the gun?"

"Yes, but more than that."

Adam went very still. "Okay. Tell me."

He couldn't meet Adam's eyes. The moored boats bobbed gently in the returning tide, gulls circling in the cloudless sky. A sob tore out of his throat. "I said I wasn't broken, but I am."

In a stride, Adam was wrapped around him, holding him so tightly. Parker's arms were folded and pressed to Adam's chest, and it was sweaty and warm and *good*, and he wanted to stay forever. Tears spilled from his cheeks, and he couldn't dam the flow this time.

"We're all broken," Adam murmured, one hand stroking over Parker's head. "We're doing our best. You're doing your best. You're always so hard on yourself."

"But—"

"But what? You shouldn't be scared? You shouldn't be affected when you're traumatized? When you lose your family? When you're assaulted by a cowardly fuck? When you have to watch a friend die? It should all roll off you without leaving anything behind?"

He knew Adam was right, but shame clung to him with barbed hooks, digging into his flesh. "I try to be strong," he whispered.

Drawing back, Adam took Parker's face in his hands. "I've told you before that you're the strongest person I know. Getting hurt isn't what matters. It's that you heal. That you pick yourself up and keep going. And you do. Every time."

"I'm scared." Shivering despite the heat, he curled his hands in Adam's ratty T-shirt.

Adam leaned their foreheads together. "We're both scared. We won't try to hide it anymore, okay? Not from each other."

Shivering, Parker pressed his face to Adam's neck, breathing in sweat and the faint whiff of leather that seemed to cling to him even when it was too hot to wear his jacket. "I thought I was over it. But seeing her, it was like I was back there again. He was making me take off all my clothes, and he was hitting me, and…"

Adam's growl vibrated through him, and he squeezed Parker closer.

"I feel like such a wuss, you know? Being scared of her."

"You're not."

With each breath in Adam's arms, the crushing weight against Parker's lungs lightened. "I think she was telling the truth. I think Damian was too. That this is a safe place. Even though I maintain that things that sound too good to be true usually are."

Smiling, Adam tipped up Parker's face and kissed him softly. "I love you so much."

"You must, since my breath has got to be all pukey and disgusting."

Laughing, he kissed him again. "You always taste like sunshine and—"

"Shut up!" Parker guffawed, which felt so warm and light and wonderful. He blew out a deep breath, getting serious again. "I want to believe her—Bethany. That she's sorry. But I don't know if I can get past it."

"You don't have to." Adam kissed Parker's head.

"I don't want to ruin things here if it really is everything they say. I want to be wrong. I want this to work out. For us to all be safe."

Drawing back, Adam rubbed their noses together. "We'll take it one day at a time, okay? Whatever happens, we're in it together."

"Okay." He looked out to sea, to the vast expanse of the horizon, and then to where the gun had been consumed. He mused, "You know, we might have needed that gun at some point in the future."

Adam followed his gaze. "Huh. Yeah, good point. I guess I

was going for the symbolism. Not so much the practicality."

The laughter that bubbled up Parker's throat took with it another chunk of weight from his chest. "Whoops."

"My bad?"

They both laughed, and Parker could breathe normally again, the sunshine on his skin soothing.

"We'll figure it all out," Adam said.

"One way or another, I guess we always do."

So far.

Parker shook off the dark thought. The world had gone to shit, and Adam was right. One day at a time. Hell, one hour. One minute. And in that minute, everything was okay. They were safe and pressed together, and Adam's breath smelled stale, and Parker didn't care.

Theresa marched up the dock with a tight smile, her dark ponytail swinging. She wore work boots and khaki shorts, a buttoned blue shirt hanging loose over a tank top. "Hey there. Calmed down?"

Stepping away from Adam, Parker ran a hand over his hot face. He was a snotty mess. "Yes. I'm sorry."

"Let's go to my office and talk about it." When Adam opened his mouth, Theresa added, "Yes, you too."

They held hands as they followed Theresa, fingers entwined. Leaving the water behind, they took a wide, well-tended path through the trees, coming upon a clearing with several one-story buildings. Parker wasn't sure where the hospital was in relation, not spotting it.

Shrieks of children's laughter filled the air, a group of kids ranging from about five to twelve kicking around a soccer ball on a small, grassy patch.

"They've finished their chores, and school doesn't start for half an hour," Theresa said, nodding toward a building that looked new, the wood beams bare without the years of dirt and wear the other structures had. "We have a couple of teachers with us now, and anyone with a particular knowledge is encouraged to lend a hand."

Parker watched the children, some with eyes the same hazel as Adam's, bordering on gold. "It's…a mix of kids?"

"Yes. We're one community now."

A little girl scored a goal, and her shout of victory was part howl. Parker glanced to Adam, who watched avidly, his expression tender, a smile playing on his lips.

"That's the mess hall." Theresa pointed to the largest building, a rectangle. The smell of buttery toast wafted on the air. "We're planning to tear down the north wall and build an extension. We serve breakfast, lunch, and dinner, and snacks are always available. As long as everyone does their share, you're free to eat as much as you'd like. And as you saw, the cabins do have kitchenettes if you prefer to cook for yourself. We encourage everyone to join in communal meals, though."

"Where does the electricity come from?" Adam asked.

"Solar panels." She pointed, and Parker thought it was north, the harbor being west. "Up on the hill, we've got panels and a lookout station. My grandfather was ahead of his time when it came to sustainable energy. We have generators as well, but we get a lot of sunshine here."

"We were at a place in Colorado that used green energy," Adam said. "Certainly comes in handy now."

Jaden and Evie's faces flickered through Parker's mind. God, he hoped they were okay. The Pines had been so luxurious and enormous compared to the structures on Salvation Island, but the fact that the island had apparently been operating for years was a comfort.

All around, people went about their tasks, smiling and chatting, sweat on their brows. One group chopped wood, a couple in their werewolf forms, powering through a downed tree, claws gleaming on axe handles.

As Theresa led them to the east side of the clearing, they walked through a copse of trees to a pasture and two barns. Cows did indeed dot the grass, chewing cud, their tails flicking at flies lazily.

"We're growing our chicken and cow populations. We have a transport ship now, and we'll be making regular trips to the mainland for supplies and livestock." She motioned across the pasture, where a dozen people worked. "We're tearing up more trees for more farmland. The gardens won't be enough."

"How many people can this island hold?" Adam asked. "If survivors keep arriving…"

"We're not sure. Several thousand. The island's about twenty-five square miles, so we have room to work with."

"Why haven't I ever seen it on any maps?" Parker asked. "Was it always called Salvation Island?"

Theresa led them back into the trees. "No. It didn't have a name before we recently christened it. We just called it 'the island' I suppose. As for maps, my grandfather was a man of influence. Even managed to have it taken off Google Maps before he died. Amazing what money can accomplish."

"If he was so rich, why isn't it fancier here?" Parker asked.

"That wasn't his vision. He wanted wolves to get back to nature here."

They passed the garden plots going back toward the main buildings, more people of all ages bent and filling baskets.

"I feel like I'm in that *Star Trek* movie on the planet where everyone wears brown and never raises their voices." Parker hadn't meant to say it out loud, and now Theresa looked back at him with a furrowed brow. "I just mean…it's trippy. Like a commune or something."

She smiled. "It is a bit. When my mom would bring me here as a kid, I loved it. Running around barefoot with other wolves, not hiding who I am. But when I was a teenager, I thought it was 'so lame.' I don't know how my mother put up with me."

Parker hurried to say, "No, it's not lame. I didn't mean that. It's—" *Weird? Suspiciously peaceful? Potentially awesome?* "I don't know. My head's kind of spinning right now."

"I can imagine." Theresa led them up a few steps into a squat little building that held a reception area and a few offices through doorways. She sat behind her desk in one and motioned to the wooden guest chairs.

Adam squeezed Parker's hand once they sat, not letting go even though their palms were super sweaty. Parker's eyes flicked around the office. A framed map of the world hung on the wall behind the desk, and on top of a row of filing cabinets to the right sat a jumble of picture frames. Theresa was in some of the pictures, and Parker could track the growth of a boy who looked about eleven in the most recent.

It was all so...*normal.* Could Salvation Island really be everything it claimed? His pulse kicked up, excitement sparking through him. He wanted it to be real so fucking badly.

Theresa sat back and watched them for a few moments. "I had a quick conversation with Bethany. She insists you shouldn't be blamed, Parker. When she joined us, she confessed that she'd cooperated in acts of aggression and cruelty, and that she regretted it. She hasn't given us any reason to think her insincere. But I understand why you might feel differently if you were victimized by her and her cohorts in the past."

He squirmed on the hard chair. "Seeing her was... It sucked. I've—I didn't want to come here. Adam and the others did. I was sure you were setting a trap. And maybe you still are." He tried to laugh, and it limped out before he cleared his throat, Theresa still watching patiently. "When I saw the boat, it all came rushing back. I didn't think. I reacted."

"I can imagine. And this is why we don't allow weapons. You

lied to us, and that's unacceptable, Parker."

Adam jumped in. "He's exhausted. He's barely slept and—"

"It's okay." He squeezed Adam's slick hand. "No excuses." To Theresa, he said, "You're right. I lied. I was afraid. Which is still an excuse, isn't it? I guess I should just shut up. I rarely do that, so yeah, I'll just…"

The smile that briefly lifted her lips seemed genuine. "I understand being afraid. But we're not your enemy. We live in a new world, and if we're going to survive—if we're going to *thrive*—we can't allow threats. Mercy is a luxury, and luxuries are thin on the ground these days."

His throat was dry. "So, what happens now?" Adam was a wall of tension at his side, and Parker clung to his hand. Would she kick him off?

Would Adam come with me if she did?

"You made a mistake, but intentions are important. You're forgiven, provided nothing like this ever happens again. We want Salvation Island to be safe for everyone. That includes you, and that includes Bethany. You don't have to be friends, but can you coexist?"

Could he? What if he said no? Parker thought of her with Shorty, laughing, and then this morning clutching the Pop-Tarts, terror rippling through her. "It's a big island. I'll try."

"Good. We have things here that others want, Parker. Food, water, medicine, stability. Hope. We want to help the survivors of this plague, and we want you to be part of that. Do you want to be part of it?"

In that moment, clutching Adam's hand and looking into Theresa's patient, gold-flecked eyes, with children laughing outside and a community being built, he really, really did.

"Yes. I won't let you down. Assuming you're not actually cannibal psychos who want to lock us in your sex dungeon."

Theresa barked out a laugh, her shoulders shaking. "You do

have a way with words, Parker. Sorry to disappoint you on that count. No sex dungeons." She grinned and lowered her voice conspiratorially. "Plenty of sex, though."

He and Adam shared a smile as footsteps pounded up the few stairs outside reception. Lilly burst inside, skidding to a stop when she noticed them through the open office door. Craig arrived moments behind her, out of breath.

Lilly strode into the office. "Is Parker in trouble?"

"Sweetheart, let's listen, not demand," Craig said, taking her hand. To Theresa, he added, "I'm sorry for the intrusion."

Lilly pulled her hand free and stepped up beside Parker. "He saved us. He would never hurt anyone who didn't deserve it."

Theresa smiled. "That's good to hear. We've discussed it, and everything's fine."

"You're not kicking Parker off the island?" Lilly's face was still creased in apprehension.

"No," Theresa said.

Lilly spun and threw her little arms about Parker. The lump in his throat was too big to speak over, so he just hugged her back, Adam releasing his hand so he could. She was warm, and her curls tickled his cheek.

Craig clapped a hand on Parker's shoulder. "Good news for a change. We could use some. We're going back to sit with Jacob. Want to come?"

Patting Lilly, Parker managed, "Yeah. I'd like that." He glanced at Theresa. "Is that okay? I'm just, like, free to go?"

"Yes. We trust nothing like this will happen again." She smiled kindly, but there was steel in her tone. He could respect that.

Trust.

It wasn't an easy word, but he had to learn the shape and weight of it if they were going to have a real home.

WITH A SNORT, Craig jerked upright in his chair next to Jacob's bed. "What?" He blinked at Jacob, who slept fitfully.

"It's okay," Parker said from his chair on the other side of the mattress. The rest of the infirmary was empty, the sinking sun casting a richly yellow glow on the white tiles through the west windows.

"I didn't mean to fall asleep." Craig rubbed his growing beard and then sat up straighter with tension, glancing around. "Where's Lilly?"

"Adam's with her. Some kids were playing Marco Polo at the beach. We thought it would be good for her to have some fun."

Nodding, Craig slumped. "Good. Thank you." He brushed back Jacob's lank hair. "How is he?"

"Seems to be getting better. His fever's down a bit. He's pretty knocked out, but he's moaning less, so I think that's good? Connie seemed happy with the progress."

She and Parker had only had a brief conversation centered on Jacob. She'd patted Parker's arm kindly, and he had to admit there was something inherently comforting and mom-ish about her. It would be interesting to get to know her better.

"Thank God." Craig's button-up shirt was open to his throat, the tails hanging out of his khakis and sleeves rolled to his elbows. A food stain of unknown origin adorned his chest.

"You want to grab a shower? I'll stay with Jacob."

"No, I should be here when he wakes up."

"You've barely slept. You need a break."

Craig shot him a skeptical look. "And how much sleep have you gotten since you woke in the middle of the night to sail our butts through the Gulf Stream? Heck, I don't even know when that was now. But I know you haven't slept enough. Those dark circles tell the tale."

"I know. I'll sleep well tonight." The day was waning, and Parker couldn't deny the weariness that settled over him like the heavy apron thingy the dentist always put on him during x-rays. "Huh. I guess I'll never have to go to the dentist again. I always hated the dentist. The downside is my teeth might fall out."

Craig's brow furrowed. "The dentist?"

He waved a hand with a smile. "Sorry, it made sense in my head. Yeah, I'm tired. I admit it. But seriously, go get a shower. I can wait."

"Are you trying to tell me something? Do I stink?" Craig teased. "Just say it, man."

He grinned. "You hella stink."

After a moment, Craig's smile faded. "Everything okay after this morning?"

Parker's belly clenched, the memory of the warm metal in his hand sending a swell of bile up his throat. He swallowed. "Yeah. It was... Before we met you guys, something bad happened. I mean, aside from all the obvious bad things with the virus and the end of the world as we know it."

Craig listened patiently, and Parker licked his lips, trying to push the words out. "Adam was ashore, and I was alone on *Bella*. I was stupid and let this other boat sneak up on me. I was worried about Adam, and I wasn't paying attention behind me. So dumb, and—"

"You're not stupid, or dumb, or any other names you might call yourself. You're human. So as my wife would say if she was here, enough of that nonsense talk. Be kind to yourself. We all make mistakes. We all forget things." He lowered his voice to a whisper. "My wife would also say, don't act like your shit don't stink. You're not perfect. None of us are but the Lord."

The smile that lifted Parker's mouth felt *good*. "Your wife sounds like she was awesome."

Craig sighed fondly. "Oh, she was. Was she ever." He gazed at

Jacob. "I've always had excellent taste in women, if I do say so myself. I miss both of them. Miss them so much."

Parker looked at his hands, almost expecting to see Abby's blood staining them the way it had the deck of the *Saltwater Taffy*. "I'm sorry I couldn't save her. I should have been faster. I—"

"Stop. You did your best. I know you can hear, but I wish you'd *listen*."

He slid his sneakers on the tiles, rubber soles squeaking. "I'm trying. I am."

"What happened to Abby wasn't your fault." Craig breathed deeply. "Wasn't mine either, and sometimes I have trouble with that. But it's the truth. And whatever happened to you that day you mentioned, it wasn't your fault."

Crossing his arms, he shivered. "I don't know why I can't forget it. I'm fine. She said herself that what they did to me was nothing compared to others."

"She being the woman here? Bethany?"

"Yeah. There were four of them, two men and two women. One of the men seemed to be in charge. Shorty, I called him. Since he was short or whatever." Parker rubbed his palms over his thighs, his cargo shorts bunching up. He breathed hard, pushing out the words. "He made me take off all my clothes, and hit me in the head with a gun. Smacked my ass hard and threatened to rape me. I was really scared. I couldn't get to the gun, and I was just…helpless."

He blew out a slow breath. Saying it out loud to Craig seemed to loosen the ever-present knot in his stomach.

"God, I'm so sorry that happened to you." Craig looked at him with compassion, no judgment shadowing his kind eyes. "Are the rest of them here? Because if this Shorty's here, I can't imagine him going very long without your boyfriend tearing his head off."

It probably shouldn't have made Parker feel good to hear that Craig thought Adam would kill for him, but it did. "It's only her left." He tried her name, the syllables sticky like molasses. "Bethany." It was strange to think of her as having a name that wasn't *redhead*. Strange to think of her as a person. But the fear in her eyes had been real. Maybe the regret was too. "She says she's sorry. I guess. I don't know. I'd rather not see her."

"Hey, no one would expect you two to become pals. I hope she is sorry, and I hope she won't be a threat to anyone else here. She was kind to Lilly this morning, but we'll see. We've got your back, Parker."

"Thank you. I just want things to be normal, you know?"

"Do I. Normal never seemed so wonderful. I think maybe we could get some here. I mean, as normal as things can be on a werewolf sanctuary island in the end times. But hey, my baby's playing Marco Polo. I'll take it." He gazed seriously at Parker. "And what they did to you? It's not something you just..." He snapped his fingers. "Get over."

"I wanted it to be. I thought if I could have crazy awesome sex with Adam like before, it meant I was okay. They didn't break me. And at first, I thought it'd worked." Heat flushed his cheeks. "And you probably don't want to hear about our sex life."

Craig chuckled, lifting his hands. "Hey, I don't judge and I don't begrudge. And I've heard bits and pieces. Sound carries really well over water."

Laughter warmed Parker's chest. "That's what Adam says. Uh, sorry. Did the kids hear anything?"

"Lilly was fast asleep, and Jacob..." Even though Jacob seemed asleep now, breathing deeply through parted lips, Craig whispered, "And I don't think he minded too much. He might have been a little jealous. Poor kid. I remember what it was like at that age. Horny morning, noon, and night."

Parker smiled. "Yup."

"Daddy!" Dripping water in a purple bathing suit with a towel around her waist and her curls in pigtails, Lilly burst in. She skidded to a stop, her face dropping as she looked at Jacob. "How is he?"

"He's doing okay, sweetheart." Craig grinned. "How was Marco Polo?"

Adam followed behind her, and Parker's heart skipped with affection and a low tug of desire just looking at him. He ached to touch.

"She's a natural," Adam said. "The others are convinced she's part wolf since her hearing's so good."

"Maybe Jacob can play soon." Lilly leaned over him and gave his hand a squeeze.

"Let's hope it's really soon," Parker said. To Craig, he added, "You guys go clean up and get dinner. I'll stay."

"I can stay too." Adam trailed his hand over Parker's shoulders, leaving warmth in his wake.

Lilly said, "I thought you were going to talk to Miss Connie."

"It can wait."

"No, go ahead. I'll be fine here." It had taken some doing to get Adam to leave him to go with Lilly to the beach. Parker took Adam's hand. "I'm okay. I'd tell you otherwise."

"Would you?" He rubbed his thumb over the back of Parker's hand.

"Yeah. I promise."

"Okay. I won't be long either."

"Go, go." Parker shooed them. "We'll be fine here."

With a gentle kiss from Adam, they left, and Parker listened to the birds outside and Jacob's even breathing. When Jacob muttered and flickered his eyes open a little while later, Parker jolted forward on his chair, almost tipping it.

"Jacob? It's Parker. Can you hear me?" He rubbed Jacob's thin arm. Eyes opening fully, Jacob blinked at him and croaked something he couldn't make out. "Hold on, drink some water." Parker poured a cup from the pitcher on a side table and held

Jacob's head so he could drink.

Sagging back against the pillows, Jacob licked his chapped lips. "Where are we?"

"Salvation Island. We made it."

He gazed around the infirmary with wide eyes. "It's okay? Not bad?"

"So far, so good. We think we're safe here." As Parker watched the relief wash over Jacob's face, he realized it was true, and he wasn't simply hiding the truth from a sick kid.

I think we're safe here.

A little voice reminded him of the Pines, but he silenced it. They had their eyes open, but maybe it was okay to hope.

"How are you feeling?" he asked.

"Shitty. But better than before." Jacob shifted and poked at his stomach. "I should have said something about the cut. It was dumb."

"We all make mistakes. It's over now. You're going to be okay. You're shaking off the infection. Well, you and the antibiotics."

Jacob lifted his arm with the IV. "Guess it's good they have all this stuff." He still looked unnaturally pale, blue veins stark under his skin and circles beneath his eyes. "Where's everyone?"

"They'll be back soon. I had to pry Craig away to go get rid of his BO, and Lilly can't wait to talk to you. Adam's with the woman who runs this island. Connie. She was a nurse, and she's a werewolf. This island's full of them. It belongs to them, but now they're letting the rest of us come here too."

Jacob stared incredulously. "*Werewolves?* We're on an island with werewolves? Like Adam?"

"Yeah. Hopefully they're like Adam. So far, they all seem really nice." *God, I hope they're not going to cook us for dinner tonight.* He was fairly confident they weren't. Mostly. A strong ninety percent sure.

"Do you think my mom would have liked it here?" Jacob

spoke so softly Parker barely heard the question.

Breathing through the swell of grief and guilt, he nodded. "I think she really would have. And I know she'd be glad you're here. That you're safe and you're getting better. She loved you so much. You know that, right?"

Tears filling his eyes, Jacob nodded.

"She—" Parker sat up straighter. "Shit, I completely forgot." He patted his pockets and unzipped the one on his left thigh. Gently, he pulled out the silver necklace, the little dove dangling from the chain, the setting sun through the high windows catching it with fading rays. "Your mom wanted you to have this. I'm so sorry I didn't give it to you before."

His hand trembling, Jacob reached for it, the IV tube trailing behind. He grasped the chain, watching the dove sway gently. "Thank you."

Parker's throat tightened, his eyes burning with the too-familiar return of tears. "Do you want to put it on?"

Crying now, his cheeks wet, Jacob asked, "But isn't it a girl's necklace?"

"Fuck gender stereotypes. It's beautiful and it's yours. It'll look great on you."

Sniffing, Jacob smiled, just a bit. "You think?"

"I know."

Adam's low baritone added, "Definitely." The door closed behind him as he crossed to the bed.

"Here, let me help you." Parker took the necklace and carefully unclasped it. Adam reached down to help Jacob lift his head, and Parker fastened the catch. The dove sat just below the hollow of Jacob's throat.

"Perfect," Parker declared. "Not too tight?"

Jacob shook his head, fingering the silver. Sniffing loudly, he swiped at his cheeks. "Thanks." His eyes were heavy again, and they chatted softly about the island for a while before his eyes closed completely. He dozed, his mouth open, chest rising and falling steadily.

Adam pulled up another chair beside Parker, and they joined hands, threading their fingers together. Parker asked, "Everything okay with Connie?"

"Yes. She wants to have breakfast with us tomorrow. Get to know us. Tell us more about the island, and what's expected of us."

"Okay." Parker exhaled. "That sounds good."

"Yeah?"

He looked back at Jacob sleeping and in the distance, heard a kid who might have been Lilly laughing. Holding Adam's hand, their palms sweaty, he smiled. "Yeah."

"GOD, I'M SO tired." Damp and naked after a wonderfully hot shower, Parker flopped back on the wide bed. The navy curtains shut out the night, the only light coming from the adjacent bathroom.

Naked as well, Adam stood at the foot of the bed half in shadow, rubbing a towel over his hair. "I know. Go to sleep."

"Mmm. I don't feel like it."

Chuckling, Adam said, "Now you're just being contrary."

"Maybe." Parker ran his fingers over his chest, brushing his tingling nipples. He'd flipped on the ceiling fan, and it sent a breeze over his drying skin with a low, rhythmic thump. His legs were splayed—not completely wide, but comfortably. His cock was soft, but as he skated his fingers over his chest, it twitched with interest.

Adam watched with interest as well, his lips parting as he followed the progress of Parker's fingers, sweeping lower and lower to his belly button and back up again. "You should rest."

"You still don't want to fuck me?" Parker kept his tone teasing, although the hurt from being rejected the night before still nagged dully.

Regarding him seriously, Adam said, "You know I always want you. It wasn't about that."

"I know." And he did. He really did, he realized. "It's just good to hear."

Adam murmured, "God, how I want you." He was still holding the towel, and he dropped it at his feet.

With a shuddering inhalation, Parker spread his legs, bending his knees. He licked his palm, his tongue rough and wet, then stroked his cock slowly. "How do you want me?"

"Just like this," Adam whispered before crawling between his legs and pressing his knees up toward his shoulders.

"Am I enough?" he blurted.

His gaze intense, Adam took Parker's face in his hands. "*Yes*. Wanting a community—a pack—it's not a judgment of you. It's not you being lacking. It's about wanting more for *us*. Having people we can trust who make us stronger. Safer."

With Adam between his legs, heavy and strong and alive, safe in their own space while the island hummed around them, Parker felt like he finally understood. Yet fear lingered in the corners of his mind.

"What if it goes wrong? What if bad people come?"

"Then we'll deal with it. Together. We never had any guarantees in life. Never will."

"That's true." He inhaled as deeply as he could and nodded. "As long as we're together, we can handle it."

"Always together. No matter what." Adam's gaze roved hungrily, a tremor rocking him, his voice dropping desperately. "God, Parker."

"What?" His breath caught at the emotion shining in Adam's eyes.

"You're so beautiful. You know that, don't you?"

Before he could answer, Adam dove between his legs, spreading Parker's ass and licking almost frantically. Parker couldn't stifle his shout, a bolt of pleasure shooting right to his dick. "Oh fuck! *Adam.*"

Growling, Adam spit onto Parker's hole, getting it nice and wet before he transformed with a rumble, letting the wolf out. His tongue lengthened, and when he fucked into him with it, Parker was pretty sure he was going to levitate and hit the ceiling.

Which meant he'd be sliced and diced by the fan, but it would be *so worth it.*

Adam's claws scraped his thighs, his fangs grazing Parker's sensitive flesh. Maybe it shouldn't have made him so hard, but it did. His cock was already leaking, and he threaded his fingers into Adam's thick hair to stop from jerking himself off.

He didn't want this to end yet. Didn't want this to end *ever.* Moaning, he didn't care if werewolves nearby could hear him, or humans for that matter. Nothing else mattered but Adam. His ass was wet with spit, Adam thrusting into it with his tongue, almost as good as a dick, his hairy face rough on Parker's inner thighs.

After another minute, Parker was absolutely on fire. "Want you inside me. Need more."

Pulling back, Adam skimmed his fangs along one of Parker's thighs. His eyes glowed gold as he held himself up over him, and he bit back what had to be a howl when he shoved his cock into Parker's ass.

The stretch and burn were incredible. Parker hoped he'd never get used to this, never stop feeling like it was brand new again every time he had Adam inside him.

"You feel so amazing," Parker moaned. His cock ached, trapped between them as he stared into Adam's golden gaze, clutching at his arms, their skin slick.

His fangs still out and claws probably shredding the sheets,

Adam pumped his hips, thrusting hard, the headboard banging the wooden wall. "Fuck, Parker."

"I hope these cabins are well constructed." Parker groaned, Adam heavy and hairy on top of him, ramming his ass mercilessly.

Adam laughed, his shoulders shaking and rhythm faltering. Breathing hard, he buried his face in Parker's neck, panting hotly. When he raised his head, his fangs were gone, his eyes a paler yellow as he transformed back. Tenderly, he brushed a hand over Parker's cheek, then started a slow roll of his hips.

The tenor changed, and now Parker couldn't look away from Adam as they rocked together—had to keep his eyes open even though the pleasure made him want to tip his head back and surrender to it.

With their gazes locked, he hooked one knee over Adam's shoulder, spreading himself as much as he could, willing Adam to take more. Take him. Keep him.

They kissed, tongues exploring and sharing, sweaty flesh slapping as they grunted softly. Adam was so thick inside him, the sensation of fullness spreading over Parker's whole body, as if his skin was too tight.

His cock strained with the brush of their bellies against it, and when Adam reached between them, it only took a few strokes for Parker to come apart, closing his eyes despite himself as his orgasm thundered through him.

When he looked again, still shaking with tremors of hot pleasure, he found Adam watching him, working his hips faster, still milking Parker's cock as he tipped over the edge.

He squeezed too hard when he did, and Parker squeaked, Adam releasing him with a deep rumble of laughter giving way to a gasp as he emptied another pulse into Parker.

Tangled together after Parker lowered his legs, they caught their breath. Parker smiled at the ceiling fan, which rotated steadily. "Okay, now sleepy time." His eyes were heavy already.

"Thought I'd have to sleep with one eye open here, but it really isn't like that."

"We're safe." Adam leaned down and whispered, his breath a warm gust, "But I always have an ear open. I promise."

"I know. Me too. Even with my sadly inadequate human hearing." He blinked slowly, dreams pulling him down.

"Wait, I just want to—" Adam eased away and padded over to the chair in the corner where his leather jacket rested. When he returned, the red glow of the camera light came to life.

"If you wanted to make a porno, you should have gotten the camera out a little earlier." Parker motioned to his spent and sticky dick. "And if you don't mind…"

Huffing with laughter, Adam said, "It's not that kind of movie." He soon returned from the bathroom with a wet cloth. He wiped Parker clean with gentle strokes and then himself.

"Thanks, baby," Parker murmured. "Can I be asleep for this shot in your movie? You need at least one scene of me not talking."

Kneeling on the bed, Adam's smile faded. He stared at the small silver camera in his hands, his face in shadow now. "I can't even cut it together. Some people here have laptops, but they won't have the software."

Parker propped himself on his elbow, shaking off the sleepiness. "Sure they will. Hello, iMovie? It may not be whatever fancy program you used in a real studio, but it'll do the job."

Adam lifted his head, a smile dawning over his stupidly handsome face, his teeth gleaming white in the darkness. "You're right."

"You really should be used to that by now. I mean, I told you that first day I was an A student." He tapped his head. "Not just a hat rack, you know."

Adam kissed him then, sweet and long.

When they parted, Parker admitted, "Although I was obviously wrong about my first impression of you. And it seems I just might be wrong about this island. So really, it's only these two times. The exceptions that prove the rule or some shit."

"Something like that." Adam urged Parker up to sitting, positioning him on the bed so the light from the bathroom hit his face.

"Why are you filming me right now?"

"To mark our first night on Salvation Island."

Parker frowned. "But we were here yesterday."

"Last night doesn't count. We fought."

"But we were here, and it was night, and—" Parker shook his head, laughing softly. "You know what? Sure. It doesn't matter."

Adam studied the viewfinder on the camera, shifting slightly. "I want to make it real. That's why I want to film you."

With his foot resting on Adam's thigh, stroking softly, Parker nodded. "First official night. Roll it."

Adam hit the button.

"Well, here we are on Salvation Island. First night of the rest of our lives. Our very long and happy, stress-free lives." Parker leaned back and rapped his knuckles on the headboard.

"How do you like it here so far?" Adam asked.

He thought about it for a few moments. "There was a rocky start, but that's kind of the way I do things. I think it's going to be good. It feels…promising."

"Somewhere we could make a life?"

"Yeah." Parker smiled, realizing he really meant it. "It does feel like that."

Adam switched off the camera and placed it on the side table. He cupped Parker's cheek, running his thumb over the stubble there. "But no matter what happens, my life is with you. Pack or no pack, island or no island. Whatever comes, you're my home."

For once, Parker couldn't find the words. As they kissed long into the peaceful night, Adam didn't seem to mind.

About the Author

Keira aims for the perfect mix of character, plot, and heat in her M/M romances. She writes everything from swashbuckling pirates to heartwarming holiday escapism. Her fave tropes are enemies to lovers, age gaps, forced proximity, and passionate virgins. Although she loves delicious angst along the way, Keira guarantees happy endings!

Discover more at:

keiraandrews.com

Made in the USA
Las Vegas, NV
19 August 2024

94040474R00152